"Literature, librarians, and love... *Roommating* has the perfect combination of all three! Schorr's bright, funny writing shines in this story of two twenty-somethings finding themselves—and each other—with the help of a septuagenarian, an adorable dog, and the vibrant NYC backdrop. When it comes to books about books, this is what the experience is all about."

—Lucy Gilmore, author of *The Lonely Hearts Book Club*

"Meredith Schorr absolutely nails it with this delightful romp that will have readers kicking their feet with delight. Told with warmth, charm, and Schorr's signature blend of heart and humor, *Roommating* is a book for book lovers and anyone else who likes their slow-burn romances served with a side of hijinks."

—Lindsay Hameroff, author of *Never Planned on You*

"Meredith Schorr's *Roommating* is a book-lover's dream! I was utterly charmed by this cozy, quirky—but also sexy!—romance in which temporary roommates battling over a sublet accidentally fall for each other. Schorr's love for libraries and books is felt in every real-life title drop and the inclusion of my new favorite microtrope—one-on-one book club meetings as foreplay. This is a feel-good comfort book that I already plan to re-read again and again!"

—Melanie Sweeney, *USA Today* bestselling author of *Take Me Home*

"*Roommating* is such a fun and creative spin on 'and they were roommates' with the most lovable characters. Meredith Schorr writes New York in a way that feels lived-in—dare I say, *cozy*? Reading her books feels like coming home. I can already tell *Roommating* is going to be one of my go-to comfort reads."

—Kate Goldbeck, *USA Today* bestselling author of *You, Again*

"All's fair in love and real estate, and nowhere is that truer than in New York City, where this feel-good romance by Meredith Schorr leaps off the pages. Heartwarming and humorous, *Roommating* is the coziest of love letters to librarians, books, and the people we choose to share our corners of the city with."

—Lauren Kung Jessen, author of *Yin Yang Love Song*

"Meredith Schorr has done it again, blessing us with another warm and cozy hug of a romance! Schorr's stories have it all: humor, pining, hilarious side characters, and so much heart. *Roommating* is both steamy and sweet, and watching Sabrina and Adam fall in love had me swooning. Schorr has quickly become one of my go-to romance authors!"

—Fallon Ballard, *USA Today* bestselling author of *Change of Heart*

"Soft-hearted and slow burning, *Roommating* is the perfect romance to curl up with and fall head-over-heals into. I was enchanted by the multi-generational storyline and even more enthralled by Adam and Sabrina's inevitable attraction. With Schorr's signature charm and the library-esque, book-lover setting, I couldn't have been more in love! Don't miss this heartwarming, soul-touching story."

—Clare Gilmore, *USA Today* bestselling author of *Perfect Fit*

"*Roommating* is not just a sizzling read containing prose hot enough to scorch your panties and pages brimming with butterfly-inducing banter, but it's also an evocative testament to the unique love between a grandchild and grandparent. I found myself rooting for both the plucky librarian and the landlord's handsome grandson as they battled to prove not only who's the worthiest roommate, but who can move beyond the mistakes of their past in order to make the most of their present. Fans will delight in this book lover's romance which proves that sharing a bathroom with a man is a lot sexier than it sounds."

—Heidi Shertok, author of *Unorthodox Love*

"With delicious forced-proximity, a surplus of tender moments, and Meredith Schorr's signature wit and charm, *Roommating* is a delightful romp of a romcom that had me laughing and swooning from start to finish."

—Heather McBreen, author of *Wedding Dashers*

"Between an utterly unique premise and delightful characters who absolutely leap off the page, Meredith Schorr's *Roommating* is the perfect book for hopeful romantics everywhere. Sabrina and Adam's chemistry is palpable, and Sabrina's journey as she learns that it's okay to ask for help and take chances is the most satisfying story you'll read all year. I never wanted it to end!"

—Sara Goodman Confino, bestselling author of *Don't Forget to Write*

"Cozy, bookish, and brimming over with charm, *Roommating* by Meredith Schorr proves that the best romances start with the wrong roommate."

—Jean Meltzer, international bestselling author of *The Matzah Ball*

"*Roomating* is a funny, sexy, and deeply romantic story about love and family. Meredith Schorr's ability to make you think even while you laugh and swoon is unparalleled."

—Stacey Agdern, author of *The Dating Contract*

OTHER BOOKS BY MEREDITH SCHORR

Someone Just Like You

As Seen on TV

ROOM MATING

Meredith Schorr

FOREVER
New York Boston

This book is a work of fiction. Names, characters, places, and incidents are the product of the author's imagination or are used fictitiously. Any resemblance to actual events, locales, or persons, living or dead, is coincidental.

Forever
Hachette Book Group
1290 Avenue of the Americas, New York, NY 10104
read-forever.com
@readforeverpub

First Edition: June 2025

Forever is an imprint of Grand Central Publishing. The Forever name and logo are registered trademarks of Hachette Book Group, Inc.

Library of Congress Cataloging-in-Publication Data

Names: Schorr, Meredith, author.
Title: Roommating / Meredith Schorr.
Description: First edition. | New York : Forever, 2025.
Identifiers: LCCN 2024059811 | ISBN 9781538758267 (trade paperback) |
ISBN 9781538758274 (ebook)
Subjects: LCGFT: Romance fiction. | Novels.
Classification: LCC PS3619.C4543 R66 2025 | DDC 813/.6—dc23/eng/20241213
LC record available at https://lccn.loc.gov/2024059811

ISBNs: 9781538758267 (trade paperback), 9781538758274 (ebook)

LSC-C

Printing 1, 2025

In memory of Nanny Tessie and Grandma Molly, and dedicated to grandmothers everywhere.

Author's Note

This book contains references to the death of a parent (off the page), parental abandonment (off the page), and homophobia (off the page). I have attempted to depict these situations with sensitivity and care. Please be safe when reading if these are triggers for you.

Chapter One

My seventy-two-year-old roommate Marcia is a ten.

I make this observation from behind my phone, primed to record her placing the first book on the black four-tier revolving bookshelf we spent most of our Sunday afternoon struggling to put together. "Are you ready?" I ask her.

Marcia shakes her head of chin-length salon-dyed blond hair. "I'm not sure. Why are there so many extra screws? Shouldn't we have used them all?" Her gaze dips to the small clear bag holding at least ten leftover screws on the dark wood living room floor of our two-bedroom apartment in Union Square.

I shrug. "They're probably spares. Ikea is generous that way."

This may or may not be true, but the bookshelf is standing, which must count for something. I tuck my phone into the pocket of my high-waisted wide-leg jeans and squat. Then I slide the bag of extra screws under one of the flattened cardboard boxes at our feet before straightening my legs. Out of sight. Out of mind. "See? No extra screws anymore."

"Clever," Marcia says, her blue eyes twinkling. With a grunt, she bends her knees and retrieves the bag. "We should store them somewhere safe, just in case."

I laugh. "It's a good thing one of us is sensible, huh?"

She blows a raspberry. "I think you mean old."

I smile fondly at her. I'd swallow a container of retinol in one gulp to look as good as Marcia in my seventies. "Age is relative. Compared to my twenty-four, sure, you're old*er*. But the guy in front of us at Trader Joe's yesterday? Ninety if he's a day. Compared to him, you're but a young grasshopper."

She waves me off and regards me with soft eyes. "Have I told you lately how happy I am that you live here?" She squeezes my forearm affectionately.

Warmth fills my belly. "Not as happy as I am," I say, meaning it.

When I first moved to Manhattan from Connecticut after graduating college more than a year and a half ago, I shared a one-bedroom apartment with two girls I'd connected with through Craigslist. Our place was party central for pre- and post-bar outings several nights a week. It was all fun and games at first, but the lifestyle wasn't sustainable while taking two courses a semester toward my master's in library and information science and working approximately fifteen hours a week as a library page at a branch of the New York Public Library. Trying to focus on schoolwork in a "bedroom" partitioned with sheets while perpetually drunk twenty-three-year-olds shout "Woo!" on repeat less than ten feet away... well, I don't recommend it.

Then I saw a segment on the *Today* show about a roommate app that matched younger adults with older people who had rooms to spare, and I found Marcia. The deal is, I pay obscenely low rent—by New York City standards—in exchange for taking care of the more physical burdens in her life, helping care for Rocket, her precious but hyperactive Jack Russell terrier, and demystifying the techie things that frequently trip her up. Even with the dismal salary I make at the library and paying my own way through grad school with loans, I can afford it. It's been a dream—both the living arrangement and Marcia, who's become one of my best friends.

"Do you like it here?" Marcia asks.

For a second, I think she's read my mind, but she's referring to the bookshelf's current placement in front of the window overlooking Fourteenth Street and to the right of the dark-gray suede sectional couch.

"It's perfect. Time to christen this bad boy," I say, gesturing to the hardcover copy of *Nothing Like the Movies* on the granite-covered square coffee table.

She chews her lip. "Maybe you should do the honors."

I cock my head. "Do you want to take the video then?"

"I'd probably cut off your head, so no."

I chuckle. "You said it, not me." Marcia is comically horrible at taking pictures with her phone. We haven't even attempted video yet.

"But I must look awful!" She stretches her royal blue sweatshirt over her cropped black leggings and smooths down her hair.

"You look gorgeous, but I won't post unless you approve it first."

She sighs and plucks the book off the table.

Victory. I clap. "Yay!" Once I confirm she's ready, I start filming. "Momentous moment here! Watch as Marcia places the first book on the gorgeous bookshelf we *just* put together. Go for it, Marcia!"

Marcia flashes a smile and hams it up, spinning the four-and-a-half-foot shelf for a full rotation before letting it come to a stop and carefully placing *Nothing Like the Movies* on one of the top shelves.

From behind my phone, I shout, "Woo-h—"

Thunk.

The slab of wood holding the book crashes to the ground, taking *Nothing Like the Movies* and the three shelves below with it.

I jump. Marcia gasps. We share a moment of silence while we survey the crash site. I turn off the video. "Well, that was unfortunate."

Marcia points at me with what I've come to recognize over the last seven months as mock annoyance. "*They're probably spares*, she said. *Ikea is generous that way*, she said."

"Fine. You win! They're not spares, and Ikea is the worst."

We burst into laughter.

Rocket barks, a piece of paper dropping from his mouth with wet and mutilated cartoon images of the Ikea instructions man pointing unhelpfully at black arrows and slabs of wood.

Since we've long passed our threshold for playing carpenter, we decide to shelve (pun intended) the project to revisit at an undetermined time in the future. An hour later, we're at the white circular table in our small dine-in kitchen sharing an extra-cheese pizza.

I take a bite of my second slice. "Is it me or does pizza taste better after hours of grueling labor *not* building a bookshelf?"

"Mm-hmm." Marcia dabs at her mostly uneaten first slice with a napkin, letting it soak up the grease.

"Is everything all right?" I ask.

She's been uncharacteristically quiet since putting in the order with Unregular Pizza using the Slice app I downloaded on her phone.

"Yes. I'm sorry. Just... thinking. But I'm glad you like the pizza. Brenda from the gym recommended the place." She cuts into a slice using her knife and fork and takes a bite, looking a bit like a child forced to eat his broccoli.

"Are you upset about the furniture? I might have oversold my skills. We should have paid someone in the building to do it." Rocket brushes against my leg under the table wanting food. I gently push him away.

She lowers her fork to her plate, the metal causing a clinking sound as it hits the ceramic. "I actually know someone who might be able to help us. I've been meaning to talk to you about him."

Him? Since I've lived here, I don't think a single man has gotten beyond the threshold of our apartment. After letting boys and partying affect my schoolwork when I first moved to the city, dating has now taken a back seat to pursuing my dream of becoming a librarian... like so far back, it's in another car. But Marcia's husband died ten years ago, and since she's retired from teaching, she has plenty of time on her hands. Maybe she's ready to date. "Tell me more about *him*!" I lean forward on my elbows.

"It's Adam."

My eyes widen while my arms drop to my sides. "Adam as in your grandson, Adam?" I don't know much about him except that her son kept them apart for the last decade. There are several pictures of Adam in the living room and her bedroom, including from his bar mitzvah more than ten years ago, but nothing more recent. "What did he want?"

"He's going through a tough time professionally. He just got laid off from his last position."

"I'm sorry to hear that."

Marcia must catch the note of sarcasm in my voice because she levels her eyes at me. "He apologized for letting his father come between us and insisted he does not share his views. He wants us to have a relationship."

"Well, that's great!" As if it weren't hard enough for Marcia to come out to her friends and family as bisexual in her sixties, her own son couldn't handle it and basically ejected her from his life, further punishing her by removing access to Adam.

She smiles timidly. "Rather than jumping right into yet another job, he's decided to take a short break to figure out what he really wants to do next. Since graduating from UPenn, he's been through several jobs trying to find the right fit. His father and stepmother refuse to pay for his 'vacation from life,' so I'm thinking about inviting him to stay with me for a little while. With us." She clarifies, "On the couch. If it's okay with you."

My mouth falls open, but I quickly snap it shut. Marcia's still speaking, and I want to hear her out.

"I hate to put you in an awkward position, but I'll make sure he stays out of your way. And it's not forever. It's just...I don't know him very well. My own grandson." Marcia's features collectively droop in barefaced sadness.

My heart splinters a little. "It's fine! This is your apartment. You can invite anyone you want to stay over." I mean every word, though I'm sure I'll have more feelings on the matter once I have time to digest it.

Rocket lets out three barks as if expressing his agreement. Then again, Rocket is almost always barking unless he's asleep or having his belly or ears rubbed. "Seriously. This seems like a great opportunity for you two to bond. I'm all for it," I say. I can't really blame Adam for allowing his father to keep him from Marcia when he was a boy. And I fully support him making up for lost time as a man.

Marcia blows out a breath of relief. "Thank you!"

I watch as she grabs her slice of pizza with both hands and bites into it with gusto. Thrilled to see her spirits back up, my mind wanders to my own late grandma, Nana Lena. We spent every day together for most of my life, and although we were close when I was super little...well, let's just say teenage Sabrina wouldn't win any granddaughter-of-the-year awards. I regret wasting so many opportunities to bond with her now that she's gone. I regret a lot when it comes to her. Even though I've never met Adam, I don't want him to have those same regrets with Marcia.

After dinner, Marcia goes to her room to call Adam, and when she returns, she's beaming. He's accepted her offer to move in temporarily and will be here on Wednesday. She retires for the night, and I stay in the living room to watch an episode of *Selling Sunset*. It occurs to me that once Adam moves in, I might have to watch all my shows on my laptop since the couch out here will now be his bed.

I toss the gray chunky-knit throw blanket off my lap and walk over to the leaning white ladder shelf set against the opposite wall. It's decorated with plants, glass figurines and other tchotchkes, and picture frames, including one of a teenage Adam in a navy-blue suit, powder-blue yarmulke over his brown hair and white prayer shawl draped across his narrow shoulders. The poor kid's got metal braces and a serious T-zone situation going on, but his light blue eyes pop against his outfit. He shares that feature with his grandma. The first time I saw it, I told Marcia he was adorable. In truth, he was about as adorable as the cast of *Stranger Things* after the first season, but I expect he's probably grown out of his awkward stage by now.

I return to the couch and search for "Adam Haber" on Instagram, scrolling through the results until I find what I guess is the right one. On his feed are some photos of the Philadelphia skyline, a few lake and hiking pics, a beer bottle against a setting sun, but none of him. He's in a few tagged photos, but they're either profile shots, taken from behind, or his face is hidden by sunglasses. I close out of Instagram assuming I'll find out soon enough.

While washing my face and brushing my teeth before bed, I tidy up the vanity to make room for Adam's stuff. I'm thrilled for Marcia to bond with her grandson, and if greatness runs in the family, maybe we'll become friends, but there's also a slight pinch of anxiety in my gut. Besides losing access to the couch and flat screen and sharing a bathroom with a dude, my dynamic with Marcia is bound to change. Will she have as much time for me now that her estranged grandson is back in her life? But I push aside these selfish thoughts. I've had Marcia to myself for almost seven months, but she's not my grandmother. I won't stand in the way of Adam bonding with his.

Chapter Two

Wednesday morning, I'm on the couch enjoying a cup of coffee before my shift at the library while listening to Harlan Coben and Jasmine Guillory recommend books on the third hour of the *Today* show when the doorbell rings.

As per usual, Rocket loses his mind. He vaults from the couch, where he's been snuggling at my side, and whips down the narrow foyer to the front door, jumping so high like he thinks he can climb over it into the hallway. "Be right there," I shout, hoping Adam can hear me over Rocket. I assume it's Adam since Marcia, who's in the shower, said he'd be here sometime today. For no reason whatsoever, I'd assumed she meant dinnertime. I place my mug on the coffee table and stride to the front door, gently shooing Rocket out of the way so I can let Adam in.

Instead, I cast my eyes upon some other twentysomething white guy who can't possibly be Adam because this guy is *hot*—like, I'm sure I've seen him in movie sex scenes with Margot Robbie or Zendaya *hot*. His hair, which is somewhere between medium and dark brown with hints of red, is cut above his ears in the front and a little longer in the back. His eyes, the shade of blue wheat, fall beneath full eyebrows, and a trace of stubble covers his flawless fair skin. I tear my eyes away from his face and take in the rest of him. Gone are the lanky shoulders of his early teenage years, replaced by ones that are broad without being at all Hulk-like. He's tall—although nearly *everyone* is tall compared to my measly five feet, one inch—and wearing a light-gray Henley under an unzipped black winter jacket—

"Does Marcia Haber live here?" he asks, interrupting my objectification to remind me he's a human being, and I'm acting gross. His lips twitch.

My face burns like molten lava. "She does. Are you Adam?" As difficult as it is to reconcile that this man is the grown-up version of the awkward boy in the photo frame, it's the only logical explanation for why he's standing outside my door on the day Adam is expected to arrive.

"I am. I caught an early train this morning. Are you—"

Before he can complete the sentence, Rocket dashes through my legs and out into the hallway like a trapped demon out of the opened gates of hell. "Shit. Rocket!"

Our apartment is on one far end of the hallway, and by now a barking Rocket has already reached the other end and is on his way back, most certainly to repeat the lap again and again until he wears himself out sometime next year. After sliding his dark-brown canvas messenger bag down his shoulder and placing it against the door, Adam squats. "Hey, Rocket. Come here, boy."

Rocket freezes and watches Adam, who slaps his muscular—not that I noticed—thighs in a "come hither" motion.

"Good luck with that," I mutter. There's no way.

And yet, there is. Right before my eyes, Rocket sprints over to Adam, who rubs his brown ears while Rocket licks his face. The display reminds me of those YouTube videos of soldiers returning from war and reuniting with a beloved dog for the first time in years. Except Rocket is only two and it's been much longer since Marcia's seen Adam.

Adam seamlessly guides Rocket inside the apartment, dragging his blue suitcase, one shade darker than his eyes, behind him.

I pick up his messenger bag, which feels like it's filled with boulders, and follow in awe.

We return to the living room at the same time Marcia exits her bedroom, running her fingers through her damp hair. "Did Rocket get out again?" It takes a moment for her to realize we're not alone, but when she notices Adam, her face breaks out into the hugest smile I've ever seen. And this is saying a lot because Marcia is generally a very smiley person. "Adam!"

"Hi, Grandma." Adam's almost shy as he scrapes a hand through his hair.

"Come here!" Marcia doesn't wait for him to act before heading his way and pulling him into a hug while I take the opportunity to release his heavy messenger bag from my shoulder as gracefully as I can, in case there's a twelve-piece set of fragile dinnerware in there.

Observing the two, I can practically feel how tightly Marcia is squeezing from here, her arms stretched to reach around him, but before long, Adam sinks into it and hugs back just as hard. I nearly choke up.

When they separate, Marcia gives Adam the once-over of a loving grandmother. "Look at you. You're all grown up." She shakes her head, clearly trying not to cry. She proceeds to ask him a bunch of questions without letting him answer: "How was the train? Did you find the apartment okay? Are you hungry?"

I'm about to make a quiet exit to my room to give them some privacy when Marcia says, "Have you met Sabrina yet?"

"Sort of." Adam faces me. "Hi again," he says with a teasing glint in his blue eyes.

I guess it was too much to hope he'd forget my initial reaction to seeing him, but I pretend *I* have. "Thanks for dog-whispering Rocket before."

Hearing his name, Rocket darts right over.

"Aw, he's a good boy." Adam kneels and grabs the chew toy from Rocket's mouth, gently tossing it across the room. When Rocket chases after it, he stands. "I actually am hungry. What's your plan for today, Grandma? Can I take you to breakfast? And if it's not too cold, maybe you can show me around the neighborhood after?"

Marcia's face shimmers with joy. "I'm yours all day. Breakfast sounds great, but it's on me. I have hundreds of meals to make up for."

Adam grins. "The unemployed and broke grandson cannot argue with that logic."

"It's settled then," Marcia says.

Adam turns to me. "Can you join us?"

My stomach flutters. A hot guy with manners. "I appreciate the invite, but I have work today." I look between him and Marcia. "And I wouldn't want to impose on your reunion."

Marcia beams. "We can all have dinner later. Do you have time to give Adam a quick tour of the apartment before you leave? I need to dry my hair and make myself acceptable for public viewing."

Adam and I say, "You're gorgeous!" at the same time.

Marcia rolls her eyes. "You'll get along well. You're both full of crap."

She returns to her room, and then it's just me and Adam again. "She's so excited you're here," I say.

Adam's eyes soften. "I'm excited too. We have a lot to catch up on."

My heart pulls, and I swallow hard. "Anyway... this is the living room. Obviously. The couch pulls out." I point stupidly at the TV like I'm a host on HSN. "The TV in here has Netflix, Apple TV Plus, Disney Plus, Hulu, Prime, Max, Peacock, Showtime. All the streaming you could possibly want. Except sports. Marcia doesn't have ESPN or Yes or any of those." I'm babbling. "You saw the kitchen. It's right when you walk in. Marcia's bedroom and bathroom are through the door she just entered, and mine is down there," I say, pointing toward the far end of the living room. We'll share this bathroom right here," I say, opening the door to my left.

Adam pops his head inside.

"Everything is off of the living room. Almost impossible to get lost."

Adam cocks his head, his eyes sparkling again. "Almost?"

"Enough tequila, and I'd get lost in my own bed."

"I hear you. One too many Jell-O shots and I'm..." He makes the "mind blown" gesture.

"J... Jell-O shots? Really?" I pegged him for more of a beer guy with absolutely zero basis for doing so.

"No." He laughs and sets his suitcase to the side of the couch. "Oh shit, my other bag is still in the hallway."

"I brought it in." I motion to where I left it against the wall.

He blinks. "Thank you."

The way he's gazing at me with open curiosity is unnerving, though I can't say I hate it. "What do you have in there anyway? Cement blocks?"

His lips quirk. "Something like that. My laptop and some books."

My eyebrows shoot up. "Books? You read?"

From his bemused expression, I suspect he thinks I just asked if he knows *how* to read. Before I can clarify, he says, "You're not at all how I pictured, Sabrina."

For some reason, hearing my name from his mouth sends my chest all aflutter. He looks me up and down, but I can't take offense because of how blatantly I did the same to him earlier. Also, my desperately-in-need-of-exercise body is too busy sweating under his scrutiny to multitask emotions. I'm in decent shape for the sole reason that I'm only twenty-four, as my fitness-obsessed older sister Audrina reminds me often. "No? How did you picture me?"

I try to see myself through his eyes. While he's objectively hot, my petite frame, wavy shoulder-length golden-blond hair, and big brown eyes usually place me in the "cute" category. This is fine with me, since cute requires less maintenance than hot.

"Older. *Much* older." His cheeks flush pink.

I touch my hair. "Oh. She didn't tell you how we connected?"

Adam shakes his head, so I explain.

"My grandma looks great. I didn't know she needed live-in help. What's wrong? Is she okay?" He fires off questions in rapid succession.

He's freaking out, which wasn't my intention. I instinctively lift my hand to provide physical comfort but lower it when I remember he's a stranger to me. Instead, I look him squarely in the eyes so he knows I'm being sincere. "She absolutely does not *need* live-in help. She's actually in great physical shape for someone her age. I'm here to make sure she doesn't overdo it. And I help with other stuff, like getting her more online. She had her own reasons for wanting a roommate my age, but I'll let her explain. Okay?"

He nods, his shoulders dropping in visible relief. "You mentioned work. What do you do?"

"I'm a library page while working toward my MLIS."

He nods approvingly. "Master's in library and information science. You're studying to be a librarian?"

My eyes widen. It's rare when someone knows what the acronym stands for. "I am."

"Do you love it?"

"I do. I have three more semesters including this one, but since I don't take summers off, I'll graduate in a year."

Adam sits on the edge of the couch and studies me again. "What kinds of things are you learning?"

"Be careful what you wish for. I can literally talk about libraries all day, but . . ." A glance at my phone alerts me to the time. "Can we continue this later? If I have any shot at getting to work on time, I need to go."

Adam winces. "Of course. Sorry to keep you."

"No worries! It's great to meet you and I'm looking forward to being your roomie."

Adam smiles slowly. "Same."

With a loud "Bye, Marcia!" I grin at Adam once more, grab my coat and bag, and head out.

Chapter Three

It's two hours into my workday at the library, and I'm placing returned books back on the shelves while briefing my co-worker and friend, Gabriel, on Adam. Gabe is the adult services librarian, but it's a slow day, and no adults are currently seeking his services.

"And it was full of books!" I say, referring to Adam's heavy messenger bag. "He even knew what an MLIS was without me having to tell him."

Gabe scratches the brown skin along his jaw. "I'm confused. Is Adam here to reconnect with this grandma, or is this some freak reality dating show where seniors set up their grandchildren with their roommates?"

"I don't know what you're talking about," I say, hiding my burning face with a large-print version of *Reminders of Him* by Colleen Hoover.

Gabe lowers the book. "*He was so good with Rocket! His bag looked so light when it was draped casually on his shoulder but nearly pulled* my *arm out of the socket!*" His russet-brown eyes twinkle.

I lean against the bookshelf and cross my arms over my chest. "Was that supposed to be me?"

"It was. I'm just missing the moonbeams shooting out of my eyes." He laughs.

"Stop." The plea is halfhearted, since he has a point. It kind of sucks that the first guy I've been attracted to in a while is my roommate's grandson and therefore off-limits.

Gabe gestures toward the circulation desk, where Lane is waving us over, and motions for me to follow.

I hesitate. The library cart is full, and when I'm finished returning books, I have a list of ones on hold to pull. Still, I follow Gabe, dragging the cart with me to appear productive in case Jenny, our branch manager, is walking the floor.

Lane, one of the circulation clerks, looks bored out of their mind behind the semicircular desk and brightens when they see us. "The place is dead today. Talk to me. Please."

"Sabrina has the hots for her new roommate." Gabe gives them the SparkNotes version of our prior conversation.

Lane's hazel eyes light up, and they lean over the desk in interest. "Show me some pics."

"I would, but his presence on IG is basically nonexistent," I say.

Lane and Gabe exchange grins.

"Checking out his social media? You're such a creeper, Finkelstein," Gabe says.

I put my hands on my hips. "I wasn't creeping. I was just curious what he looked like, so I checked his socials."

"And what *does* he look like?" Gabe asks.

"He's a cross between Dylan Sprayberry and Kevin Zegers."

"You're not helping your case," Lane says, scratching their shaved head.

Gabe chuckles.

I scrub a hand over my face. "Please stop. It doesn't matter how hot he is. Nothing's going to happen between me and Adam. He's here for Marcia, not me."

"Marcia's the roommate you met on that app, right?" Lane asks.

"That's her," I say, happy for the change of subject.

Gabe smirks. "With her strapping young grandson around to flip her mattress, show her Snapchat filters, and be her emergency contact, she might not need you anymore."

"Wait. What?" Lane looks confused, but then understanding washes over their face. "*Riiiight.* You're supposed to help her out in exchange for cheaper rent." They clench their teeth. "Gabe has a point."

My stomach hardens. "Give it a rest. Adam is only here temporarily to mend his relationship with Marcia. It has nothing to do with my housing situation." My phone flashes with a calendar reminder to start working on my application for a school scholarship that's due next month, but I dismiss it. It's not like I can work on it from here anyway.

"It always starts out temporary. I know someone who moved back in with her parents 'temporarily' after college to save enough for three months' rent. Six years later, she's still there. And she's a lawyer now!" Gabe raises an eyebrow.

The more-empathetic Lane smiles softly at me. "I'm sure Adam will be long gone before six years."

"But just in case, my friend Brandon's roommate just moved out if you're interested. Real cheap. As long as you're okay with the bathtub in the kitchen."

I tuck my phone back in my pocket. "Thanks for this heartfelt pep talk, *friends*. I'll be off now."

"We're just teasing." Gabe's eyes crinkle in the corners.

A patron approaches Gabe to ask for thriller recommendations featuring septuagenarian main characters at the same time Lane's phone rings. After providing my own recommendation, I leave my colleagues to their work and drag my library cart back to the fiction section.

I aggressively push *Love and Other Words* by Christina Lauren between *Josh and Hazel's Guide to Not Dating* and *My Favorite Half-Night Stand*, but Sita, the other page, packed the books so tightly, there isn't enough room. Cursing to myself, I remove half the books from this shelf and the one above it, rearranging everything and leaving some breathing room for future me.

I twirl a lock of hair around my finger. As much as I hate to admit it, Gabe has a point. Marcia might not need to rely on me as much while Adam is here. But I know she wouldn't kick me out because of it. Our arrangement *began* because of what I could do for her in exchange for lower rent, but it's evolved into a real friendship.

As if the universe knows I'm desperate for validation, my phone pings with a text from Marcia.

> **Marcia:** Hi Sabrina. I hope you're having a good day at work. I'm making dinner and thought it would be a nice time for the three of us to spend together. Are you free? Marcia.

I recall what Adam said about wanting to learn more about my library program and smile to myself. I only talked to him for a few minutes, but I *liked* him. Was there *also* a physical attraction? Yes, but it's not my fault he had a major glow-up since his bar mitzvah. It doesn't mean I'm looking at this temporary living arrangement as some sort of dating setup. *Gabe*. I roll my eyes. But I also don't think Adam's a threat to my relationship with Marcia. Whatever connection we'll form will fall somewhere in between those parameters, and I'm looking forward to it, which is exactly what I write when I text Marcia back about dinner.

Chapter Four

The apartment smells like a steak house when I get home, and my stomach rumbles with hunger. Marcia and Adam are at the table playing cards with old rock music playing softly in the background from Adam's phone. They greet me with smiles when I join them.

"How much has she taken you for so far?" I ask Adam before draping my bag over the arm of a free chair and sitting down.

He grins. "Three hugs and one hair tousle."

I laugh. "You're getting off easy. I lost an entire box of Ferrero Roche chocolates once."

"I've got a great poker face." Marcia flips her hair and grins playfully. "How was work?"

I shrug noncommittally. I can't very well tell them about my conversation with Gabe and Lane. "It was fine. I was glad to have your recommendation of *The Thursday Murder Club* when I helped a patron today. What did you guys do?"

Marcia's cheeks glow with happiness. "We spent an hour in Academy Records and had lunch at the Grey Dog. It was a perfect day." She stands, using her hands to push off the chair. "The roast beef is in the oven. I should get started with the side dishes." She looks between us. "Mashed potatoes and asparagus okay with you?"

"Sounds great, Grams."

"I agree. I'm excited!"

I typically eat dinner with Marcia only a couple times a week, and it's rarely a large meal like this. The effort tonight is clearly because of Adam. Cooking is a Jewish grandmother's love language. Nana Lena cooked almost all our meals when I was growing up because my mother worked full-time. I took it for granted, but what I wouldn't do now for one more serving of her famous sweet-and-sour chicken and meatballs fricassee. I feel the familiar pang of regret and put on a happy face. "Do you need any help?"

"Nope," Marcia says with her head in the refrigerator before bringing a bunch of asparagus and a cutting board to the small island. "In fact, why don't you two go out for a bit? Dinner will be ready in about an hour and a half."

"If you're sure." I look at Adam. "Do you want to take a walk with Rocket? I can show you the dog park." I note the absence of barking, which means only one thing. "He's sleeping?"

Adam nods. "Yeah. But I could go for a walk."

We stand at the same time, and when our arms accidentally brush, I can feel the heat of his skin on mine. I pick up notes of grapefruit wafting from his body. Whatever it is will probably join my Lush Rose Jam body wash in the shower by this time tomorrow. My body flushes with warmth at the thought of Adam in my shower. *Our* shower.

"I just need a minute to drop my bag in my room." I bolt to the bathroom first, cursing at my red cheeks in the mirror, then race to my bedroom, dropping my bag on the floor and flopping backward on my bed.

My bedroom isn't huge, but there's decent closet space, and it's big enough to fit my double bed, pale green eight-drawer dresser, and small white corner desk and chair without being too cramped. The walls were originally painted a neutral beige, which made sense for a guest room, but they're now a very soft pink that's just slightly feminine without feeling like a child's bedroom.

When I'm confident the excess color has left my face, I enter the living room and do a double take. *Nothing Like the Movies* greets me from the top shelf of the revolving bookshelf. Adam and Marcia were out for most of the day, which means he accomplished in a short time what I'd failed to help Marcia do in an entire afternoon. I hear Gabe's voice in my head again. *She won't need you anymore.*

Adam appears at my side. "Most of the work was done already," he says, making me question if he can read my thoughts.

I turn to him. "Thanks for finishing it." And I mean it. What's important is not that Adam swooped in and completed what I couldn't, but that the bookshelf is finished and stable. Besides, Adam is a guest, unlike me, who lives here permanently. If helping his grandma out around the house makes him feel useful and takes the responsibility temporarily off of my shoulders, what's there to complain about? I relax a fraction.

His eyes travel around my face. "I hope you don't mind. I don't want you to think I'm coming in and taking over all your projects."

I suck in a breath. How did he know I needed to hear those exact words? My body loosens up the rest of the way. "I was doing a crap job of it, so I definitely don't mind."

He gives it a spin. "Do you know what books you're going to fill it with?"

I grin. "I do." I also know exactly where I'm taking him on our walk.

When we hit Broadway, Adam points to his left. "Mount Sinai?"

I give him side-eye. "You think I'm taking you to a hospital?"

He pulls the hood of his black jacket over his head. "I just met you, Sabrina. Maybe you're fascinated by them. A *Grey's Anatomy* enthusiast. But fine. No hospital."

I refused to tell him where we were going when we left the apartment, just that it wasn't far. His earlier guesses included Whole Foods and a Capital One bank. Either he's joking or has zero confidence in my tour-guide abilities.

He slows his pace as we approach the corner of Twelfth and Broadway. "The Strand."

"Ding ding ding!"

He stares up at the red awning and the historic loft-style building where the iconic bookshop is housed. "Can we go in?"

"We sure can. But all these books here?" I gesture at the carts on the sidewalk outside the entrance. "They're discounted." Since my budget doesn't align with my reading addiction, I take most of my books out from the library, but sometimes I get lucky here.

I shiver when a blast of February wind slaps against my face, making me wish I hadn't left my itchy but warm scarf at home. My black puffer coat and matching purple knit hat and gloves aren't cutting it today.

"Bargain books can wait. It's cold." Adam angles his head toward the entrance. "Let's go in."

Inside, it's packed as usual. Customers hover around the "best of the best" and "modern classic" display tables, and a line ten people deep waits for the register. I observe Adam as he takes it all in with a look of wonder. I can't hold back a smile. I *knew* the Strand was the right call.

His fingers brush the books on the table in front of us. "I don't even know where to start."

"There's no right or wrong way. I usually go straight to young adult on the second floor." I point to the staircase to our left.

"Graphic novels are there too. And romance. I think the top floor is where the old and rare books are. I never go there unless there's an event," I admit with a sheepish shrug.

Adam's lips quirk. "Do they test you on the layout of famous bookstores in school?"

I giggle. "Don't I wish! That is research I'd happily do." We both step back in opposite directions to let someone pass... three someones. Once there's a break in traffic, I say, "Go wander," immediately worrying it came across like I'm trying to ditch him. I'm not. But I also don't want to assume he wants to hang out with me here. It's not like this is a date, and I've known the guy for less than twenty-four hours.

"Okay. I'll come find you in young adult in a little bit."

"Should we exchange numbers?" I ask at the same time he says, "Maybe I should get your number."

"Great minds! We can definitely get lost in this place," I say.

"For sure. Even without tequila," he deadpans.

"Or Jell-O shots."

We exchange grins and phones. I put my number under Sabrina Finkelstein in case I'm not the only Sabrina in his address book. He returns my phone open to his contact—Adam. Not Adam Haber, just Adam... like it didn't even occur to him he wouldn't be the first. On someone else, it might strike me as presumptuous and cocky, but those are not the vibes I get from Adam.

We part ways and he heads toward the back while I trudge upstairs to the second floor. I spend some time touching the spines of books I've read and reread in the young adult section and then, feeling nostalgic, I segue to the children's section and do the same.

His grapefruit scent gives him away first. I look up from my book just as he says, "What are you reading?"

I show him the book I'm holding: *Betsy's Little Star*. I'm already a quarter into it. "That was fast."

Adam's eyebrows crinkle. "It's been almost forty minutes."

"It hasn't." I check my phone. "It has!"

He gestures to the book. "Interesting choice."

"It was one of my favorites when I was little. My grandma introduced me to it."

"Are you close?"

"We were." I swallow hard. "She died about six years ago."

He sighs deeply. "I'm sorry."

"She's the reason I fell in love with reading and wanted to be a librarian. She'd take me to the library every weekend and I'd pick up one or two books for the week that we'd read together." Besides *Betsy's Little Star* by Carolyn Haywood, she introduced me to the Ginnie and Geneva series by Catherine Woolley and the All-of-a-Kind Family series by Sydney Taylor. These were classic books I read over and over again as a little girl. I've thought about Nana Lena so much over the last few days, which I'm sure is because of Adam and Marcia's reunion.

"You must miss her."

I drop my gaze to the wood-paneled floor. Adam doesn't want to hear my sob story—that I ruined my special relationship with my grandma by spending the last few years of her life holding her accountable for the actions of my deadbeat father—and I definitely don't want to tell it, so I quickly change the subject. "I've heard all good things," I say about the book in Adam's hand: *The Midnight Library*.

"You haven't read it?"

I shake my head. "I mostly read young adult."

He gazes at me with focus. "Any particular reason?"

"I could say it's because I want to be a youth librarian and need to keep on top of new releases in the genre, but it's also because I really enjoy them." I lift my chin and hold eye contact, almost daring him to judge me.

He nods. "Cool. Maybe you can recommend one to me."

"I'd be delighted to! Maybe we can read one at the same time, like a buddy read." I cringe. Talk about coming on too strong. As if Adam has nothing better to do than start a book club with me.

"I'd be down for that."

"You would?" My eyes must be the size of silver dollars.

He grins. "Sure. Maybe my grams will want in too."

"Yes! Let's definitely ask Marcia."

Since dinner will be ready soon, we head downstairs. The line is short enough for Adam to buy *The Midnight Library.*

"Did you know that Patti Smith worked at the Strand?" Adam asks on our walk back.

"Is she a friend of yours?"

Adam freezes, causing a collision with the pedestrian behind us. He apologizes and we resume walking. "Are you serious? You don't know who Patti Smith is?"

"She's in a Taylor Swift song, right?" I stuff my hands in the pockets of my coat.

He sighs. "Oh, Sabrina. You didn't just say that."

I chuckle. "But I did." I suspect I'm supposed to be embarrassed and possibly ashamed by my ignorance, but I'm mostly humored by Adam's reaction.

We stop at the light on University and Fourteenth, and Adam gently nudges his hip against mine. "You have so much to learn about music. It's a good thing I'm here."

As the light changes and we cross the street toward the apartment, I hope he can't see the goofy smile on my face.

Chapter Five

We get home right as dinner is ready. I set the table, and a few minutes later we're at the circular kitchen table enjoying a home-cooked meal of roast beef, mashed potatoes, and white asparagus.

Across from me, Marcia takes a sip from a glass of red wine. "Did you see Adam finished putting together the bookshelf?"

I swing my gaze to the right and meet Adam's eyes for a beat. "I did." My feminist side is still bummed that our combined efforts weren't enough, but my lazy side is happy it's done. "We should post an updated video."

"Did you upload the original one?" Marcia blinks slowly. "I don't think I've ever used 'upload' in a sentence before."

Adam glances between us, his fork with a bite-sized piece of medium-rare roast beef an inch from his mouth. "What did I miss? What video?"

"I captured Marcia placing the first book on the shelf for my Insta. Or rather, I *tried* to, but then the shelf came crashing down with the book on it." I open my phone to the camera roll and play the video for Adam.

As he watches, I hear my own voice saying, "Momentous moment here" and cringe. My voice sounds completely normal to me as I'm speaking, but on video it's so husky, almost crackling. It takes me by surprise every time.

"I didn't share it," I tell Marcia. "But if we film again, I can post them simultaneously. First as a fail and then as a success."

Adam glances between us. "You guys do this often? Post videos on Instagram?"

Marcia waves her fork. "Sabrina does. I just act in them."

Adam gawks. "Act?"

I shrug. "I get more likes when I post something with Marcia than I do solo."

"Young people are fascinated by anyone over sixty. They think we're 'cute.'" Marcia rolls her eyes.

"They like you because you're a breath of fresh air," I say, quoting a comment I got on my last Marcia video word for word.

Adam studies me. "Are you an influencer or something?"

I throw my head back and laugh. "Not even close. I have less than a thousand followers." I laugh again. "My close friend Carley is though. Well, she's technically a theatrical makeup artist, but she's taken her expertise to TikTok and Instagram and taught me some tricks to at least make my grid more appealing."

I met Carley at summer camp when we were thirteen, but we lost touch. We ran into each other at Trader Joe's a few months after I moved to the city, and our friendship continued where we left off, as if the ten years we hadn't seen each other had never happened. I'm so grateful we did, since New York can be a lonely city of eight million.

"How is Carley?" Marcia asks.

"She got her first off-Broadway show!" She's only worked off-off-Broadway until now, and I'm so proud of her.

Marcia raises her glass. "Cheers to her! Soon she'll be on Broadway using Patti LuPone for her old-lady makeup tutorials and won't need me anymore."

Adam's eyes bug out. "This just keeps getting more and more interesting. What is this about makeup tutorials?"

I clamp my lips together to repress a laugh. The look of absolute bewilderment on Adam's face right now is adorable. "Carley does makeup videos where she gives advice on how to apply certain makeup techniques depending on your age. She uses Marcia sometimes for boomers." I smile fondly at my roommate. "The one on how to make blue eyes pop got close to ten thousand likes!" I turn to Adam. "Marcia was the model for that one too."

Adam shakes his head again. "My grandma, the model."

Marcia snorts. "Yes, the scouts for *Vogue* AARP edition will be knocking on my door any minute now."

Adam's own blue eyes twinkle. "You two seem to have a lot of fun together. Sabrina told me how you found each other, but I still don't know why you were on that app in the first place. You dodged my questions all day."

Marcia purses her lips. "I did not *dodge* your questions. I was just more interested in hearing about *you*."

I sit up straighter, wishing I too had heard about Adam. All I know so far is that he's currently out of a job and that he likes to read. *Fine, Gabe. I also know that he's hot.*

"And I caught you up. Now it's your turn," he says.

Marcia places her napkin on her plate. "After your grandfather died, I lived alone for several years, but I was lonely. I thought a roommate would be fun. Like a mini-*Golden Girls*, only in New York."

"If you were Blanche, I'd rather not hear the stories," Adam says.

I press a fist to my mouth.

Marcia rolls her lips. "What stories? The tales from all the times

I suggested going out, and Linda said no? She was sixty-eight going on a hundred. All she did was eat, shit, and sleep, and she was healthy as kale! She started almost every sentence with, 'When you get to be our age,' this happens and that happens." She scoffs. "Speak for yourself. I'm not dead yet." Marcia sighs dejectedly. "When the year was over, I told her that I didn't want to renew her lease. Extra money is nice, but not if it comes with all that negativity. And then one morning, I was watching the *Today* show and saw the segment on multigenerational roommates."

"We were watching it at the same time. Kismet." I beam.

"*Beshert.*" Marcia smiles at me affectionately. "It gave me the idea to have a younger roommate this time. Someone to infuse more light in my life. And so I asked my neighbor to help me download the app." She grins. "I've used *upload*, *download*, and *app* in the same thirty minutes. What is happening to me?"

"You're practically a woman in STEM," I say.

Adam chokes on his drink.

I make an innocent face at him. "What?"

"Anyway, I completed my profile and heard from Sabrina within twenty-four hours."

I take over from here. "My roommates partied constantly, but I didn't want to do a complete one-eighty and live with someone like Linda. Marcia's profile was so high-energy compared to the others I read." I knew immedately she was "the one" and recall my heart fluttering as I shot off a response, praying no one had beaten me to it. "Most of the other ads were for people in their eighties or nineties. I wasn't sure what Marcia would even want from me in exchange for the lower rent."

"I wondered about that too. You seem incredibily independent," Adam says.

"Because I am! My doctors encourage my active lifestyle, but they also caution me to listen to my body and not push it because of my high blood pressure and the fact that I'm on the dark side of seventy." She blows out a breath. "Sabrina picks up the slack of the more physical activities and, more importantly in my opinion, helps me keep up in the digital era. She set me up with reminders to take my pills so I don't need to stick notes to the refrigerator! And I'm up on pop culture thanks to her. We even listen to Taylor Rodrigo."

Adam says, "I think you mean Taylor Swift. Or Olivia Rodrigo?"

Marcia raises her palms. "See?" She winks.

Adam narrows his eyes. "You were joking?"

"Give her some credit." I chuckle.

"Like I told Linda: I'm seventy-two. I'm not dead."

Adam snorts.

"I'm not the only one doing the educating." I tell Adam how Marcia got me hooked on the Rolling Stones, Aerosmith, and early Genesis. "She's a wealth of information about classic rock."

"Now I know where my good taste in music comes from. Dad's karaoke go-to songs are 'Never Gonna Give You Up' and 'Wannabe.' " Adam curls his lip.

"Spice Girls? That one's so catchy." I clear my throat and sing, "*If you wanna be—*"

"Please stop." He shudders.

I whisper-sing the next line, only stopping when Adam sticks his fingers in his ears. I don't know the rest of the lyrics anyway.

"How *is* your dad?" Marcia focuses on cutting the long spear of asparagus on her plate into tiny child-safe pieces in an obvious and failed attempt to pretend she's not at all invested in the answer. It's heartbreaking.

Adam refills his wine. "Still an uptight son of a bitch."

"Did you just call me a bitch?" His grandmother raises an eyebrow, even as her lips twitch.

"Sorry!" He grimaces. "I didn't mean it literally. But he *is* uptight. You disagree?"

"No..." She laughs. "But he's your father."

"Whatever."

Marcia's face clouds over, and it breaks my heart. To finally make the choice to be her true self after decades of withholding a huge part of herself, only to be rejected by her own son, the person she brought into this world and loved unconditionally. A pain like that never goes away. Even though she knows this is a Jeffrey problem and not a Marcia problem—just as I know that Audrina and I are not to blame for our dad's abandonment—it must still hurt.

The room is only silent for a few seconds, but it feels longer, so I swerve the conversation back to music. "Do you know who Patti Smith is, Marcia?"

Marcia looks at me like I'm an alien from Jupiter.

Adam groans. "This ends now." He opens his phone to his music app, and within seconds, familiar music fills the air. "Have you ever heard this song?"

"Only hundreds of times." I have the urge to bop my head. *Because the Night*. "This is Patti Smith?"

"Ding ding ding." Adam does a perfect imitation of me after he guessed we were going to the Strand. "Although many bands have covered it."

I duck my head, duly embarrassed, before changing the subject. "Dinner was delicious, as always."

Adam swallows the last bit of food on his plate and leans back in his chair. "I agree. Will you make your potato pierogies while I'm here, Grams? I haven't had them in ten years."

Marcia beams. "It will be my pleasure!"

"And please make extra for me!" I say.

Adam turns to me. "Do you cook?"

To avoid incriminating myself or lying, I counter with, "Do you?"

"No."

"Me neither."

This earns a well-deserved chuckle from Marcia, who stacks some dirty dishes and walks them over to the sink.

"My last attempt was congee, which ended up in the garbage, and the time before that..." I can't remember. "What disaster came before the congee?"

"Honey-glazed salmon," Marcia says, returning to the table.

"Oh yes. The glaze cooked at a much faster rate than the salmon. It was a disaster." I shrug sheepishly.

"Nonsense. You made salmon tartare with a lovely burnt-honey sauce."

As she brings more dirty dishes to the sink, I turn to Adam. "Your grandmother is too kind."

Adam looks over his shoulder at Marcia, still at the sink. "Relax, Grams. Come sit."

I scoot my chair back and stand. "I'll handle the cleanup from here."

Marcia sits, and while I finish clearing the dishes, Adam returns the butter and horseradish containers to the refrigerator. "Do you have family in the area?" he asks me.

"My mom and sister live in Connecticut."

"Why Manhattan then?"

"Because it's the best city in the world. You'll find out soon enough." I empty the contents of a plate into the garbage can. "I considered Boston, but my school has a great library science program. Library jobs are hard to come by, and I secured mine before I moved. I've also made new friends here." Thinking of Carley, I add, "And reconnected with old ones. Given how expensive this city is, I'm so grateful I don't have to share a pea-size room with fourteen roommates." I toss a fond glance at Marcia.

She laughs. "Yes. Sabrina showed me some of the roommate ads for apartments here. I can't believe people live that way," she says before excusing herself to the bathroom.

Adam sits back down. "Your mom and sister though—do you miss them?"

"I see them on holidays and live close enough to make spontaneous trips if I'm homesick."

My mom climbed her way up the corporate ladder of a pharmaceutical company and was always working when I was younger, leaving me and Audrina in the care of Nana Lena and Grandpa Lou. She had no choice, since my dad was a deadbeat and someone needed to put food on the table and keep me and Audrina clothed in the latest trends and up-to-date with the newest phone, but it's hard to miss something I never had. And as much as I love my sister, we're so different—she's all about exercise and fashion and I'm into books and pop culture. Small doses work best for us.

I'm about to ask Adam about his friends' reaction to his temporary relocation from Philadelphia, but Marcia rejoins us and changes the subject to Adam's and my respective plans for the night.

"Homework for me." A master's in library science involves a lot of reading. I also have to choose the subject of my young adult author study due next week.

"What about you, Adam? Going to explore the city more?"

Adam covers his mouth and yawns. "Not tonight. I'm too old. When you get to be my age..." He grins.

Marcia wags her finger at him. "I never want to hear that phrase again. Consider this your warning."

Adam laughs. "Understood. I'm going to stay home and relax tonight. I've been wanting to watch *One of Us Is Lying*, although I doubt it's as good as the book."

"It's not," I confirm. "But it's worth watching."

He exhales audibly. "The book is always better."

"Agreed!" I beam at him.

"Netflix and chill. Great idea," Marcia says.

I choke on a laugh, assuming she hadn't meant to encourage her grandson to have casual sex in her living room. Adam and I share a knowing smile across the table. The bonding moment hits me below the waist, and I might be the first person in history to speculate if her roommate's grandson has chest hair under his Henley.

"I need a break from Jeffrey's constant nagging to figure out my life," he says.

Marcia frowns and kisses the top of his head. "My poor boy. Take all the time you need."

"You're a lifesaver, Grams."

While I run the dishwasher and scrub the soiled pots and pans, Adam helps finish clearing the table. Marcia lingers in the kitchen and watches Adam as if she's afraid he'll disappear in a poof of dust.

I stop what I'm doing to observe them hug again. Marcia's eyes are closed, and a soft smile plays on her lips. Her joy at being reunited with Adam couldn't be more obvious if she screamed it out the window. I'm truly happy for both of them, which is why I'm taken aback by the sudden desire to flee the room and cry into my pillow. When they break apart and catch me watching, I straighten my back and smile despite feeling like a third wheel in their sweet reunion.

Chapter Six

When my alarm goes off almost a week later, I press snooze with a groan. Tuesdays are rough because I have a shift at the library followed by both of my classes in the afternoon and evening. I lie flat on my back with my arms over my head and my legs stretched out. My eyes are closed, but it's no use. Even if I could fall back asleep, the nine extra minutes will haunt me later when I'm running late and missing every single light on my walk to work. Because that's how it goes; if I get stuck at one red light, they're *all* red lights from then on unless I'm willing to sprint across half a city block to get ahead of it. Usually, I'm too lazy.

I drag my miserable ass out of bed and into the living room. The couch is open and the sleeper bed is unmade, but there's no Adam-shaped blob under the covers. I don't know how late he usually sleeps, but he's always still dead to the world, all cozy and tucked under a blanket when I leave for work. Before my brain has the chance to contemplate his current whereabouts, I step into the bathroom and bang right into his back. The first thing I feel is cool wet skin and muscle against my palms. My tired brown eyes meet Adam's alert light-blue ones through the bathroom mirror. And just like that, I'm wide awake. And mortified. "Oh my God. I didn't mean...I didn't see you there." My hands are still on his bare back. I drop them like they're on fire.

"You're fine." Adam turns around so we're face-to-face.

I suck in a breath. The bathroom we share is not big—more spacious than an airplane bathroom, but much smaller than Marcia's en suite. Between the toilet, blue single-sink pearl-granite vanity, and glass-door standing shower, there's enough room for one person, but two is cutting it close. Real close. Adam can probably see the line of sweat forming on my forehead. It's easy to avoid continued eye contact since he's so much taller than me, but it leaves me staring at his torso.

I take in the light dusting of dark hair on the top of his chest, the smooth skin below, and the happy trail beginning at his belly button and leading under the towel...*my* towel. I consider telling him he got the short end of the stick, since the cheap blue and pink towels in the closet are mine and the bougie, fluffy white and green ones are Marcia's. But it's not a big deal. The idea of us sharing the same towel is kind of hot. Heat pools below my belly. Kind of ironic that I need a cold shower because he just took a hot one.

"Do you need to use the bathroom?" He's so close I can smell the mint from his toothpaste.

I try not to look at his bare triceps, but that leaves my view open to most of his other parts, which are equally naked. "Um...Yes."

He either has no idea what effect his almost-naked body is having on me or he's a very good actor. "I didn't want to change in the open living room, but it's so hot and steamy in here so I left the door half open to let the air in."

I nod stupidly. It's definitely hot and steamy in here.

He frowns. "I should have checked with you before showering. I don't usually get up this early, but I have plans today. Are you in a hurry? I'll just be a few more minutes."

"It's okay. Take your time." My voice comes out breathy. I want to ask what plans he has *so* bad.

I realize I've been staring and rub the back of my neck. "Just give me a shout when you're done."

I return to my room and flop back on the bed, awash with need to be touched by someone other than myself. My relationship history consists of two steady boyfriends, one in high school and the other in college. Both ended mutually and amicably at graduation. Since then, I've only had a handful of first dates and hookups, the most recent with a guy I met at a Halloween party four months ago. He was dressed up as Sherlock Holmes and I was Nancy Drew. With tequila-induced optimism, I'd hoped we'd bond over iconic detectives in literature. The only mystery we solved together was just how awkward the morning after a drunken hookup can be... *excruciatingly*. When I left his place in the morning, he called me Serena and wished me the best of luck in my nursing program. I'm in no hurry to do that again, but I'm also in no rush to settle down with boyfriend number three. Which leaves me a horny single girl living with a delectable and extremely well-built, book-loving, age-appropriate man... who happens to be my roommate's grandson.

Other than my inconvenient crush, it's been an easy transition so far. The modest apartment is more crowded now and I'm not fully comfortable with the new dynamic yet, but I have no complaints about Adam. He doesn't leave the television on too loud after I've gone to sleep at night, and I don't feel like I'm not allowed in the living room during the day. I try to be equally considerate by blow-drying my hair in my room with the door closed and not banging around in the kitchen when I make my coffee in the morning. Rocket, who must be asleep on Marcia's bed now, has one more human who worships him, and it's mutual. And Marcia is still in heaven enjoying her renewed relationship with Adam.

I try to give them space to bond one-on-one. I'm not home much anyway during the day, so it's only in the evenings when we're all together—except for one night when I went out with Carley, a couple where he was out, probably exploring, and one when the two of them went out to dinner without me. I don't feel like a third wheel too much, but when I do, I remind myself that Marcia missed out on so much of Adam's life when he was a teenager. She deserves this quality time with him now.

Adam calls out, "All yours!"

I quickly undress, putting on my rarely used soft pink bathrobe to guard against another encounter, this time with *me* half naked, and head back to the bathroom.

Adam's sitting on the now-closed couch but looks up from his phone when I exit my room. He looks up at me. "I hope I didn't make you late. Next time I get up early, I'll check with you first."

I wave him off. "I'm not too behind schedule yet, so it's fine." Since he's now fully dressed in dark blue jeans and a black T-shirt, I can make eye contact without fear of bursting into flames. I take a closer look at his shirt and do a double take. In the center is a black-and-white screen-printed image of a woman with the name *Patti* in script underneath. "Is that Patti Smith?"

Adam's lips curl up on the sides. "Yu*p*."

"Are you wearing it for my benefit?"

"Yu*p*." He laughs.

I shake my head. "Don't forget to get me that list." Adam surprised me by actually following up on my proposed young adult book club, so I asked for the titles of some of the adult books he's read and enjoyed lately to try to get a sense of his taste.

"Will do." His gaze drops to my chest and back up quickly, a flush now painting his cheeks.

I look down at the exposed skin on my chest where my robe is just barely hiding my tits. I quickly pull the corners tighter against my body. "I should..." I swallow. "Get ready." I step inside the bathroom and close the door behind me. A quick check in the mirror confirms that my blush matches his.

The living room is empty when I get out of the shower, and thirty minutes later, I'm ready to leave for work. I pass the kitchen and call out a quick bye but freeze at the sight of Adam standing on a step stool, changing a bulb in the ceiling light. Rocket jumps up and barks repeatedly like it's a game while Marcia leans against the counter in her pajamas, watching her grandson with a cup of coffee in her hand.

"You heading out?" she asks.

"Yeah." The word comes out at half the volume of my normal voice. Changing that bulb was one of the first things I did for Marcia because her doctor discouraged her from climbing ladders to reach high spaces if she doesn't need to. And she didn't because I was there. But now Adam is here too.

Adam turns to face me and his eyes light up. "Have a great day."

I manage a smile, thanking him and saying it back, while reminding myself that two people making Marcia's life easier is better than one.

Chapter Seven

"That was so good," I say to Marcia as we join the crowd exiting the AMC Village 7 movie theater the following Sunday afternoon. I'd been dying to see the new Henry Golding and Selena Gomez rom-com, which was only in theaters. Marcia and I were just putzing around the apartment, so I asked if she wanted to see it with me for a girls' day out, and she happily accepted. "Did you love it?"

Marcia grins, tossing her empty bag of popcorn and small Coke Zero cup into the trash can. "It was cute. Nothing tops the trifecta of *When Harry Met Sally*, *Sleepless in Seattle*, and *You've Got Mail*, but I'm still glad rom-coms are making a comeback."

"The grand gesture gets me every time. I don't know anyone in real life who has been the giver or receiver of one, but the fantasy lives on! Especially when it involves one of the characters racing somewhere to surprise the other and declare their love." I throw a hand to my heart. "Swoon!"

We wordlessly head to our apartment—me making an effort to walk at Marcia's slower pace—but I place a hand on her arm and stop us both in our tracks. "Are you full from the popcorn, or do you want to get some ice cream?" I'm not quite ready to go home yet. It's Sunday, which means tomorrow is Monday, and even though I love my job and even my classes, I like the weekends more, when my time is my own.

Marcia twists her face in contemplation. "Sweets are a different part of my stomach than salt, so let's do it."

"I love your logic! How about Van Leeuwen? Their vegan mint chocolate chip is amazing, and we'll feel less guilty."

"I won't feel guilty anyway, but I like *your* logic!"

A few minutes later, we're sitting across from each other at a table in the back of Van Leeuwen, both eating two scoops of cookies and cream—neither of them vegan—and gushing over Henry Golding.

"He's exceptionally good looking," I say.

Across the table from me, Marcia nods. "Cheeks sculpted from glass. Abs too." Her grin morphs into a grimace. "I'm glad Adam isn't here to witness this conversation. Aren't they the same age?"

I do a quick search for Henry on my phone. "He's thirty-eight. Way older than Adam. You're safe!"

Marcia spoons ice cream into her mouth. "Still younger than my son."

I wave my plastic spoon. "Age-gap romances are on trend. And no one would bat an eye if you were a man. Fuck the patriarchy!"

Marcia chuckles. "Isn't that the truth!" She swings her head from side to side, taking in the crowded shop and the hordes of people outside walking along East Seventh Street. "This was a great idea. Much better than being cooped up at home."

I rub my lips together. "Do you think Adam will be insulted we didn't invite him?" When he moved in, I worried that I would lose out on time alone with Marcia and am glad that's not the case. But even on his first day, he invited me to join them for breakfast. He wasn't home when we left, but we could have texted him to meet us.

"He's out exploring. Did you know he's been doing that for a few hours almost every day since he's been here? He has no fear! Just jumps on the subway and takes off to parts unknown." She beams.

I repress a giggle. Adam's a grown man, and Marcia's proud of his independence like he's a teenager. My stomach dips at the reminder that she didn't get to see this transition firsthand. I spoon the last bit of ice cream into my mouth and slump against the back of my plastic yellow chair with a groan. "Why do weekends go by so fast?"

Marcia shrugs. "Sundays are like every other day when you're retired."

I huff a breath out my nose. "Show-off!"

She grins. "I'd rather be young again, but this retirement thing is a nice perk." She glances out the window again and back to me. "Shall we?"

I agree, and less than a minute later we're on our way out the door. "Let's take a picture first."

I wait for Marcia to smooth down her hair and refresh her lipstick. When she's ready, I position us next to the giant ice cream cone hanging from the entrance and take a selfie that I post in my IG stories with the caption, "Rom-com and ice cream date with my roomie." At the last minute, I add Taylor Swift's "It's Nice to Have a Friend" as background music.

On the next block, I check my notifications and a tingle rushes through me.

Marcia bumps against me and looks over my shoulder with her eyebrows raised. "What are you smiling about?"

"Just getting lots of likes on our picture." I shove my phone in my jacket pocket before she can see that it was only one like, and it was from Adam.

Chapter Eight

"I can't believe how seriously you take this show."

I remove my intense gaze from *Love Is Blind* on the flat screen and turn to Adam, who's sitting next to me on the opposite end of his couch/bed with an amused expression on his face. We're exactly two weeks into his stay. "Why wouldn't I?"

He pulls a face. "Because I seriously doubt most of the contestants are really in it for 'the right reasons.'" He chomps on a Cheeto from the bag on his lap.

I shift so I'm leaning against the arm of the couch and facing him, knees pulled into my chest. "I, personally, have zero desire to go on television to find love, but the impressive success rate of *Love Is Blind* speaks for itself."

He lifts an eyebrow. "Tell me, Sabrina. Do *you* think love is blind?" The serious tone of his voice is in contrast to the twinkle in his eyes.

"Not necessarily. But I *do* think building the emotional connection without preconceived assumptions getting in your way is a good idea."

"What do you mean by preconceived assumptions?" He extends the bag of Cheetos to me.

I shake my head, declining to partake in what I've quickly discovered is Adam's favorite snack. I can practically hear my sister going on about the dangers of filling your body with processed cheese. "I think people have preconceived notions about what they're attracted to based on their dating habits. If I've always dated guys with blond hair, I might assume someone with brown or red hair isn't my type and immediately swipe left. But I might be surprised to find that I am wildly attracted to a ginger if we talked for weeks with a wall between us and formed a blind connection first."

Adam mutes the TV. "*Do* you only date guys with blond hair?"

I chew my cheek. If we were at a party or on a first date, I would assume he was flirting and ping back something like, "Not *always*." Or, "I make exceptions sometimes." Or, "My type is brown hair with red highlights." All with accompanying sultry eye contact. But I don't know if Adam *is* flirting. He might just be making conversation. Whether I *hope* he's flirting is not something I'm prepared to examine at the moment, even though the answer is a resounding yes. But this living arrangement is not about me and Adam. It's about Adam and Marcia. The dynamic is tricky, so I simply say, "No."

He faces the TV again like he's reluctant to make eye contact. "What *is* your type?"

And now I'm 95 percent sure he *is* flirting. Despite my better judgment, my heart skips a beat as the word *you* begs to fly out of my mouth.

"Sabrina!" Marcia's voice shrieks from inside her room, blessedly negating my need to answer the question while freaking me out at the same time.

I vault off the couch with my heart in my throat, but I'm not fast enough for Rocket, who comes flying out from the kitchen, where he's been gnawing on the new toy Adam bought him for being a good boy at the groomer. He whines and scratches at her closed door.

Adam also beats me to Marcia's door, gently pushing Rocket away and throwing it open. "What's wrong?"

Marcia's in her pajamas with her back to us at the small desk in the corner of her bedroom. She rotates her black swivel chair so she's facing us. Her blue eyes are wide. "They found my information on the dark web! What does that mean?"

My tight muscles relax in the knowledge she's not having a heart attack or being held at gunpoint by a robber. "Let me see." I lean over the desk so I can get a good look.

She points to the open email from McAfee—an identity-monitoring report. After I'd lived with Marcia for about a month, she mentioned all the pop-ups she was getting from McAfee and Norton about protecting her computer from viruses and hackers. She referred to them as "junk mail," and that's when I realized she had zero protection on her computer and helped get her set up.

"Was my identity stolen? A fake sex tape emailed to all my friends?" Her voice is shaky.

Adam's eyes bug out.

"No," I say, trying not to laugh. "It just means some of your passwords have been breached. We just need to change them. Let's see what they say."

Marcia stands and gestures for me to take her place on the chair. With Adam and Marcia hovering over me—Adam's arousing grapefruit scent mixed with her comforting floral—and Rocket circling in and out of my legs, I wait while McAfee generates a summary of all the breaches. I nod. "It's what I thought. Your password has been exposed on three sites." I jot them down on the yellow Post-it notepad on her desk. "Let's go to these websites and change your passwords." I flash a stern look at her over my shoulder. "Something besides Adam0925, please."

Over the next few minutes, she gives me some stronger options. I suggest adding hashtags and random numbers, and when we're satisfied, I go to the sites and make the changes for her.

"You need a password for everything these days," Marcia says from behind me. "But what's the point if they're so easy to steal?"

"That's why you don't use your birthday!" I say while changing her password on a flower-delivery website. "Or your grandson's."

"I don't know what I'd do without you," she gushes.

Adam, who's been otherwise quiet, says, "I didn't realize Sabrina helped you with this sort of thing."

"She sure does... even set me up with a password manager app so I don't have to worry about memorizing them all! She's a godsend." She squeezes my shoulders.

My chest swells. "I'm not sure about that. I'm just happy I can help." I keep my stare straight ahead while I continue to type so they don't see that I'm on the verge of silly, choked-up, feeling-validated tears. When I'm confident my complexion has returned to its regular pallor, I spin around. "We can update the password manager next."

Marcia is beaming at me. "Thank you."

"It's not a big deal!" I give a bashful glance to Adam, but he's staring into space, all contemplative. "Everything okay, Adam?"

He shakes out of his trance and blinks at me. "Yeah. Fine." He smiles but it doesn't reach his eyes. "Just glad everything is straightened out." He pats Marcia's arm.

I cock my head and study him. I don't buy that everything is fine, but I'm also not confident he'd confide in me even if I pressed him. I decide to move on for now. "Meet you back on the couch to resume *Love Is Blind* in five?"

He scrubs a hand through his hair. "Actually, I'm exhausted. You mind if I turn the TV off?"

My shoulders drop an inch before I hitch them back up again. "Oh. That's fine. I should get ready for bed anyway. Big day tomorrow with work and school." I stop short of faking a yawn, hoping my disappointment isn't obvious.

After I finish helping Marcia fight the good fight against the villainous dark web, I spend the rest of the night in my room, reviewing the discussion board from my youth literature class and reading the required articles. Before I know it, it's time to get ready for bed.

When Adam first moved in, I didn't change into my pajamas until I was in my room for the night, but I've since decided that it's perfectly acceptable for me to walk around in shorts and a tank top in my own home. I keep my bra on because my nipples have a mind of their own, especially around hot guys. But it doesn't matter that I'm still wearing my nude front-clasping bra under my pink ribbed tank top because Adam isn't even in the living room. I assume he's either in the bathroom, in which case I'll have to wait my turn, or the kitchen, when I hear his voice. It's coming from Marcia's room, where the door is open just a crack. Marcia tells him how happy she is to have him there. She still says some version of this at least five times a day, but I love to hear it. Then Adam says he wishes they didn't waste so much time letting his dad keep them apart. He says this at least *once* a day.

My throat thickens at this touching moment, as it always does, until a wave of guilt crashes over me for eavesdropping, even though it's not on purpose. It's a two-bedroom apartment, not a mansion.

The talking stops and there's a faint "squish" sound. I'm guessing Marcia went in for a hug. She does that a lot too. I close the bathroom door behind me. After washing my face and brushing my teeth, I'm about to return to my room when I hear my name mentioned. On instinct, I take a step closer. In case they see me, I pretend to look for a new container of body moisturizer in the closet next to Marcia's room where we keep our unopened toiletries.

"Sabrina keeps me young. We have fun together."

Warmth rushes through me and I smile to myself. I think we make a great pair—my youthful perspective balanced with Marcia's more experienced and mature one—but it's validating to hear it directly from her. It's a dynamic I'm not used to, since my mom wasn't around much and my grandma...well...if I let my mind go there, I'll never fall asleep.

Adam says, "I'm happy you have a roommate you like, but you do have to be smart."

I frown. Smart about what?

"Seriously, Adam. There's nothing to worry about," Marcia says.

My muscles tighten. Worry? What is he worried about?

Adam says, "You can't just go around sharing your passwords with people, Grams."

I gasp and throw a hand to my mouth. Is this about me? Am I *people*?

"I only shared them with Sabrina."

"Who was a virtual stranger. She could have done anything with them. Robbed you blind."

"But she hasn't."

My pulse speeds up. Does Adam really think I would do something so horrific? I only want to help her! I curl my fists and blink back the tears building behind my eyelids, my insides torn between anger at this ridiculous accusation and disappointment that the accuser is Adam, who I thought was becoming my friend.

"Thankfully, but don't give her the opportunity. If you need help, I'm here too."

"You're as much of a Luddite as me!"

Ha! You tell him, Marcia.

"Just promise me you'll be more careful with your personal information. Don't respond to any weird emails from Nigerian princes asking for money either."

"What does a prince want from me?"

"A real prince wants nothing. A fake one wants your life savings! Your identity can be stolen even if you do everything right, but your risk increases if you're careless with your personal information."

I don't stick around to hear what Marcia says next. I quickly dash into my bedroom and close the door behind me as quietly as possible.

Chapter Nine

"What's with the resting bitch face?"

I'm in front of the romance shelf pulling books from the hold list about an hour into work the next day but jerk back and face Gabe, who's reorganizing the March Madness display by the window. "What are you talking about?"

Gabe waves a hand in front of my face. "You look like you're auditioning for a role of sucking lemons."

I sigh and tell him about the conversation I overheard between Adam and Marcia the night before. "While Marcia was all, 'You're a godsend, Sabrina,' and practically bringing me to tears with her gratitude, *his* gut reaction was that I might be trying to steal from her." Exhausted from tossing and turning all night, I scrub a hand over my eyes.

I can't even pinpoint what upsets me the most. It stings because I thought Adam and I were bonding. I like him and genuinely thought the feeling was mutual, but now I know we're on vastly different wavelengths. And then there's the anger. Where has *he* been for the last ten years to now show up, a virtual stranger himself, and warn Marcia against *me*? For all I know, *he's* the one after her money.

He was sleeping when I showered this morning and in the

bathroom when I left for work. A blessing because I don't know how to act around him now. "It was just so unexpected because we'd been bonding earlier that night."

Gabe's eyebrows shoot up. "Bonding *how*?"

Heat whips across my cheeks as I remember our questionably flirtatious banter about my type. "All PG."

Gabe chuckles before switching the positions of *Long Shot* and *Sooley* on the display. "I was worried something like this would happen when he moved in, but I didn't want to say anything."

I address the second half of his sentence first with an eye roll. "You didn't want to say anything? You?" This has never been Gabe's problem.

He flashes a devilish grin.

"And what do you mean by 'something like this'?"

His face turns serious. "It all sounded too good to be true. Adam goes to live with his grandmother, becomes besties with her twenty-something roommate, and the three of you live happily ever after?" He shrugs. "Maybe in one of those cheesy made-for-TV movies, but in real life, you and Adam would either want to bang it out or he'd be threatened by you. In this case, both happen to be true."

"No comment on the banging-it-out part, but why would he be threatened by me?" I pull *Before I Let Go* off the shelf and toss it in the cart with more force than is required.

Gabe gives me a pointed look. "You're a threat to his relationship with Marcia *and* his bed." My confusion must be obvious because he sighs. "Imagine if your grandma invited you to move into her luxury apartment building rent-free, and you thought you had it made except there's already someone in the guest bedroom, a surrogate granddaughter, while you're stuck on the couch."

"Someone who is paying rent!" I ignore the surrogate granddaughter part of his hypothetical, not needing yet another reason to be sad this morning.

"Exactly. And the good news is, she can't terminate your lease without cause. You could take her to court if she tried."

My mouth drops open. Before getting his MLIS, Gabe went to law school for a year, something he drops into conversation two or three times a month—except I don't need his legal advice. "Who said anything about terminating my lease? You're getting carried away." I almost wish I hadn't said anything. Gabe loves drama. "Marcia knows I'm trustworthy, and she told him so."

He shrugs. "I'm just saying, you should watch your back. If Adam really wants you out, he can try to trap you into breaching the contract...frame you for illegal activity. Plant drugs in your room."

"Stop it! You're watching too much *Law and Order*!" When an older woman playing solitaire on one of the public computers turns around, I remember where I am and lower my voice to a whisper. "You're ridiculous. *Plant drugs in my room*. Ha!"

"Laugh all you want, but who are you to assume the lengths the man will go to get a good night's sleep?"

I snort. "He sleeps just fine." A vision of Adam crashed out on the couch with his mouth slightly open all cuddly with Rocket springs to mind, but I push it aside. I slouch against the bookshelf. "What should I do?"

"You gotta let him know you're not going anywhere." He wiggles a finger in my face. "But don't show any sign of weakness. If he smells fear, he'll pounce."

"He's not a wild animal." I press two fingers to my now pounding temples. Even though I doubt Adam will pounce *or* try to get me thrown out, we should probably get his concerns out in the open. I don't delight in confrontation, something I blame on being the younger child with a headstrong older sibling who was always right…kind of like Gabe…and a mom who was too busy working overtime to intervene. But I can't live with all this tension indefinitely.

Gabe returns to his desk and I continue pulling books, but I can't focus. While organizing the DVD shelves in the young adult section later that afternoon, I imagine what a confrontation with Adam would look like. Will he try to deny it? Will he double down and accuse me to my face? Or will he apologize for doubting my character? If the last one, I would forgive him. He's being protective of his grandma, which I can appreciate. But if he doesn't back down, I'll be forced to defend myself. It could turn into a full-blown fight, which would upset Marcia. She was so afraid of how I'd react about Adam coming to stay with us. It would kill her to know I'd overheard their conversation and lost sleep over it, especially since she already set him straight. For her sake, I should just let it go and not say anything.

Except I'm not sure I can.

My phone pings with a text from Carley.

Carley: Can I come over tonight and meet the grandson?

I smile softly. Carley isn't an actual psychic, but she can read my mind sometimes. It's both irritating and comforting. Right now, it's comforting. I've kept her in the loop about Adam since the very beginning but haven't had a chance to share the latest yet.

Sabrina: I have class tonight after work but you can come by after 8. Something happened and I could really use your advice. It's too long to text

Carley: 🌶️

I've tried to keep my pesky attraction to Adam on the DL, but clearly I'm failing miserably. This is where the mind reading shifts to irritating.

Sabrina: Nothing like that!

Carley: 👀

I breathe out a laugh.

Sabrina: I'll see you later

She hearts my text, and I tuck my phone into the pocket of my jeans and get back to the business of organizing DVDs.

After work and school that night, I stop by the mail room in the lobby on my way to the elevator. I'm leafing through the unusually large stack when I freeze. Among junk mail for Marcia Haber and Sabrina Finkelstein is a bank statement from Chase for Adam Haber. Further thumbing reveals a Visa bill also addressed to Adam at our address.

I'm shook by this...so much so that I stand unmoving in the middle of the mail room clutching today's letters, only semi-aware of the strange looks several neighbors are throwing my way as they weave around me to retrieve their own mail. It's just...I didn't realize Adam would be staying here long enough to forward his mail. Also, I don't know anyone under the age of forty who doesn't do paperless billing. Even Marcia is almost exclusively online, now that I've helped set her up. The only reason we even *check* the snail mail on a regular basis is because our mail slot is tiny relative to the amount of junk mail we receive. Twenty-five-year-old Adam is more of a boomer than Marcia!

When someone accidentally brushes my side on her way past me, I finally spur my body back into motion and head to the elevator. The door is closing when I approach, but I stick my hand inside to stop it. Upon entry, I utter an apology to the other riders with my head down. I'm not aggressive by nature, but there are only two elevators in the building, not including the freight. If you miss one, it could be a while before the next one arrives.

"Yeah, yeah, yeah. Some people are so pushy."

I lift my head at the familiar voice and meet Adam's teasing smile. Wearing his black windbreaker, open at the front to reveal the top of a dark gray T-shirt, and dark jeans, he's the only other person in the elevator. My temperature rises. "Hu...hi." How is he acting so normal—joking around with me like we're best friends today after warning Marcia not to trust me last night? The nerve of him flashing his Harry Styles dimples.

I shrug halfheartedly. "These are for you," I say, handing him his mail.

"Thank you, Sabrina." He takes it from my hands and, without a second glance, shoves it into the black tote bag from the Strand draped over his shoulder.

"No problem." I stare straight ahead at the elevator buttons, rubbing my palm to smooth out the zap of electricity from our brief skin-on-skin contact. "You know, you can save a lot of money on stamps if you pay your bills online."

"Maybe I'm a stamp collector."

I give him a side glance. "Are you?"

His lips quirk. "No. I just have the basic Forever stamp twenty pack."

"I can get you set up if you want... like I did with Marcia," I say on a whim. The door opens to our floor and I rush out first, surprised by my own boldness.

We walk down the hall in the direction of Rocket's barking. Ignoring my offer, Adam says, "Do you think he knows we're home, or does he bark whenever the elevator opens on our floor?"

Either he has no idea I'm onto him or he has a superb poker face, but I'm relieved because I haven't decided how to play this yet. I ignore him right back, even though I know that Rocket barks every single time the elevator opens on our floor unless he's asleep, something Adam would also know if he paid any attention.

The second we enter the apartment, I hang my winter coat in the hall closet and try to make a mad dash to my room until Carley gets here. Only Rocket intercepts my plan and hurls himself at me, seemingly to get his mouth on the stack of mail I'm holding. I let my school bag fall off my shoulder onto the living room rug.

"Not for you," I say lovingly, patting his head with my free hand. Playing nice doesn't work as Rocket tries to climb my legs. I pose like I'm about to toss the mail for him to fetch. When Rocket's eyes follow the direction of my hand, I race to the kitchen and drop the stack on the table. Although anything on the warm oak hardwood floor is up for grabs, even Rocket knows the table is off-limits.

"How was your day?"

I take a deep breath through my nose and turn around.

Leaning against the wall where the living room meets the kitchen, Adam grins. "What's the most interesting thing that happened at the library?"

I have told him some of the more entertaining stories from work, like the time the fire alarm went off because a staff member burned their macaroni and cheese in the microwave. Everyone willingly evacuated except one patron who wanted to stay back to retrieve his print job...coincidentally a recipe for homemade mac and cheese. I initially basked in Adam's seemingly sincere interest about the library, but now I just feel duped.

Nothing *interesting* happened today aside from Gabe's warning to "watch my back" in case my new roommate plants drugs in my room. Maybe I should tell him *that*. I'm still contemplating when Rocket dashes back into the living room and I see him chew on the school bag I dropped on the lavender-and-gray shag rug. "Rocket. No!" The Herschel Little America Backpack, the same shade of blue as Adam's eyes (not that I noticed) with pastel-pink straps, was a gift from my mom for Hanukkah. At over a hundred dollars, I couldn't afford to buy it for myself. My love for Rocket is unconditional, but he's testing the boundaries of my devotion right now.

Rocket pretends he can't hear me and continues to gnaw on the strap of my beloved bag like it's a bone from a rib eye steak.

"Rocket!"

At the sound of Adam's voice, Rocket releases the strap from his mouth and darts over to him.

"Thanks," I mumble grudgingly. How does he *do* that?

The doorbell rings.

"Who is it?" Adam and I ask at the same time.

"Me."

"Helpful." Adam chokes out a laugh and heads for the door.

"It's for me," I say, racing in front of him to let Carley in.

My friend's long, straight dark hair is tucked under a sparkly blueberry winter hat that matches her eyes, and she's wearing a leopard-print puffer jacket and baggy Levi's. She smiles brightly between me and Adam crowding her at the threshold. "I feel so welcome!"

I take a step back to let her in the apartment. "Carley, meet Adam. Adam, this is Carley."

I lead us into the living room where Carley appraises Adam slowly, like he's a painting at the MoMA. "So you're Marcia's grandson."

He grins. "I am. And you're the makeup artist slash influencer. Congrats on the off-Broadway gig."

Her eyes slide to me. "You've been talking about me?"

"You've come up once or twice." I glance toward my bedroom, anxious to get these introductions over with.

"She's proud of you," Adam says, looking at me not at all like someone who would plant drugs in my room.

Carley throws a hand to her heart and beams. "I'm proud of my punk-ass book jockey too! And I'm proud of you too."

Adam cocks his head. "What did *I* do?"

"I'm sure you've done many things deserving of pride, but I'm talking about that." She points to the revolving bookcase now fully stacked with my collection of YA novels.

He ducks his head. "Sabrina and my grams laid all the groundwork. I just finished it."

"And he's humble!" Carley looks around the room. "Where's Marcia?"

There's no sound coming from her room, and I wonder the same thing.

"She's at a co-op board meeting and a wine tasting at a neighbor's," Adam says. "She told me about it earlier."

Carley's eyes widen. "We should crash the wine tasting!"

"There are almost five hundred apartments in this building. We'd have to go door-to-door like trick-or-treaters to find the right one." I take her by the elbow. "Let's go to my room." I lead the way but stop walking when Adam calls my name. I turn to face him, immediately noting the furrow in his brow. "Yeah?"

"Is everything okay?"

I chew my lip. This would be the perfect opening to come clean with what I overheard, but I want Carley's input first. "Why wouldn't it be?"

He shrugs. "No reason."

I nod and follow Carley into my room, closing the door behind me.

Carley plops her butt on my pink beanbag chair and fans herself. "Time has been good to the grandson. He's transformed from awk-weird to hot-dorable, à la Josh Peck." She removes her jacket to reveal the neon-green shirt she's wearing underneath and shakes her hair free from her hat.

I sit on the edge of my bed and kick off my sneakers. "I guess."

Carley narrows her eyes. "What's going on? You said you needed my advice?"

I fill her in.

She twists her mouth thoughtfully. "I don't buy it. That boy out there"—she points at my door—"does not look like someone who is concerned about you stealing from his grandma."

I bite my cheek. "I'd agree if I hadn't heard him with my own two ears."

"Are you going to say anything to him?"

"I don't want him to know that I was eavesdropping." He's entitled to a private conversation with Marcia, even if it is about me.

"When someone speaks your name in the same context as a Nigerian prince, you listen!"

My lips twitch, but the doubts linger. "What if Adam keeps putting ideas in Marcia's head and she ends up hating me?"

Carley smirks. "She's not going to hate you."

I lie back and spoon my pillow. "You don't know that."

She sighs. "I know you're scared because you think of Marcia as a surrogate grandmother, but—"

I shoot up. This is the second time today I've heard this phrase. "Marcia's like fifteen years younger than my nana was when she died." The age difference between my grandma and Adam's isn't so odd; Marcia had Jeffrey in her early twenties, and he had Adam in *his* early twenties. On my side, Nana Lena was forty when my dad was born and in her late eighties when she died of a sudden stroke. She was whatever generation came before boomers.

"If you say so." Carley somewhat awkwardly lifts herself off the chair to a standing position and paces my pale wood floor. "Marcia already put out that fire. You said yourself that she defended you."

My heart plumps recalling the kind things she said about me. "You're right. I just needed the outside validation."

Carley's expression softens. "I think you should tell him what you overheard and clear the air. Otherwise, it's going to be a really awkward living situation with you all passive-aggressive toward him and him all confused and wounded following you with his puppy-dog eyes."

"He doesn't look at me with puppy-dog eyes."

"Fine. Siberian husky eyes."

I choke on a laugh. "They're pretty, right?"

"So pretty!" She pulls me off the bed. "I'm sorry for the mad dash, but I should get out of here. I'm meeting my own blue-eyed boy later."

"Frank?" Carley met Frank, a production electrician, at Bar Centrale when they were both there for post-show cocktails one night a few weeks earlier.

"Yes." A flush crawls up her neck.

She must like him because she doesn't blush easily. "Have fun!"

"I plan to. Walk me out and then talk to the grandson."

"Fine. It's better to do it while Marcia is out." Given that I asked for her advice, I should probably take it. And she's right. We can't continue living with the current vibes.

"Agreed! No time like the present." She puts her hand on the doorknob. "You've got this?"

I nod.

"Tits up." She lifts her chest.

"Tits up." I do the same.

She opens the door.

The light in the living room is off and the apartment is empty. I'm alone.

Chapter Ten

When I made the decision to confront Adam, I had no idea it would be so hard! He was sleeping when I left for work on Friday, watching *Begin Again* with Marcia on Prime that night, and basically impossible to catch out of earshot from Marcia at all times in between. I work a ten-to-five shift on Saturday, but when I get home, he's alone in the living room, quietly reading on the couch with the television off. *Finally.*

I say a quick hello and drop my purse in my room before joining him again. "Hey, Adam?" I peer closer to see what he's reading but he blocks it with his large hands, almost like he knows how curious I am and is mocking me. "Is Marcia home?" I don't want to risk her walking in on our conversation.

He raises his head. "She's in her room." A shadow crosses his face.

I immediately panic. "What happened?"

He grimaces. "I came home as she was wrestling with folding the couch. I took over, but it was too late. She pulled her back."

My stomach lurches. "Oh no."

"It's my fault. I didn't make the bed before I left for the Y. I don't know what I was thinking." He looks pained.

Fuck. Though I could pile on the guilt, I'm not that cruel. "How bad is it? Does she need a doctor?"

Adam places his book on the coffee table. *The Ferryman*. "I don't think so. I set her up in bed with some painkillers and a heating pad. She's resting."

"I'm going to check on her." I turn my back on him and knock gently on her door.

"Come in."

My stomach drops at the sight of Marcia lying in bed in a two-piece pajama set at six on a Saturday evening. The cord from the heating pad stretches from the bed and disappears behind her nightstand. She looks twice her age. I gulp. No. She looks precisely her age, which sometimes I forget is almost fifty years older than me.

"I'm so sorry about your back."

"Why are *you* sorry?" Marcia props herself up against the pillow. Rocket, who is sprawled across her legs and docile, like he knows she needs tender loving care and is in no condition to deal with his usual shenanigans, looks up at her before resting his head again.

I curve my body inward to make myself smaller. "I'm supposed to do the heavy lifting around here so you don't have to."

Marcia sucks her teeth. "You were at work. Last time I checked, it wasn't possible to be in two different places at the same time. *Adam* should have done it, and I should have left it for him."

"You should have." I twirl a hair around my finger. "Why didn't you?"

She averts her gaze. "Because he left the living room a mess, and I didn't want to wait until he got home."

I playfully slap a hand on the bed and giggle-yell, "Marcia!"

Rocket growls; whether it's because I raised my voice or slapped the bed, I'm not sure.

A part of me—an evil part I'm not proud of—gets a small thrill that Adam didn't take care of her the way he should have, because maybe it means she still needs me in that role. I just wish this validation didn't come at the expense of her comfort. "While we're on the subject . . . sort of . . . am I doing everything I should to deliver on my end of our arrangement? Do you have any concerns about my um . . . performance?" Why is this so hard? My fingernails dig into my palms. Even though I heard her defend me to Adam, I crave direct reassurance that she trusts me.

The wrinkles in Marcia's forehead deepen. "No! You're wonderful. Ten out of ten, no notes, as you kids say." She frowns. "Maybe I should be asking you the same thing. My grandson moving in wasn't part of the deal either. Are you adjusting okay?"

I wave her off. "Absolutely." This was the truth until recently, and I definitely don't want her to know that I overheard their conversation. "It's great you two are becoming so close."

Marcia smiles for the first time since I walked in. "I do love that boy."

Something warm tugs in my belly. "It's obvious he loves you too."

"He promises he'll never leave the apartment without folding the couch again, and I promised to leave it alone if he breaks his promise."

"And I promise to subject you both to my cooking if either of you break your promises!"

She chuckles. "Rain check on the dueling pianos tonight?"

"Absolutely." Marcia's other friends refused to trek to a bar in Hell's Kitchen, but I thought it would be fun.

I take a shower to scrub remnants of peanut butter and jelly from the half sandwich a junior patron left between the pages of *Cloudy with a Chance of Meatballs* off my skin, then retire to my room, avoiding eye contact with Adam on my way to and from the bathroom.

Since my plans with Marcia have been postponed, I have nothing to do tonight. Adam's in the living room, which means if I stay home, I'll be trapped in my bedroom all night. I could use the opportunity to confront him as planned, but I've already talked myself out of it and don't have the energy to talk myself back in. My eyes dart to my laptop and folder of printed reading assignments, but I don't want to study on a night I reserved to have fun. I could text some friends or even tap into my apps to find a last-minute date and redirect my misguided sexual attraction to Adam toward a stranger. It's been months since I've put effort into my love life. But I'm not convinced I want to be social. I decide it's still early enough to play it by ear but blow-dry my hair so it's not stringy and flat, just in case I decide to go out later.

When I turn off the blow-dryer, the first thing I notice is how eerily silent the apartment is. Even the near-constant din of the television seeping through my walls is absent. I step into the hallway in shorts and a T-shirt just as the front door to the apartment closes. The lights are all off. Adam's gone out. Marcia is resting in her room. This feels like a sign from the universe to stay in and take advantage of what's supposed to be communal space while I can.

After heating a frozen pizza for dinner, I get comfy on the couch, which I try to forget is also Adam's bed, and watch Kimberly, Leighton, Bela, and Whitney slam shots and dance at a Kappa party on *The Sex Lives of College Girls*.

I'm suddenly nostalgic for my own carefree days of college, when I wasn't solely responsible for my finances, and everything didn't... I don't know... *matter* so much. The answer to my earlier internal question hits me: I *do* want to be social. In fact, I *long* to be with friends. I chew my lip, wondering what Adam's up to.

While Bela makes an inappropriate but hilarious sexual comment on the TV, I text my own inappropriate friend.

Sabrina: Drinks later?

Even if Carley wants to hang out after the show she's working tonight, it will be past ten by the time the performance is over and she's finished assisting the cast with makeup removal. I place the phone back on the coffee table assuming it will be a while before she responds, but within thirty seconds, my phone pings.

Carley: Keybar. 11:00

Chapter Eleven

Both Lyft and Via are charging premium Saturday-night rates that I can't justify when public transportation is right outside my door. After standing in the cold for ten minutes, the crosstown bus finally shows up and crawls its way down Fourteenth Street until I get off on First Avenue. On my walk to Keybar, I text Gabe to see if he wants to join us. He says he'll meet us there.

The place is packed. For every drink you buy at Keybar, you get a ticket for a free one of similar value that never expires. Naturally, it's popular with the young and broke. I tuck my coat under my arm and weave my way through the crowd until I spot Carley at the bar at the far end. She's facing the other way, but I know it's her thanks to the tiny rabbit-shaped birthmark on her upper back, right above the line of her black satin slip dress. The first time I saw her birthmark when we met at summer camp, I dragged her into our bunk's damp and mildewy bathroom and privately revealed the nearly identical birthmark on my left butt cheek. Convinced we were related in another life, we became instant best friends for eight weeks until camp was over. I switched to the more affordable day camp the following summer, and although we followed each other on social media, real life took over and we lost touch until we bumped into each other at Trader Joe's ten years later and continued from where we left off.

Tonight, when I tap her shoulder, she turns around and beams. "Sabrina's here. Rolo shots!" Next to her at the bar are Peter and Amy, two of the costume attendants for the show she's currently working on. They have their heads bent toward each other in what looks like an intense conversation, but briefly greet me with smiles and waves before turning back to each other.

Carley looks me over and nods approvingly. "That look is fire."

Glad I put more than minimal effort into my outfit—a low-cut black bodysuit top, high-waisted straight-leg jeans, and silver ankle boots—I do a small twirl.

Amy and Peter finish their private chat just as Gabe arrives. After brief introductions, the five of us do a round of the bar's trademark Rolo shots and order five drinks, all free, three of them from the trio's earlier round and the other two left over from the last time I was here. Not long after, thanks to loud deep house music and bordering-on-preposterous conversation with friends, I'm positive my night is even better than the one the suitemates were having on *The Sex Lives of College Girls*.

"Mia screamed like her hair was on fire," Peter says, referring to an actress who went ballistic after tripping over a shoe in the middle of tonight's performance because someone left it onstage during a scene transition.

I find their backstage stories fascinating and lean in to ask a follow-up question, but I completely forget what I'm going to say when *he* walks through the door.

My heart throbs. I forcibly grip my Keybar's Lemonade like it's a pole on a fast-moving subway. It's probably not him. There must be thousands of cute guys with multishades-of-brown hair. And lots of them own black windbreakers. He turns his head slightly toward me, and I gasp. It's 100 percent Adam Haber. Adam is *here*... at the same bar as me. I take a huge swig of my cocktail.

Carley hands me her drink and says something about going to the bathroom. I don't respond.

Adam blessedly hasn't seen me yet. Is he alone? There's a girl practically up his ass, but they could be strangers since we're packed in this bar tighter than pickles in a jar. He glances over his shoulder and his lips move. I can't hear what he's saying given the DJ has the music turned up high enough to entertain bars all the way down in Brooklyn. The girl's eyes light up at Adam's attention. They're definitely here together.

Adam reaches the bar a second before she does and gets the attention of the female bartender immediately. His date... friend... *whatever*, also blonde, slips into the small space to his right. Adam orders something and looks behind him. This time his eyes meet mine and stay there. It's almost like he's not sure who I am... like I look familiar and he's trying to place me. But then his mouth slowly curves into a crooked grin.

My cheeks burn, and if I weren't holding a glass in both hands, I'd wipe the sweat from the back of my neck. Why is he so damn smiley, and why am I so freaked out that he's here?

"Are you eye fucking someone?"

I whip my head to face Gabe. "What? No! It's..." I whisper—not that Adam could hear me from this far away and over the music—and duck my head because he might be able to read lips. "Adam's here." When I glance back at the bar, he's no longer there. "Well, he *was* right there."

"Adam? As in your roommate?"

"*Marcia's* my roommate. He's just the grandson."

"The *hot* grandson. You said it yourself. And don't deny it. Your face is doing that thing it did when Channing Tatum did a reading of his picture book at the library."

"My face is doing nothing. And if it is, it's because it's hot as balls in here."

Carley rejoins us. "I think I just saw Hot Grandson. Either that, or his doppelganger is here."

"Sabrina *likes* him," Gabe teases.

I give Carley back her drink and lightly punch Gabe, second-guessing my decision to invite him out tonight.

"Hey!" He grimaces even though he's still wearing his jacket and probably felt nothing.

"Have you talked to him yet?" Carley asks.

"No. I was planning to after work today but Marcia hurt her back, and I—"

"Chickened out," Gabe answers for me.

I glare at him. "I didn't chicken out. It just seemed unimportant compared to Marcia's pain."

"You need liquid courage. Rolo shots!" Carley says, dragging me to the bar.

Over the next half hour, my friends manage to distract me enough that I barely think about Adam being in the bar somewhere. I don't see him and wonder if he left after the one drink. And then I have to pee so bad, Adam could be right in front of me and I wouldn't care.

"Oh my God. What are you *doing* in there?" The girl in front of me yells at the bathroom door, echoing my thoughts.

I shift my feet. "I know, right? She better not be touching up her makeup while I'm out here dying." I repeat. "*Dying*." We chuckle. Despite my bladder pain, I love bonding with strangers in bar bathroom lines.

"I'm afraid they're puking or—"

"Taking a dump!"

We bend over in laughter.

Adam materializes at my side like a hologram and smiles like he's thrilled to see me. "Someone gets foul when she's drunk."

"I can't be held accountable for what I say when my bladder is about to explode." I work to keep the tone of my voice from being overly friendly, since I can't unhear his warning to Marcia that I might rob her blind. But I don't want to cross into hostile without getting his side. Now that I finally have a chance to confront him, it's literally the last thing I want to do. The first is relieve my bladder.

"I read that there are over ten thousand bars in Manhattan. Kind of wild that we both came to the same one tonight."

"I guess." I look pleadingly at the closed bathroom door.

"What is up with you lately, Sabrina?"

I turn to face him and bat my eyelashes innocently. "Whatever do you mean?"

He grunts. "You've barely spoken to me in days. I'd understand if you were upset about what happened to my grandma... entirely my fault... but you were cold to me way before today. What did I do?"

When he follows the question with serious puppy-dog... correction... *Siberian husky* eyes, it takes all the restraint I can muster to keep calm.

The bathroom door opens and the girl who was in front of me gives me a toothy smile. "All yours!"

I return a grateful grin before turning back to Adam with the door open. "I can't have this conversation with you right now because I *really* have to pee." I enter the bathroom and close the door behind me with force. The latch doesn't engage. I grunt, "Motherfucking *close*!" and try again. This time it works.

Peeing is sweet relief, but it's short-lived. When I open the door after washing my hands, Adam is still there, waiting for me.

He taps his foot. "You've peed. Now can we talk?"

"For the love of..." It must be liquid courage because suddenly I can't hold back another second. I grab his hand, pull him inside the bathroom with me, and slam the door shut again. "I overheard you tell Marcia that she shouldn't trust me with her passwords because I might... and I quote... rob her blind." I raise my chin.

His face drains of color.

I smile smugly. "So excuse me if I don't want to watch trashy television or start a book club with someone who thinks so little of me." The alcohol in my system does nothing to slow my heart.

Adam scrubs a hand through his hair. "I'm sorry you heard that."

"But not sorry you said it. Gee, thanks."

"I just don't think my grandma should share her passwords with a stranger."

I get up in his face, which is obscenely close to my face. How did I not notice how small this bathroom was sooner? A bead of sweat drips between my boobs at the realization. The one we share at home is a mansion in comparison, but that's beside the point. "I'm not a stranger! In fact, *you're* more of a stranger to her than me. Some grandson you've been for the past ten years. And now you think you can swoop in and try to play hero against an imaginary villain?" I feel immediate guilt when Adam's eyes go heavy and the corners of his lips pull down. *Who am I to talk?*

"You're right. I haven't been around, but I am now, and maybe I'm overly protective of her to make up for it. I know you wouldn't steal from her, but the thing is, she didn't know that when she first met you, and I wanted to stress the need to be more careful in general."

My pulse slows down marginally. "I get that."

He scratches at his stubbled jaw. "I'm sorry I hurt your feelings."

"I'm over it." I said I would forgive him if he provided a valid reason and apologized, and he's done both.

His eyes soften. "I'm glad."

"Me too."

"Because I like you, Sabrina. And you smell—"

"I smell?"

His face turns red. "Good. You smell good."

My eyes widen. His are unblinking. He's so close, I wouldn't even need to move to kiss him. I could just lean forward slightly and...

Someone bangs on the door. "Hurry the fuck up in there!"

We both jump.

Adam locks his jaw. "I forgot we were in a bar bathroom with a line outside."

My breathing slows. "Same. I guess we should..." I step around him in the limited space to open the door. My hand is on the knob when he gently pulls on my arm.

I turn around to face him.

"We good?" he asks.

I smile softly. "We're good."

When we step out of the bathroom together, there's a mix of wolf whistles and suggestions to get a room. Mortified, I keep my head down and rush back to my friends under the assumption Adam will find the girl he came with. Will he leave with her? My ribs squeeze tight at the thought.

"I still say we go to Brooklyn this year. Manhattan is tired," Peter is saying.

Carley shakes her head. "But Manhattan doesn't require being on the subway on St. Patrick's Day. Last year someone puked an inch from my sneakers. My green, sparkly Allbirds were nearly green, *chunky* Allbirds."

"We're making plans for St. Patrick's Day? Already?"

My friends gape at me.

"What do you mean *already*?" Gabe asks. "It's next weekend."

I hitch a breath. "What? No! What's today's date?"

"March ninth."

"March ninth, March ninth, March ninth." I repeat the date because it feels important. Then I remember why. My blood turns cold the way it does when I momentarily misplace my phone and freak out that I've lost it. Tonight, my phone is safe in my purse, but I have a different, *worse* problem. I pull it out and check the calendar. March eighth was yesterday. March eighth was the deadline to apply for a fellowship through my school that would have saved me thousands in tuition. I started filling out the application but never finished. When I dismissed my last reminder, I must have turned it off completely.

"You okay?" Carley asks me, concern apparent on her face.

"You look whiter than usual." Gabe's thick dark eyebrows furrow, belying the mocking tone of his voice.

"I'm fine. I just... I need to go. I'll call you later... tomorrow!" My realization rendered me completely sober, and I weave my way through the crowd of people like I'm playing—and winning—Frogger. I rush through the door, although I'm not sure what the hurry is since the deadline passed and it's not like I can do anything about it at two in the morning anyway. I just know I can't be here anymore.

I inhale air I wish I could say was fresh, but it's stale, post-rain, lingering smoke air. But the cold feels good... for a second... until my arms break out in goose bumps. I left my jacket inside. *Fuck.*

"You forget something?" My black quilted coat appears as if I summoned it. Only it's attached to Adam's hand.

I focus on slipping my hands through the sleeves to hide my surprise and pleasure that he followed me outside. "Thank you."

"Carley gave it to me. You left in a rush without it. It's March. Who will manage my grandma's online payments if you catch pneumonia?"

"She pays them herself. I just..." Then I notice the cheeky grin on his face. *Oh.* "Too soon, Adam. Too soon."

He laughs.

I step toward the curb. There are no cabs. I might have to walk to Fourteenth Street to catch one. It's only a few blocks, but I consider trying Lyft again. It might not be as expensive at this hour. There's no way I'm taking the bus home. It will take forever.

"So why the rush out of the bar?"

"I'd rather not talk about it." I can't believe I missed the deadline. "Why did you follow me outside?"

"You looked upset." His ears turn red. "And I was leaving anyway. Figured we could share a cab. Here's one." He raises his arm to hail it like he's lived in Manhattan his entire life. We get in and he tells the driver our address.

We're silent as the cab heads west on Fourteenth Street. "You're not still mad at me, are you?"

"No." I almost wish I still was because then we could just make up again and the problem would be solved.

"My mom's identity was stolen when I was a kid."

I swing my head to face him. "What? For real?"

He nods. "My parents spent months trying to straighten it out. It was hell."

"I'm so sorry." I've heard nightmares about this, which is one of the reasons I set Marcia up for so much protection in the first place.

"My grandma knew all about it and so it made no sense to me that she would be so careless." He clears his throat. "Nothing personal again. I just mean in general."

"I understand." I pat his thigh and quickly bring my hand back to my lap. Something occurs to me. "Is that why you pay your bills with a check like a boomer?"

He shrugs sheepishly. "A lot of Gen Xers do that too."

"Yeah, and they're still twice your age." I chuckle. "Thanks for telling me, but that's not why I ran out of the bar."

"Why then?"

I gulp. "I missed the deadline to apply for a fellowship that would have saved me $7,500 in tuition." The deal for a fellowship is that the school sets you up to work somewhere, a museum or library probably, once a week for nine months. The payment comes in the form of a scholarship. I'm already busy with school and work, but I could handle a second job for one day a week. "It would have made a huge difference since I'm not eligible for other scholarships because I'm part-time." Getting the fellowship wouldn't be life-changing since it only comprises a small portion of the total cost of tuition. But it would have been *something*.

Adam's eyes widen. "Will you have to drop out of school?"

My mind wanders to Gabe. "Don't pack up my things just yet."

His expression is soft. "Never even crossed my mind."

I tuck a lock of hair behind my ear as my throat thickens. "I'll manage... like I have been... but it would have been nice to catch some sort of financial break. Things are very tight right now. I go to school year-round to make up for my part-time status, but I might not be able to this year if I need to pick up more hours at the library or take another job this summer. It will delay my degree. At this rate, I'll be thirty by the time I get a job as a real librarian."

My mom paid for my undergraduate degree but said grad school was on me. She got her business degree while working a full-time job *and* as a divorced mother of two with minimum child support that she had to pay a lawyer to chase down every month until she gave up trying. She did it all on her own. I understand why she'd want to instill the same work ethic in her daughters, but the challenge is real.

"That sucks." Adam's blue eyes are gentle and sympathetic.

I appreciate that he's not trying to make me feel better by minimizing it or offering up solutions. He's simply listening. "I'm going to talk to my advisor on Monday and see if they'll let me submit a late application." This idea came to me just now.

Adam nods. "Decent plan. Sometimes deadlines aren't as fixed as they say. They're just motivators to get people to move."

I chew on a chipped nail. "Yeah, well, I hope this is one of those times."

The cab stops at our building, and we ride the elevator and enter our apartment in silence. I'm exhausted. A second after my head touches the pillow and the second before I fall asleep is when it first occurs to me that Adam left the bar without his date.

Chapter Twelve

Monday night, I'm on my bed reading for school when my phone rings.

I drop the book to my side and scooch my body up so my back is straight against the headboard. "Hi, Mom," I answer.

"How are you, sweetheart?"

My shoulders relax and my legs go soft at the warmth in her voice. We've never been Rory–Lorelai close, but we haven't spoken in a couple of weeks, and I miss her. The call starts out as usual. I'm fine. So is she. Her job is good... busy. School is going well. It's the same basic catch-up as always since neither of us ever have anything earth shattering to share.

"How's Marcia?"

"She's great. Well... she had a little issue with her back this weekend, but she's fine now."

"I'm glad it's nothing serious."

"So am I. She bounced back like a boss." I smile to myself. I still can't believe she went to yoga class the next morning.

"How are things going with her and her grandson?"

"Really great. Her face is permanently lit up around him. It's adorable."

"How about you two? Are you getting along?"

I shift on the bed. "Me and Adam?" A flush whips across my face as I flash back, for at least the twentieth time in as many hours, to dragging him into the tiny bathroom at Keybar where, thanks to multiple Rolo shots, I finally blurted out what I'd overheard. I'm so glad I did because things are back to normal between us again. After witnessing his mother go through a stolen identity experience at such a young age, of course he's more cautious and would want to warn Marcia against trusting strangers with personal information. My combination of anger and sadness disappeared once I knew it was less about me and more about making sure Marcia was aware of the dangers out there. I don't think she's naïve enough to get catfished, but it's not the same world she grew up in.

"How are you coping with living with a man?" Mom asks.

It's a valid question since my households have been exclusively female for most of my life. I was only four when my dad left. My grandparents moved in with us, but after my grandpa died when I was nine, it was just me, Audrina, Mom, and Nana. I had female roommates in college and again when I moved into the city. "No issues on that front." *Anymore.* He thinks I smell good. He *likes* me. Whatever that means. If someone hadn't banged on the bathroom door, would we have kissed? A fluttery sensation crops up in my tummy at the thought.

"As long as you're okay."

"Why wouldn't I be?"

"I just thought it might be hard to see them together. I know how much you miss Nana," she says softly.

I close my eyes to fight the memory of Nana crying the morning I left for college for the first time. She held me so hard, and I wiggled out of her embrace in a rush to get to the dorms. I didn't come home for Rosh Hashanah freshman year because I'd only been at school for two weeks, and she died from a sudden stroke before Thanksgiving break. I never got to say I was sorry, not just for cutting our hug short but for the teenage angst that destroyed our close relationship. Unfortunately for me, being kind to someone else's grandmother doesn't make up for being ungrateful to my own. I swallow down the lump in my throat.

"Sabrina?"

I jolt and wipe the tears from my eyes. "I'm here."

"Anything else new?"

I scrape my fingers across my comforter. I asked my advisor for an extension for the fellowship this morning, but he said the deadlines are airtight because only ten fellowships are available. My only hope for a loophole is if fewer than ten students applied on time. As this is unlikely, I'm screwed.

I'm at a crossroads. If I tell my mom I dropped the ball, she might drill me about my game plan like I'm one of her subordinates at work. Except there's also a possibility she'll reassure me it's not the end of the world. She knows I'm serious about my future and not about to let hiccups derail me long-term. She might even offer to loan me money for my living expenses without interest. I can already imagine her devising a formal scheduled payment plan to ensure I don't feel entitled to it or take it for granted. Like it's possible given the example she showed me. It's on the tip of my tongue to spill the entire story.

Then I think of how tirelessly she worked to get where she is all on her own with two little girls to clothe and feed on an entry-level salary thanks to a deadbeat husband and father. My life is easy in comparison, and I have no excuse for missing the deadline aside from dismissing my reminder, which never should have happened. Do I want to come clean, or is it better to keep my shame a secret?

WWMD? What would Mom do?

She'd figure it out on her own, and so will I.

"Nothing else is new." I twirl a lock of hair around my finger while my mind justifies the decision to lie. The fellowship was never guaranteed even if I'd submitted a timely application. I'm not any worse off than I was before I missed the deadline. I merely lost out on an opportunity to be *better* off. Unfortunately, I *need* to be better off…even a little bit. I decide to ask for more hours at the library. If I have to delay graduation by an extra semester to make more money to pay my living expenses, so be it. It seems so important now, but no one is going to ask how long it took to get my master's when I'm Marcia's age.

The conversation wraps up and I tell Mom I'll be home for her birthday and Passover the following month. We end the call. Then I lose myself in a study on cultural diversity in young adult literature for school until my eyes refuse to stay open any longer.

Chapter Thirteen

The next morning at work, I head straight to my library branch manager Jenny's office to ask for more hours. She's my only co-worker with private space, but she's the boss so it makes sense. The room is small, only about 150 square feet, but there are space-saving cabinets on the wall and she keeps her desk tidy, with fresh flowers weekly. This week's batch is a combination of yellow daffodils and forsythia.

I haven't had much one-on-one contact with Jenny, a fortysomething white transplant from Kentucky, aside from my interview, but she seems fair. She doesn't complain about the occasional personal call at work or chatting when the floor is quiet. She'll either tell me there's some wiggle room for additional hours or there's not. She won't fire me for asking. With that silent pep talk out of the way, I knock on her door.

She looks up and jerks her head back in surprise, her long brown curls swaying with the movement. This is to be expected since I've never come by her office before without being summoned, and even that's only happened once or twice. "Everything okay, Sabrina?"

"Do you have a minute?"

She tells me to sit, except there's only one chair and an enormous box of books is taking up all the seat space. I chew my lip. Do I remove it? Try to squeeze in next to it? Sit on top of it? I try lifting it first. "*Umph.*" It doesn't budge.

Jenny chuckles. "Sorry about the box. Someone left it there this morning and I haven't had time to do anything with it except confirm it's too heavy to relocate without the help of a bodybuilder."

"No problem." I sit with three quarters of my butt dangling off the seat.

"What can I do for you?" she asks with a slight Southern drawl.

I take a calming breath. The only way to guarantee failure is to not even try. "I was wondering if there was any way I could take on more hours."

Her eyebrows draw closer. "You're working while studying for your master's, right?"

"Yes. That's kind of why I need more hours. Living expenses combined with paying interest on my student loans, well, it isn't cheap." I technically don't need to start making payments until six months after I graduate, but my mom urged me to start earlier to lower the total cost. She's the budgeting wizard; I just do what she says.

Jenny's brown eyes soften, and she nods in understanding. "I remember. I just finished paying off my loans a few years ago. The cost of living here... well, let's just say I could buy a four-bedroom house back home in Kentucky for what I'm paying for my two-bedroom rental here in Park Slope." She exhales deeply as if it's something that keeps her up at night. "How many hours are you working now?"

"Approximately fifteen a week."

Jenny taps her pen along the scratched wooden desk, the diamonds from her engagement and wedding rings sparkling. "Hmm. You might just be in luck. Nancy gave her notice."

My eyes widen. "She did?" Nancy is one of the branch's two part-time library assistants. She focuses mostly on youth services but sometimes assists Gabe in adult as well, much to his displeasure. "I had no idea." Clearly, Gabe didn't either, or he'd be dancing down the library aisles. He can't stand her for featuring mostly books by white cis male authors on her displays and consistently misgendering Lane. I'm not a fan either but try to avoid drama at work.

"It's only been a few days. I figured she'd tell everyone herself... or not." She wrinkles her pixie nose. "I know there's some tension between y'all. Anyway, I haven't had a chance to go through regular channels about her replacement, but would you be interested?"

I don't need to think about it. "Yes!"

Jenny smiles. "That was easy. I'd need to formally interview you, but you have my support. It's twenty hours a week with a small bump in salary." She leans forward. "Part-time still, so no benefits."

I nod. This is fine since I'm still on my mom's health insurance.

"You'd have more direct contact with patrons and be involved in programming, creating displays, et cetera. But you'd also be expected to assist with circulation generally. It's a natural progression from page given your intention to stay within the library system after graduation. I think you'd enjoy it."

"I know I would!"

"Nancy's here another week and then we'd need you Monday through Saturday, at least until we find your replacement. But we can still work with your school schedule. Most of your classes are in the evenings, right?"

"I have one late afternoon class two days a week but otherwise, yes." My other class is in the evening after the library closes. I itch to do a victory lap around the floor. A promotion doesn't make up for missing out on the fellowship money, but from a professional standpoint, it's even better. I wonder but don't ask if Jenny would have offered it to me rather than putting out a formal ad if I hadn't requested more hours. It feels like fate, so why question it?

We schedule the formal interview for the following day, I thank her again, then go find Gabe. After I sum up my conversation with Jenny, he plays it cool on the floor but then drags me outside onto the street, into the cold, and yells, "Fuck yes. Fuck *yes*!" before calmly walking back inside completely composed. I accuse him of being happier about Nancy leaving than my hopeful promotion, but he insists he's equally thrilled about both. I don't believe him, but it doesn't matter.

After work, I head to school, where I find it hard to contain my toothy grin. It's one of those days where the air is sweeter and the future looks bright. I'm pausing to hold doors open for people, looking for reasons to offer up my seat on the subway, and stopping to give tourists directions. With Jenny's support, and assuming I don't fuck up the interview, I'm getting a promotion! The possibility didn't cross my mind when I woke up this morning. It wasn't on my radar at all. I assumed I'd hold the lowest position at the library at least until I graduated, and I was fine with that. It was a job at a *library*, my favorite place since I was a little girl and got lost in the latest of the Avalon High or Gallagher Girls series while Nana hunted down new books by Jennifer Weiner and Eileen Goudge. And now I was climbing my way up the ranks and making more money to boot.

I'm still drunk on happiness when I get home. Adam and Marcia are in the kitchen, side by side with their backs to me at the breakfast nook with a laptop on the counter between them.

"What are you guys up to?"

They both jolt at the sound of my voice, their shoulders lifting slightly and heads swinging to the right like a choreographed dance. I smile at their identical reactions. *Genetics.*

"Nothing much. What's up?" Adam swivels his stool and lowers the laptop cover before facing me again. "How was your day?"

"Yes, how was work and school?" Marcia asks.

Adam's smile is a little too bright to be real and Marcia is wringing her hands nervously. It's cagey, but nothing can mess with my mood right now. "It was excellent! I'm up for a promotion at work!" It's been about ten hours since my conversation with Jenny, and I still can't keep the exclamation point out of my voice. "My interview is tomorrow, but my boss says it's basically a formality."

Marcia's mouth drops open in sync with her eyes widening to full moons. "That's wonderful, Sabrina!" She stands and hugs me. "I'm so proud of you."

My chest swells as I squeeze her back. I'm almost as thrilled to make her proud as I am about the promotion itself. "Thank you!" I work to relax my jaw from its permanent smile.

"Congratulations!"

I separate from Marcia and beam at Adam. "Thanks!"

He extends his hand. I instinctively take it, not knowing where this is going, and before I realize what's happening, he's pulled me to him, squeezing me like a papa bear.

"Oh! Um. Thank you!" I murmur into his chest while breathing in his Cremo Pacific Sea Salt and Grapefruit exfoliating bodywash. I squeeze him back while also running my hands up and down his strong back because... hello muscles! The hug is over all too soon, and when he pulls away, I feel the absence of his touch.

"Hopefully, you feel better about missing out on the scholarship now," he says.

I smile softly. "I do."

Marcia beams between us. "When a door closes, a window opens."

I nod enthusiastically. "I need to text Carley and call my mom!"

"They'll be delighted. Go and come back with details when you're finished," Marcia says.

I tell her I will before heading to my room. I've barely taken five steps when I overhear Marcia hiss, "How are we going to fix this?"

"I don't know. Let me think," Adam says.

I backtrack to the kitchen. "Fix what?"

Marcia blinks rapidly. "Nothing."

Adam dips his head.

Cagey.

"Spill," I demand, but then my stomach knots. What if this is a personal family matter? I swallow hard. "Never mind. It's probably none of my business."

"It's not that. We're just in a bit of a pickle, but we'll figure it out, right, Adam?"

"Uh..." Adam shrugs weakly and rubs the back of his neck. "Sure?"

A swarm of butterflies takes flight in my belly. "You're making me nervous. Please put me out of my misery."

Marcia slides into a chair at the table. "I'm locked out of my banking website."

I let out a breath of relief. "That's it? What happened?"

She darts her eyes to Adam, who leans against the island looking guilty. "I wanted to transfer money to my IRA but forgot my password. Adam told me to click 'reset your password,' which sounded simple at the time, until I answered the security question wrong three times and I got locked out." She scrubs a hand down her face. "Why did I think the name of my first-grade teacher was a good security question? It's been sixty-five years!"

"Why didn't you just look up your password or wait for me to help you?"

She pushes out her lips. "I figured you'd be tired from working and school. Adam volunteered to help."

"Oh he did, did he?" I level my eyes at him with a hand on my hip. *Not this again.*

He grimaces. "I was only trying to be helpful." In a lower voice, he adds, "No other reason, I swear." He raises his palms. "But I fucked up."

I chuckle. "First of all, calm down." I glance between them. "I can fix this. Hand me the laptop."

He does, and I sit down at the table with both of them on either side of me. Within a minute, I'm on the phone with the bank. Within five minutes, Marcia has verified her identity and her account has been restored. Ten minutes later, her password manager has been updated. I log out of her computer and lower the lid. "In the future, just wait for me to get home, okay?"

Marcia slides her chair closer to me and gives me a one-arm hug and a kiss on the cheek. "You're the best."

I make a gloating face at Adam, but he looks so sheepish, I burst into laughter. "I'm sure you are great at many things, but please leave the computer stuff to me. Okay, boomer?"

He chuckles. "Lesson learned."

I stand, prepared to go to my room and finally share the news about my promotion with my mom and Carley. Before I go, I say, "If you want to be useful with all the free time on your hands, my library will be looking for a page to replace me. Maybe you should apply for the job." I imagine Adam discovering a PB&J sandwich inside a book and repress a laugh.

Since this is obviously a joke, I'm not at all prepared for his next words.

"Actually, I like that idea a lot. How do I do that?"

Chapter Fourteen

I wasn't serious about Adam applying for the library page job, but *he* was. It turns out he did a teen internship at the Free Library of Philadelphia in high school, which included a crash course in the Dewey Decimal System. When Marcia reminisced about taking little-boy Adam to the library where he discovered and devoured Marc Brown's Arthur series, my heart pinched thinking about Nana, and I said I would put in a good word for him once the promotion was official.

Two days later, I'm in the workroom at the library sorting through supplies for an upcoming program for teens when my phone pings with a text.

Adam: I'm at the library. Is this an okay time?

My pulse speeds up and my heart slams against my chest. I wish I had thought things through better before I joked about Adam applying for my job. Now I'm afraid that regardless of the outcome, I'm fucked. If he doesn't get the job, I'll feel horrible... like my good word meant nothing to Jenny. And if he *does* get the job... well, that's even scarier, if I'm being honest. Seeing gorgeous Adam all day surrounded by books and all night cuddling with Rocket and bonding with his grandmother? Seriously, how much can a horny, single girl take before her panties spontaneously drop to her ankles?

Ping.

Adam: I'm on the second floor—early readers

Determined to pull myself together, I leave the text on read and meet him one floor up. I find him running his fingers along the spines of the Arthur books. He's wearing khaki stretch corduroy pants that fit his ass like they were tailored for him and a chambray button-down shirt rolled up to his forearms. He's dressed more formally than most of the staff here. We're all super casual and comfortable because we spend a lot of time bending and kneeling to return and remove books from the shelves. I assume he's dressed to impress Jenny, but she won't be the only one. He wins best-looking patron of the day (so far, at least) and I'm tempted to covertly snap a photo for #hotguysreading on Insta.

My footsteps must alert him to my presence because he turns and smiles. "I'd forgotten about these until my grandma mentioned them." He shows me the one he's pulled off the shelf, *Arthur Meets the President*, before putting it back. "I hope this is a good time."

"It's exactly eleven thirty, so your timing is perfect," I say while double checking to make sure he's reshelved the book in the proper spot. When I told Jenny my roommate's grandson was interested in taking over the part-time page position, her head had flinched back comically and understandably, since most people my age don't live with someone old enough to have a grandson, and if they did, hiring said child would probably break some labor laws. But after I explained, she said to have him come by today between eleven and twelve.

"You nervous?" I shove my hands in the front pockets of my high-waisted blue jeans and rock on my toes. Perhaps he should be asking me this question.

Adam's tongue darts out to lick his lower lip. "Not really. If I don't get the job, it will give me more time to help Grams with all that tech stuff."

"At this point, she could probably teach you a thing or two," I joke, working hard to focus on my sarcastic delivery and not his tongue.

His eyes dance.

I shake my head. "Let's go."

Jenny's on the floor talking to Penny, the youth services librarian, by checkout. "Stay back a second," I tell Adam. I don't want to put her on the spot in case she's not ready. I apologize for interrupting them and ask if Jenny has time to see Adam now. When she says yes, I call him over.

"Jenny, this is Adam. Like I mentioned yesterday, he's interested in the page position." To Adam I say, "Jenny's the branch manager and in charge of hiring."

They shake hands and Jenny suggests we continue downstairs in her office, where she tells Adam to have a seat.

Adam points to the single chair. On it sits the same heavy box from two days ago. "Here?"

"Darn. That's still there. I forgot."

While Jenny scans the room like another open chair will miraculously appear, a nonplussed Adam uses both hands to grab the box from the bottom and with one movement, lifts the monstrosity off the chair. Then he holds it like it's the weight of a thin picture book. "Where do you want it?"

Jenny blinks, seemingly too shocked to speak. "The . . . uh . . . over there is good," she finally says.

Adam gently places the box on an empty spot on the cabinet Jenny pointed to.

"You're hired," she jokes. At least I think she's joking.

I cover my own swooning with a laugh and while Adam sits, I lean against the closed office door for balance.

"Where in the South are you from?" he asks her.

"How'd you guess?" She chuckles. "Northwestern Kentucky."

"Ever been to the Moonlite Bar-B-Q Inn?"

Jenny's eyes go wide. "You're familiar with Owensboro?"

Adam smiles. "College friend grew up there. We've lost touch, but I'd go back just for the barbecue mutton."

I must make a face because Jenny howls. "It's so much more delicious than it sounds!" She gestures toward Adam. "You don't have to babysit him. Why don't you give us a few minutes to chat, and I'll send him back to you when we're finished?"

"Oh. Of course!" The tone of her voice is so friendly, I can't take offense to being kicked out. Besides, most people don't take chaperones to interviews. I'm still in shock that this is really happening. "Come find me when you're done, Adam." My face burns. "If you want."

I leave them to it and return to my sorting from before, but it's hard to focus on anything but the conversation between Jenny and Adam happening in my absence. Presumably, once they stop gushing over barbeque mutton...gross...Jenny will ask the typical interview questions. I imagine the interview will go something like this:

What inspired you to apply for this job?

Adam will *want* to keep it light and admit that it was my idea because he has too much idle time, but he's too smart to take the risk of sounding apathetic. He'll say something about his love of reading and how much time he spent with his grandmother at his local library as a child.

Why should I hire you?

I bet he'll say he's a hard worker who believes that libraries are more than big rooms with books. He might talk about wanting to pay it forward to the community. I said both of these things in my interview.

What are you reading now?

Last I saw, he was reading *The Ferryman* by Justin Cronin, but he might be finished by now.

An incoming text jolts me out of my imaginary interview.

Adam: I'm finished

The necklace cord I'm holding, part of our jewelry-making event, slides out of my clammy hands.

Sabrina: Where are you now?

Adam: Young adult

Sabrina: I'll be right there

For the second time in an hour, I leave the box of supplies unattended and find Adam. This time, he's thumbing through the pages of *This Lullaby* by Sarah Dessen. "This one's on the bookshelf at home."

This isn't how I expected him to greet me minutes after concluding his job interview with my boss. It's also strange to hear him call the apartment "home," but not a bad weird, just weird. "She's one of my favorite authors."

He grins. "I got the job."

"Way to bury the lede. Congratulations!" As the word comes out, I realize that, despite my anxiety over spending so much time with him, I truly mean it.

"Thank you! I can start training on Monday, but there's paper-work to fill out. Jenny has a lunch call so I'm going to come back later. In the meantime, you get a lunch hour, right?"

I laugh. "You haven't started yet, and you're already concerned about your lunch breaks?"

"No. I'm asking if you want to grab lunch with me today. Like now."

My breath catches. I figured he'd go home after the interview and I'd have time to ease my way into the reality of us living *and* working together. But now he's asking me to lunch. Will this be a regular thing?

"I'll come back with you after to complete the forms, but I have some questions about the job you can probably answer best."

I feel a mixture of disappointment and relief that this is about the job and not because he wants to spend even more time with me.

"She also said you'd be the one training me during your regular shifts."

This catches me off guard and my skin heats up under my T-shirt as my frisky imagination conjures up a scenario where I'm forced to discipline Adam for returning a book to the wrong shelf or some other egregious library act. Then my stomach growls, reminding me to stay in the moment. Adam's asked me to go to lunch, not be the domina-trix to his subordinate.

He points in the vicinity of my belly. "Feed me," he says in an otherworldly voice.

I press both hands over my stomach and feign confusion. "Huh?

That wasn't me." *Rumble. Rumble.* I sigh. Why is my digestive system such a bitch?

Adam's eyes twinkle. "Seriously. Let's eat."

We go to Citizens of Gramercy, an Australian café a few blocks away that serves "brekky" all day. Although there's plenty of seating, either at two communal tables by the entrance or one of the six smaller tables deeper inside the narrow space, I follow Adam to the counter, where we sit on two of the four open stools. Aside from a patch of floral wallpaper, the walls are painted white. On the far end of the café, the phrase, "Stay gorgeous, Gramercy" is lit up in hot-pink script.

I flip through the laminated menu. It's a vegan/gluten-free/dairy-free paradise. "Too bad they don't have mutton."

"Don't knock it until you try it."

I drop the menu onto my lap. "No, thank you. I might not celebrate Christmas, but that doesn't mean I'm okay with eating Rudolph the Red-Nosed Reindeer."

Adam freezes with a glass of water at his lips and squints at me.

"What?" Do I have ink on my face or something?

He cocks his head. "Do you think mutton is deer, Sabrina?"

"Isn't it?" I know nothing about mutton aside from it not being very popular in Northern Connecticut or New York City, the only two places I've lived.

Adam's face turns red, the flush of amusement. "It's sheep, Sabrina. Meat from a mature sheep. Marcia made lamb chops last week. If the little lamb is a baby lamb, then Mary is the sheep, aka mutton. You wouldn't be eating Rudolph. You'd be eating Mary."

How he says this with a straight face is beyond me. I shrug off my initial misassumption—it could happen to anyone who's not an adventurous eater or in the culinary business—and focus on the second half of his statement. "I thought Mary was a child and the little lamb was her pet. Are you saying Mary was the little lamb's *mother*?"

A wrinkle forms between Adam's icy blue eyes. I've stumped him. "Huh. I have no idea. I just assumed." He takes a sip of water. "You think my grandma knows?"

"*Pfft*. Marcia knows everything!"

We laugh, then turn to the server to place our orders: the Smashing Avocado and a Golden Latte for me, and Banana Bread French Toast and an Americano for him. "Congratulations again," I say a few minutes later after an awkward silence while we sipped our warm drinks and scrolled through our phones. "Not gonna lie, I was totally joking when I suggested it. You've got a pretty sweet deal right now. Are you sure you want to join the world of the employed so soon, especially for a few dollars more than minimum wage and no benefits?"

His lips quirk. "I can't say I haven't been basking in this break. It's just... I haven't enjoyed any of the jobs I've held since graduation. And I know most people don't have the luxury of loving to work, but it would be nice to feel *some* passion, you know?"

I nod. I've known what I wanted to be when I grew up for so long, it's hard to imagine not having a specific plan.

The server places our food in front of us. My avocado toast, topped with feta, sunflower seeds, pumpkin seeds, and watermelon radishes, is set atop a pink beetroot hummus. It looks like a neon culinary delight, but I worry the interruption will signal the end of this topic of conversation, and I want to hear more about Adam's passions.

"Studying comes easy to me, but working, not so much. I have a degree in business, but 'business' is so vague, I didn't know what was waiting for me in the real world. So far, I've worked for a bank, a cruise line, and a beer distributor. The last one wasn't nearly as intoxicating as it sounds." He smiles sheepishly.

I chuckle at the pun but neglect to mention I've already stalked his LinkedIn profile and know where he worked before. "I think it's unfair to expect us to know what we want to do with the rest of our lives when we've barely lived. I always knew I wanted to do something with books, but it doesn't happen like that for everyone, and there's nothing to be ashamed of." I cut into my toast and take a bite.

He drinks from his mug. "Working in a library appeals to me. So many of my favorite books from middle school are now being banned, and I love that the NYPL has started the Teen Banned Book Club. Anything I can do to give back, even if it means an entry-level job." He grimaces. "No offense."

"None taken," I say honestly. Most grad students aren't CEOs or even midmanagement. I'm lucky for any job in my field that works with my school hours. Besides, how could I be offended by someone who's grateful that the library is fighting back against book bans and wants to give back? It's a direct line to my heart and my unmentionables.

His gaze has been mostly focused straight ahead until now, but he turns to me. "So thank you again for hooking me up. This is on me." He gestures toward our dishes.

I snap my fingers. "I wish you'd told me ahead of time. I was too cheap to spend the three dollars for the poached egg on top of my toast."

In a more serious tone than mine, he says, "I thought it was a given. I know you didn't sign up for me moving in with you guys, and you've been extremely cool about it. I appreciate it."

The expression he's wearing is so genuine that I can't help but feel touched. My face flushes with heat but I try to play it cool. "It's not a big deal. Just don't make me look bad in front of Jenny."

He raises three fingers in the Scout's-honor sign.

"But seriously, I would never deny Marcia this time with you. What does your dad think?"

He stares down at his plate. "I haven't really spoken to him about it. I'm on his shit list for several reasons, the least of which is reconnecting with his mother. He's more upset that I'm wasting the Ivy League education he paid for to take a vacation from life."

I *think* "fuck your dad" but take a bite of my toast to avoid *saying* it out loud. "Well, now you can brag to him about your big job and tell him you'll be able to pay him back any day now."

Adam brings a forkful of French toast to his mouth and grins. "With that salary? In about two hundred years maybe!"

Chapter Fifteen

"I'm starving. I want everything." Marcia scans the expansive spiral-bound menu at the Cosmic Diner on Eighth Avenue and Fifty-Third Street with the focus of Meredith Grey during surgery. We came to the small diner near Times Square straight from the Westside GI Center, where she had a morning colonoscopy. "I must have lost at least five pounds last night with the prep. Thank God I have my own bathroom." She wrinkles her nose.

I grimace. "I will *not* be counting the years until I turn forty-five. No offense."

"What I wouldn't do to go back." She looks dreamy for a moment. "Anyway, the prep is awful, but the drugs are top-notch. I feel fantastic!"

"I'll have what she's having," says our waitress, a white woman around my mom's age with chin-length dark brown hair, with a grin.

I giggle. Marcia's been talking about the drugs since the moment she found me in the waiting room after her procedure. The receptionist explained they take a bit to wear off.

"I've never seen such shiny floors in a diner. Have you ever seen such shiny floors in a diner, Sabrina?" Marcia ogles her feet like a naked Chris Evans is sprawled across the admittedly very shiny hardwood.

"I'll send the compliments to the staff." Amused, the waitress gestures to the mugs on the table and when we nod, pours coffee into both of them before taking our food orders.

"Thank you again for picking me up," Marcia says for the fourth time when we're alone again. She's definitely still loopy and effusive with her gratitude.

"Of course." Adam wanted to do it, but we agreed it was better for me to take the morning off from work than him since he just started last week.

After a sit-down on his first day, during which I described the basic responsibilities of a library page in detail, he watched me while I worked for the next two days. Then we turned the tables and I shadowed him, making sure he was well and truly prepared for the job before finally deeming him ready to work independently, like a child going off to kindergarten.

"You are a gem taking a PTO day to escort me today! I definitely think I got the long end of the stick with you as my roommate."

I shake my head. "I respectfully disagree. You could charge three times as much money for that room!" A wave of panic whooshes through me in case she decides that, yes, she absolutely can. But I also have a feeling she won't remember much of this drug-induced conversation. "Besides, I did it because I care about you, not because of some sort of obligation." I leave out that as a nonunion part-timer, I don't get paid time off. "I hope you know that I don't think of you as some sort of job and that I'm more to you than a mattress flipper slash computer lesson." I cringe at what feels like fishing, but she'll probably forget this part of the conversation too. At least I hope so.

She reaches across the table and squeezes my hand. "I love living with you. And having Adam too is the cherry on top of the whipped cream." Her face clouds over for a second. "He doesn't talk about it, but he had a difficult childhood."

"Really? How so?" I ask, eager to learn more.

Before she can answer, the waitress drops off our food.

Marcia pours maple syrup into every crevice of her waffle before cutting a square and taking a bite. She closes her eyes like it's a Michelin star–quality breakfast.

I assume she's lost track of the conversation, but then she swallows, places her fork on the ceramic plate, and leans toward me like she's about to share the meaning of life. I brace for her next words.

"He was very close with his mother and lost her when he was only twelve."

My throat goes thick. He only mentioned his mom once, when he told me her identity was stolen. I should have asked more about her. "How'd she die?"

"Breast cancer. She was only thirty-eight."

The piece of bacon I just swallowed feels trapped in my throat. That's so young. "I'm so sorry!"

"Me too. Renee was wonderful." Marcia closes her eyes for a beat. "If she'd been alive after Robert died and I came out as bisexual, things might have been different in many ways." She shakes her head slowly. "His reaction would have been the same, but Renee would have said congratulations and moved on *and* made sure that my relationship with Adam didn't suffer because of Jeffrey's biases. Instead Adam was raised by a man who expected him to follow in his footsteps. But Adam is an independent thinker, like me and like his mother. From what he tells me, they disagree on so many things, but unfortunately I wasn't around to take his side after the age of fourteen or fifteen." She sips her coffee. "I'm just glad he had more open-minded people in his life, like his classmates and teachers. Like I had my community."

Marcia told me that when she first came out, she joined a local support group for LGBTQIA seniors—people who could truly relate to the experience of coming out later in life. "Did you ever have a girlfriend?" I feel a pang of guilt like I'm taking advantage of her buzzed condition, but I'm curious because she hasn't dated anyone—man, woman, or nonbinary—since I've moved in.

"I had the one Jeffrey met, but it didn't last and then I just got frustrated and bored with the whole thing. Menopause also wreaked havoc on my hormones." She screws up her face. "But that's even worse than colonoscopy prep, and I won't depress you with the details!"

I smile softly. "I'm always here to listen if you want to talk!"

Her lips form a straight line. "Sometimes there are things you wish you didn't know about the people you love. That's how I feel about my son. Sometimes ignorance is bliss. I wasn't sure what I was going to get when Adam showed up, and boy am I pleased with the man he's become."

I picture the awkward bar mitzvah photo and think the same thing.

She peers at me. "He likes you."

I pick at my omelet. When the drugs wear off Marcia might regret being so forthcoming, so I decide not to press more or tell her that I like him too . . . a lot. Across from me, she attacks her breakfast with gusto while I contemplate what things must have been like for Adam after his mom died. He was raised by someone with a belief system completely mismatched with his own, no siblings, and kept apart from his grandmother.

My own family isn't perfect. When my parents first split, my dad would take us out maybe once a month, and I couldn't wait to see my daddy! But then it slowed down to every six months, once a year, two years, and so on. And we never knew if he'd actually follow through. I still remember staring out the living room window with Audrina for hours one day, waiting for our dad's car to pull up the driveway to take us to an amusement park. He never showed up and didn't bother to tell Mom he wasn't coming until hours later, when it was already obvious. It wasn't the only time he stood us up. Eventually, he stopped bothering to make plans altogether. Mom never let us down like that. I might have resented how much she worked, but I respected the heck out of her. I knew she loved me, and Nana made sure all my needs were taken care of. My Nana was my best pal and reading buddy. There was no one whose company I enjoyed more.

Growing up, people always assumed Nana was my mom's mother—friends who came over, teachers Nana met with at school conferences she attended when Mom was working—but she was my father's mom. His parents moved in after he left to help take care of us while my mother built her career.

Only I ignored all the good stuff in my rebellious teenage years. As I learned more about how fathers are *supposed* to act versus the inaction of my own, my relationship with Nana changed. I was angry, and since I couldn't take it out on him directly, his mother became my scapegoat. I directed the brunt of my attitude toward my nana. I stopped spending time with her that wasn't forced and snapped at her constantly. How could she just *allow* her son to abandon his wife and children? Why didn't she hate him like I did? Those years, it was all about me and my loss (well, mine, my sister's, and our mother's). It didn't occur to me that Nana had also lost a son. By the time I got a clue, she was gone, and it was too late to apologize and try to reclaim our closeness.

I look across the table at Marcia and am struck by the parallels between her relationship with Adam's dad and Nana's with mine. The specifics are different, but they share disappointment and anger toward their son along with the stubborn enduring love *most* parents feel toward their children no matter what.

"Are you okay, Sabrina?"

I realize I've been too lost in my own thoughts to carry on a conversation. "I'm fine. Just dreading going back to work and then class later. You should get colonoscopies more often." I force a smile.

"Yeah, except the drugs wore off and now I'm nauseous."

I look at her empty plate, once filled with waffles, two eggs, bacon, and sausage. "I wonder why."

Chapter Sixteen

Over the next week at the library, I spend a few days training for my new position, rotating between Penny and Gabe. Right now, Gabe's showing me how to create promotional materials for an upcoming book club event while Adam is shelving books in the aisles reserved for adult mysteries.

"Canva Pro is free for all public libraries, so we have access to all the fancy graphics," Gabe says, gesturing at the computer in front of us.

I nod, eager to learn everything I can, when I spy a patron approach Adam. I can't hear what the patron says, but Adam's eyes grow wide, and he turns my way with a pleading expression.

I don't have time to be embarrassed he busted me watching him. "You mind if we take five? I think Adam needs me."

Gabe looks up from the graphic and raises his eyebrows suggestively. "He *needs* you, huh?"

I huff. "*With a patron*. You're super professional, aren't you?"

He grins. "You're the one shirking your training responsibilities, Finkelstein. But go help your sexy roommate. Holler if you need me. At a library volume, obviously." Looking pleased with himself, he says, "How's that for professional?"

"Professional with a side of snarky. The Gabe Jackson story." I leave him with a chuckle and join Adam and his new friend. "Is everything all right here?"

Adam's posture visibly relaxes at my approach. He turns to the man. "This is Sabrina, sir. She's been working here much longer than me and will be able to answer your question."

I can't help beaming at him for putting my basic customer-service training to good use. I told him patrons can't distinguish between the roles that exist within the library—to them we all just work here. People will ask him questions often, from the location of the bathroom, to book recommendations, to computer and printer assistance. If he doesn't know the answer, he's to politely inform the patron he'll find the right staff member to take over.

The patron is an older white man with gray hair and a matching mustache. He's carrying a huge red umbrella even though the weather report doesn't call for rain and the sun is shining through the windows of the library. I like him already. "How can I assist you?"

"I'm looking for a book like *The Hunger Games*."

"I can absolutely help with that. Are you interested in young adult dystopian generally or is there something specific about *The Hunger Games* you enjoyed?"

He smooths his mustache. "I'm not sure. We watched the movies with our granddaughter last weekend, and it was the happiest she's been since she came to stay with us." His face clouds over before he tells us that his ten-year-old granddaughter is visiting from Maryland while her mother—his daughter—is on her honeymoon. "Chloe isn't taking her mom's remarriage well. Her dad passed away a few years ago, and she's afraid her mom is forgetting about him. This isn't true, but she won't listen to us." He removes his glasses and rubs at his eyes.

I think about what Marcia just told me about Adam's mother

and wonder if it's hard for him to hear stories like this. Even though we've watched TV a few times and commuted together to and from work since then, I haven't brought it up to him, figuring he'd be less than pleased if he knew his drugged-up grandmother had confided in me about his past. I sneak a glance at him, but his expression gives away nothing.

The man puts his glasses back on. "Before we watched the movie, Chloe told us all about the great Katniss Everdeen and her entire face lit up. She's Team Gale. My wife and I are Team Peeta. What about you?"

I grin. "Team Peeta."

We both turn to Adam expectantly.

He shrugs. "I never read the books or watched the movies."

My jaw drops. "What? How?" I could *almost* understand if he hadn't read it when it was published in 2008. He was only nine. But even after the movie came out, he *still* didn't read it or even watch it? I bet he'd love it since he seems to enjoy adult dystopian like *The Ferryman*. "We'll talk about this later."

Adam's lips twitch.

The man breathes out a laugh and glances between us. "My wife wears the pants in our relationship too."

"Oh we're not..." I say as Adam says, "Bossy women are the best. Am I right?" before winking at me.

I'm sure my body temperature increases by at least a couple degrees. "Hilarious." I gulp then turn to Chloe's grandpa like the professional I am. "So you're hoping to recreate the experience you shared watching *The Hunger Games* together with another book?"

He nods. "My wife, her grandmother, suggested that we read a similar book together, and if there's also a movie, even better. If we need to watch more kids kill each other, it will be worth it to keep that light in Chloe's eyes!"

I melt into a puddle, and it takes all my self-control not to declare, "*Aww*!" Instead, I rattle off a few recommendations like *Divergent*, *Uglies*, *The Fifth Wave*, and *The Selection*. The last one isn't a movie, but it's also not as violent as the others, and I think a little girl Chloe's age would love a *Bachelor*-type book.

"Are any of these available to take out now? We'll buy it for Chloe for her e-reader, but my wife and I will want to read the hard copy together."

I picture Chloe's grandparents reading side by side in bed and my heart grows a size. "Let's see!" Although we could check online, it's easy enough to walk to the young adult section in the back and see what's there. We get lucky with *The Selection*.

With his book in hand, Chloe's grandpa beams at me and Adam. "Thank you so much for your help."

"Our pleasure! Please come back and tell us what Chloe thought of the book," Adam says.

"I will!" And with a salute, he takes his red umbrella and leaves.

I turn to Adam. "We're reading *The Hunger Games* as our buddy read, and since 'bossy women are the best,' I expect no argument."

We hold our first book club discussion a few nights later after Marcia goes to bed. We asked her to join us, but she had no interest in a book about "kids killing each other." We're both dressed comfy for a night-in, me in beige drawstring pants and a plain white cotton tee and Adam in black sweatpants and a gray UPenn sweatshirt.

"How can you be Team Gale?" I say to him while curled on one end of his couch/bed.

From the other side, Adam says, "I'm not team *anyone*. I'm just calling it like I see it."

"Fine. The jury will hear your case, counselor." I kick my foot against his.

He catches it and holds it in place. "I think Katniss feels loyal to Peeta given what they've been through, but the kiss in the cave was fake. She's in love with Gale. This is not me shipping them. It's a fact."

I open my mouth to argue but nothing comes out because Adam is still holding my foot, gently massaging it through my socked toe, and it feels amazing. Better to say nothing than moan in pleasure.

I detect the exact moment he realizes what he's doing because the color drains from his face and he drops his hands like the sole of my foot has sprouted painful and poisonous needles.

I quickly hug my legs to my chest and carry on as if nothing happened. Hiding my flaming face with my hair, I say, "I don't want to give anything away, but you're wrong. I won't say more since you haven't finished the trilogy."

His eyes dance. "Fair enough."

I smirk. "I knew you'd love it."

"And you were right."

Don't you wish you'd read it earlier?"

He shakes his head softly. "No. Because we wouldn't be reading it together now."

I slowly melt.

Blissfully unaware of my liquification, Adam vaults off the couch. "Cheetos?"

Before going to sleep later, I text Carley from my bed.

Sabrina: How was the show tonight?

I close my eyes. This could be a while. My phone dings. Or not.

Carley: The makeup was *chef's kiss*

Sabrina: Because who cares if the leads are tone-deaf if their makeup application is flawless, right?

Carley: Wrd. What did you do?

Sabrina: The library's first Mahjong for Beginners lesson was today. And I had book club with Adam

My heart rate speeds up as it does whenever I mention Adam. *Rude*.

Carley: What's this about book club?

Sabrina: No comment on the mahjong? You're the one who dragged me to that mahjong club last year

Carley: that was just a decoy. You really want to talk about the book club

I sigh. There she goes reading my mind again.

Sabrina: Can you believe Adam never read THG?

Carley: Does THG stand for The Hot Grandson?

I shake my head and laugh.

Sabrina: THE HUNGER GAMES

Before I can stop myself, I text again.

Sabrina: He might have accidentally given me a foot rub

Feeling scandalous, I drop the phone upside down on the area rug at my feet and cover my eyes.

Ping.

Carley: It must be serious if there's been hand to foot contact. You're playing with fire, Finkelstein

Sabrina: Nothing is happening. It can't. Too weird

Carley: Who r u trying to convince?

Good question. I wish I had an answer.

Chapter Seventeen

The following Sunday, I'm in the apartment alone aside from Rocket, who's dozing on Marcia's bed. Marcia's getting her hair done and Adam . . . well, I have no idea where he is. Contrary to what Chloe's grandpa might think, we're not in a relationship, which means where Adam goes when he's not at home or at the library is none of my business. He could be at the gym or on a date. I push the Swiffer WetJet across the wood floor with a heavy hand and brush a sweaty lock of hair off my face. I'm seizing the opportunity to clean the living room without anyone around to get in my space.

My phone pings with an incoming text message, giving me the excuse I need to banish Adam's whereabouts from my mind, at least for now. It's from my sister.

Audrina: You're coming home for Mom's bday/ Passover, right?

Sabrina: Why wouldn't I?

Our mom's birthday is tomorrow, April seventh, but we always celebrate it at Passover whether the holiday falls in March or April, since it changes from year to year. This year it's later than usual, in the second half of the month.

Audrina: It's a yes or no answer

I roll my eyes.

Sabrina: Yes

I watch the screen as my sister types out a response, but when the dancing bubbles disappear, I place my phone on the coffee table to resume my cleaning, assuming the text exchange is over.

Ping.

Audrina: There's something else

Sabrina: Go on

Audrina: I'm moving in with Mom

My muscles tense. I blink and read the words again to make sure I'm understanding correctly. After the fourth reread, my heart leaps into my throat.

Sabrina: Why? When? Are you okay? Is she okay?

Although Audrina and I have friends well into their twenties who still live with their parents, Mom made it clear before we went away to college that she expected us to fend for ourselves after graduation, even if meant rooming with a stranger three times our age or sleeping on an air mattress in someone's bathroom. Clearly something big has gone down if my sister is moving back home.

My phone rings. Apparently, whatever it is cannot be shared over text. *Shit.*

"Tell me."

Audrina snorts. "We're both fine. I asked if I could move in temporarily to save money."

Save money. What a novel idea. Between my rent, tuition, and a social life limited to buy one, get one free ladies' nights and happy hour specials, I'm lucky if I have an extra hundred dollars in my bank account at any given time. And that's with my raise.

"Since Kevin moved out, all the rent falls on me. And there's really nothing else out there much cheaper."

I twirl my hair. Audrina married Kevin, her college sweetheart, right after graduation four years ago. We all assumed they were a real-life OTP until things fell apart and they legally separated last year.

"I agreed to pay for groceries and other incidentals, so it's not a free ride."

I feel for her. Of course I do. But along with sympathy, there's also envy, bitterness, and resentment. Audrina asked for help and got it. Just like that. But it's not fair for me to be angry with her for asking Mom for help just because I didn't. Nothing stopped me from telling her about the lost fellowship except my determination to prove I could do this on my own, like she did. And I am. I pay all my bills. I'm not starving. I go out with friends. I don't *need* help.

"Are you still there?"

I jolt out of my contemplation. "Yup."

"At least with me doing the food shopping there'll be more fruits and vegetables in the fridge and less of the processed crap she loves."

"The processed stuff is cheaper." Growing up, Mom bought whatever was on sale, even if it was something we didn't typically eat like Crunch Berries cereal or Yodels.

"Cheaper initially but more expensive in the long run when it leads to heart problems."

I sink into the couch cushion, prepared for her to regale me with her latest TED Talk on the importance of organic fruits or the magic of intermittent fasting, but she says she has to go and ends the call.

I return my attention to cleaning. I dust and polish all the furniture and water the plants.

As I'm straightening up Adam's personal items, careful not to touch anything I shouldn't, like his underwear, I spy the edge of a book beneath his messenger bag. By now he knows (or should know) you can't leave a book mere inches away from me and not expect my curiosity to be piqued like a doomed character in a horror flick. Without even thinking, I pull the book from underneath the bag. It's a mass-market paperback copy of *The Outsiders*.

I haven't read this book in *years*... maybe even a decade. I've never seen this cover before. I run my thumb along it. Against a black background is a photograph of a man in a leather jacket looking down so you can't see his face. S. E. Hinton appears at the top in big white block letters, and the only real color is the title on the bottom, also in big block letters but bright yellow.

The copy is old and dog-eared. I flip to the copyright page and see this edition was released in 1988, more than ten years before either of us were born. As I flick through the chapters, I see it's an annotated copy with chapter names and sections highlighted in multiple colors with comments in the margins, like when something is a flashback or an analogy. I make myself comfy on the couch and start reading, immediately drawn into the world of Ponyboy Curtis, his brothers, and the rest of the greasers. I don't know how much time has passed when the apartment door opens. Adam joins me in the living room with a smile that disappears as he hovers over me.

"What are you doing?" He grabs the book from my lap, his blue eyes pinned to mine accusingly.

I recoil at the aggression in slow motion like I'm being awakened from a deep sleep. I gesture at the book now in his hand. "I was straightening up your things and saw it. I forgot how much I love it! Are those your annotations or did you buy it this way?"

Ignoring the question, he shoves the novel in his messenger bag and kicks it under the couch.

I frown. He seems angry. "Is something wrong?"

He leans slightly forward with a pointed gaze. "Do you always go through people's things and sit on their beds?"

I have no idea what is happening here, but my pulse is racing when I stand. "First of all, I was sitting on the *couch*. Your bed is the mattress currently folded inside the couch. Second of all, I didn't go through your *things*. It's one thing... a book." The words and tone of my voice match the aggression of his, but at least they disguise my confusion. I don't know where Adam's sudden hostility is coming from.

"*My* book. As in not yours. Not the library's. Mine."

I gape at him. "Wow. You look really old for a six-year-old." I wait for him to say something to explain away his bizarre reaction, but he stares at the television like I'm not even there.

"Fine. Be that way." I hug myself to disguise my tremoring body. Surely he'll apologize for being a dick for absolutely no reason whatsoever.

Except he doesn't.

I have an hour before I'm supposed to meet some classmates at the university library to work on a group project, but I can't get out of here fast enough. After hightailing it to my room for my things, I rush through the living room to the front door without a word and slam it behind me.

Chapter Eighteen

My bad mood follows me to the university library. Who does Adam think he is, going off on me for no reason?

I didn't creep over to the couch in the middle of the night and remove his kidney while he was sleeping. I wasn't snooping in a private journal. I read a book (not mine, not the library's, *his*!) and I dared to do it while sitting on his "bed." Arrest me. Lock me up and throw away the key. Hang me from the gallows!

I'm thankfully able to put it aside just long enough to work on my group presentation on adolescent literacy and why analog instruction is still relevant in an increasingly digital society. But the minute I say goodbye to my classmates and head home, the knots in my body tighten to the point it would take a twenty-four-hour massage to loosen me up. I hope Adam isn't home when I get back because I refuse to make the first move, but he's roughhousing with Rocket on the living room floor. Since I'm not ready for the awkwardness of our first words post *whatever the hell that was* this morning, I grab Rocket's leash from the hook near the front door and call out, "Rocket Man! C'mere, boy."

At his name, Rocket abandons Adam and races over to me. *Take that!* I bend and love him up for a few seconds before hooking him to the leash.

"I just took him out an hour ago."

Still focusing on Rocket, I say, "I need some puppy time." I clench my fists. Why am I justifying myself to Adam? I knew Rocket first, and based on the way the dog is frantically running around me, he might not *need* to go out, but he *wants* to. That's enough for me. Without further explanation or details (because I'm under no more obligation to keep Adam updated on my whereabouts than he is to me about his), I leave the apartment and lead Rocket over to the small dog run in Union Square Park. When I release him from his leash, he immediately makes friends with a shaggy gray sheepdog while I sit on an empty brown wooden bench and watch.

Other than the convenience of being around the corner, Marcia isn't a fan of this dog park. It's small and Rocket has the personality of a much larger dog. She also claims there's a constant cloud of dust hanging over and it smells like pee. I don't notice either of these things today, maybe because it's empty aside from the owner of the sheepdog talking on his phone on the bench next to mine. The air is cold and wet like it either just stopped raining or is about to start. It's not pleasant, but I'm happy to be anywhere besides home with Adam.

Almost like I summoned him, the devil himself appears two minutes later. "Why does it always smell like piss in this place?" He sits down next to me.

I stiffen and shift an inch away from him. "Do you not trust me to take Rocket? I was doing it long before you moved in." I don't look at him as I say this. My gaze remains on Rocket. He's slapping his front legs repeatedly with his butt in the air, initiating play with a new arrival, some sort of poodle mix.

"Of course I trust you."

"Then why did you follow me here?"

"To apologize. I didn't mean to snap at you earlier."

I turn away from the bouncy dogs to look at him and nearly wince.

He's so handsome, it's almost painful. Even in his gray sweater fleece jacket, and loose jeans, he's ready for a casting call for *Emily in Paris* or a *Bachelor* spin-off. If a stranger as hot as Adam initiated conversation with me in a dog park, it would be a brag-worthy moment.

"So why did you?"

He shoves his hands in his jacket pockets. "It was the book you were reading... *The Outsiders*. My mom gave it to me. Her mom gave it to her. The annotations are from all three of us scribbling in the margins in real time while reading."

A blast of heat creeps across my face. Oh shit, it *was* a little like reading a diary. "I'd never have purposely invaded your privacy if I'd known. For what it's worth, I was entirely focused on the story itself. I barely read the annotations."

"It's not top-secret, classified stuff or anything. It's just..." He stares down at his scuffed white Vans and kicks a pebble with his foot. "I don't have many tangible reminders of my mom. The book is old. If it gets damaged, there'll be one less." He shrugs into himself. "But whatever, it's my problem, not yours. I should probably keep it somewhere safe instead of bringing it with me everywhere I go."

I imagine losing my mom so young and having only a handful of her personal items to cling to. I'd be protective of them too. My heart aches for Adam. "I get it. I'm sorry."

He scoffs. "This is *my* apology, Sabrina. *I'm* the sorry one." His intense glare morphs into a cheek-splitting, dimple-twinkling grin that I can't help but return.

"When was the last time you read it?"

"Last night actually. I do a reread about once a year around her birthday."

"It aged well! Even today, teenagers deal with bullying, social classes, stereotyping based on socioeconomic factors. All of it."

"Do it for Johnny!"

"Nothing gold can stay." We exchange silly grins again.

The wind rips through me and I lift the hood of my red windbreaker over my head. "Marcia told me about your mom. I'm so sorry."

He nods solemnly. "Me too."

"I haven't seen or heard from my dad in almost twenty years." I don't know why I say this, and I instantly wish I could take it back. A deadbeat parent is not the same as a dead one.

"I sometimes wish I didn't know mine," he says, tapping his foot along the sparse grass.

If ever there was an opening to ask for more details about his father, this is it. "Marcia said he kept you from her when he found out she was bi. What was that like?" My shoulders tense up as I brace myself for his reaction to my prodding. "No pressure to talk about it, of course."

Adam shifts in his seat. "It wasn't like I saw her every weekend before my grandpa died either, but she stopped being there on holidays and birthdays. I'd get cards and gifts in the mail and the occasional phone call instead, and he never told me why." He looks at me with wide eyes. "I had no idea it was his doing until I reached out to her directly last year."

All too familiar with blaming a grandparent for a parent's failings, I'm tempted to squeeze his hand.

"When I confronted him, he said he was shielding me because I was too young to learn about sex." He breathes out a laugh. "I was a teenager! It's not like I didn't already know just about everything.

Some of my close friends were queer." He rubs aggressively at a speck of dirt on his palm. "I already knew my dad was socially conservative. We fought about it all the time, but I didn't think he'd shun his own mother. I asked why it bothered him and why it was any of his business in the first place."

"What did he say?" I hold my breath.

"He brushed me off like he didn't know himself. There were no antiqueer slurs, but there was no apology or ownership of his homophobia either." He lets out a heavy sigh. "The worst part is that he's not a bad father and he loves me. How can someone be a good father but a bad person?"

I figure it's a rhetorical question and don't offer an answer.

Adam smiles over at Rocket, who has one end of a piece of tree bark in his mouth while the poodle mix bites onto the other side, *Lady and the Tramp* style. "That dog," he says with obvious affection.

"He's the best. Marcia told me about him at our first meeting for coffee as if it might be a deal-breaker. It just made me want to move in more." We're both still watching the dogs when I say, "I hold a lot of guilt for the way I treated my own grandmother. She was older than Marcia... mideighties... and died my freshman year of college." The confession comes out before I even realize what I'm saying. I've never talked to anyone about this before, but something about Adam makes me want to open up. Or maybe I just want to reciprocate his own transparency.

"What did you do? Push her down the stairs? Withhold her medication?"

I gasp. "Of course not! I didn't *kill* her!" I shudder at the thought. Although it might also be the decreasing temperature outside.

Adam chuckles. "Your voice got all serious... I thought maybe it was criminal."

"Not at all, but it wasn't right."

I explain how I completely disregarded all the wonderful things she did for me and acted like it was her who abandoned me and not her son. "I slept over at a friend's house and saw the way her father doted on her. He was the one who drove us home from the movies and secretly got us ice cream even though we were having dinner soon. He looked at my friend with such love. The love of...well, a father. And all of a sudden, I was hit with what I'd been missing all that time, and it was like someone changed the Spotify playlist from soft rock to rage. I went from wanting to cuddle with my nana in her bed to muttering under my breath and slamming doors. It wasn't her fault. It was his. But he wasn't there to take it, and she was." I wipe my eyes. My *God*. Why can't I talk about my grandma without crying? Even so, it's cathartic to say it out loud.

Adam's eyes go soft. "I'm nearly positive you weren't as bad as you think you were. All kids rebel against their parental figures. I bet your nana expected it and understood."

I shrug. "Audrina was always perfect. I had anger issues I'll never be able to make up for."

"Even so, your grandma loved you and more than likely knew it was a phase you had to go through and would eventually come out of. Grandmothers are wise that way. Parents are too. It's how they survive those hormonal teenage years instead of locking their bratty children in the basement until they're twenty-one. You need to forgive yourself and focus on the good memories."

I nod. "There are a lot of those. She'd organize game nights every few weeks." I raise my gaze toward the sky and smile like she's up there.

"Tell me about them."

I lower my head to find him studying me like he's searching for annotations on my skin. My face warms under his scrutiny. "We'd play Scrabble, Life, even the *Survivor* board game. And Nana kicked ass at Jenga. She had the steadiest hands until the end. Probably from all the knitting."

"See! Focus on that and not the other stuff." Adam lightly swipes his shoulder against mine before quickly pulling back. "I have my own guilt about Marcia. We spent so many years apart and maybe I should have asked my dad more questions about why she never came around anymore. I waited way too long to reach out on my own."

"You were a kid!"

He gives me side-eye. "So were you. Anyway, I'm glad I'm here now. I was a little jealous of your bond with her when I first moved in. Like maybe you're the grandchild she wished she had." He blushes.

"Well, we're even because I'm *still* a little jealous that you get a second chance to make things right with her. We have an amazing relationship, but you're her grandson. She *adores* you."

"So much that she gave you the guest bedroom and stuck me on the couch."

"I pay rent!"

"I know. I'm joking." He brushes his side against me again but doesn't move away this time. I shiver again... the full-body kind. I hope Adam doesn't notice.

His lips quirk because, of course, he notices. "It's cold and..." He gestures toward Rocket, who's inched himself away from the small group of other dogs in the run and is curled on his side. "We should get him home before he falls asleep."

I don't argue.

Adam calls him over. Rocket raises his head and trots over at a significantly less energetic pace than usual.

"You tired, boy?" In answer, Rocket buries himself in between Adam's legs. When my first thought is "lucky dog," I vault off the bench. "Let's go."

We're back on our block before we know it, and I'm considering splurging for a sampler box of cupcakes from Baked by Melissa for the three of us to share at home when I see a familiar blond head outside Le Café Coffee next door. "Marcia!"

Adam blocks my way with his arm. "Wait."

"What?"

"She's talking to someone." His arm is still against my chest.

"So?" I know many of Marcia's friends from the gym and just living with her for the last eight months. Maybe I want to say hello too. At further glance, I decide the woman she's talking to—petite with shoulder-length reddish-brown hair that has the glossiness of a fresh professional blow-dry despite the damp but humid air—does not look familiar.

Marcia throws her head back in a laugh and smooths down her own hair.

The other woman blushes and takes a step closer to her.

Are they *flirting*?

"Is my grandma flirting?"

Marcia plants a playful tap on the woman's wool-blend mod coat.

"She's totally flirting." My surprise is not judgment. There's nothing wrong with Marcia getting her flirt on; I've just never witnessed it before. My already pleasant mood ticks up a notch at the sight. "Your grandmother is so pretty. She should be dating!" She blurted at the diner that menopause had messed with her hormones, but maybe she's ready to get back out there now. Would she even still have sex at her age?

Just then, Marcia looks in our direction and waves. We watch as she says goodbye to the woman and walks over to us with a bright smile. "I was wondering which of you had Rocket." She bends to pet the dog, who stops licking the ground at his feet in favor of Marcia's face.

"Who was that woman?" Adam asks as we enter the building and head toward the elevator.

I shake my head. He is so not slick.

Marcia, who is in the lead, looks over her shoulder at us. "You've never met Lois? She's a neighbor... She lives in the other wing."

"You seemed to like her."

I jab him with my elbow.

"What? She did!"

Marcia whispers, "Can we table this conversation until we're home?" and gestures toward the two other people in the elevator.

I swing my head toward Adam. *I* can wait. I'm not so sure about him.

The elevator stops on our floor. The door is barely open before Rocket is off like a bat out of hell with a renewed burst of energy. Marcia calmly saunters down the hall, while Adam and I work to match her slower stride.

"So what's the story with Lois?" Adam asks not a second after we're inside the apartment.

"It's not what you're thinking. She's straight." Marcia frowns.

I chew on my lip. "Do you wish she weren't?"

Marcia blushes. "Kind of." She busies herself switching the positions of two figurines on the ladder bookshelf in the living room.

"Have you thought about dating again? She's not the only fish in the sea, and you shouldn't waste the pretty! Right, Adam?"

She turns and points a pale-pink manicured finger at me. "You're one to talk."

Heat flushes my face. I can feel Adam's gaze on me but don't dare meet it head-on. "I date! Some. It's hard to juggle with school and work. But we're not talking about me right now."

Marcia sits on the side of the couch. "I've actually been thinking it might be time to try again, but I wouldn't even know where to begin."

Standing in front of her, Adam and I say, "The apps," at the same time.

"But not Tinder!" Adam says.

Marcia looks up at us. "What's wrong with Tinder?"

"It's mainly for hookups." Adam's ears turn red like uttering the word "hookup" in a conversation with his grandma is outside of his comfort zone.

I giggle, and he grunts in response.

I flash him a teasing smile, then turn to Marcia. "Not necessarily. I know several people who met their significant others on Tinder. Sita from work. One of Carley's cousins. That said, it's definitely known for hookup culture."

"Maybe that's what I want," Marcia says quietly.

Adam and I freeze.

"Why is it young people assume sex is for the under-forty crowd?"

I lower my gaze. I don't think this. But I also don't *not* think it.

"Leonardo DiCaprio is fifty and has no problem getting laid," Adam says. "But his partners are all under twenty-five, so it doesn't count." He points at me and laughs. "You're almost too old for him."

I roll my eyes.

"Truth be told, it's not all I want. I miss companionship with people my own age." Marcia darts her eyes between us. "No offense."

"Understandable," I say.

"But I also want sex." She smiles. "When I first lost Robert and tried dating, I used dating sites like Match, Jdate, and eHarmony, but everything is on our phones now. I'm intimidated by this swipe culture!" She stands and paces the room.

"We'll help you!" I bring up Google on my phone and search "best dating sites for retirees." The top three results are OkCupid, OurTime, and SeniorMatch. All three have website options too, but I'm confident between me and Adam, we can get Marcia comfortable with "swipe culture."

"I'll do it under one condition," she says.

I look up from my phone.

Adam, who's now sitting on the side of the couch Marcia vacated, freezes with his finger on the remote. "What condition?"

There's a glint in her blue eyes. "You two set up profiles too."

"Already done," Adam says.

My stomach dips. He's on dating apps? I wince inwardly. Of course he is. Why wouldn't he be? "I'm already on them too, but I haven't been active in a bit...preoccupied with other things." I swing my gaze toward Adam, hoping he'll say the same thing.

He's silent.

It occurs to me he might have met the girl from Keybar on an app, and my heart quickens in jealousy. Has he seen her again? Is he with her when he's not at home or at work? Desperate to change my focus, I wave my phone at Marcia. "Now that your conditions are sorted, let's work on your dating profile." I gesture for them to join me in the kitchen, where I scoop a large handful of green grapes from the refrigerator, rinse them with water, and set them in a bowl on the table.

When the three of us are seated together, I take ownership of Marcia's phone to fill in her basic preferences. She tells us she's open to men and women between the ages of sixty-five and seventy-five who live within a ten-mile radius of the Union Square zip code.

I'm about to ask if she's looking for new friends, long-term dating, short-term dating, or hookups—I won't make assumptions—when Marcia says she's happy to be able to openly search for both men and women. "I don't care what anyone else has to say about it." A relaxed smile crosses her face. "That's the best part of getting old. I have no more fucks to give."

Adam whispers, "Did she get that phrase from you?"

I shiver at his breath on my ear. "No comment."

He shakes his head but laughs. "I assume by *anyone*, you mean my dad."

"I mean everyone, but that includes your father."

"I still can't believe he cut you off when you told him you were bi. What century is he living in?"

"In your father's defense, I didn't take his feelings into consideration when I came out to him," Marcia says.

"It's not *his* feelings that mattered!" Adam and I say at the same time.

Marcia's eyes crinkle at our loud twin protest. "True. But I brought a woman to his house as my date without any warning. Since he didn't know I'd started dating again at all, it was a double whammy."

"I remember that day. It was July fourth, right? We had a pool party." Adam scratches his neck. "It's the last memory I have of you from before times."

Marcia pops a grape in her mouth. "That's right. Wendy was the first woman I ever dated. I had my crushes in high school and college, but it wasn't something anyone talked about back then, and because I was also attracted to men, it was safer to lean into that side of my sexuality. But it didn't go away, and after your grandfather died, I had a crush on my female dental hygienist. It occurred to me that the world had changed. I was afraid, of course... after you hold something in for so long, it's very scary to say it out loud, but I saw an advertisement outside a temple of all places for an LGBTQIA support group for seniors, and that's where I met Wendy. I knew my son well enough to predict he wouldn't be thrilled, but I didn't think he'd shut me out the way he did." She inhales deeply and whooshes out a breath. "I thought he'd come to his senses, and *he* thought I was going through a phase or a delayed midlife crisis. It turns out we were both wrong. And then he stopped taking my calls." A blanket of sadness crosses her face as she looks at Adam. "I often ask myself if I should have kept it a secret from him to have those ten years with you."

"Please don't give that another fuck." Adam shakes his head. "I'm sorry, Grams, but screw my dad. I'm so glad you stayed true to yourself. Basically all you missed were my gangly, surly, pubescent years anyway."

"And what exactly has changed since then?" I joke.

Adam tosses a grape at me, but the tension is gone, which was my intention. The conversation closed for now, Marcia takes back her phone to write her bio, Adam cuddles on the couch with Rocket and a bag of Cheetos, and I read for class.

All things considered, the day turned out not so bad.

Later that night, after a quick dinner of leftover build-your-own salad from Chopt over the sink, I buckle down in my room with classwork on quick reads. When I finish, I immediately reread one of my own favorite quick reads in teen literature, *Kindred Spirits*, an oldie but greatie by Rainbow Rowell.

I close the book and check the time. It's almost one in the morning. I decide to shower before bed so I can sleep a little later tomorrow morning. Thanks to blackout shades, I can barely see where

I'm going in the living room as I carefully tiptoe to the bathroom. I don't want to risk waking Adam, so I wait until the bathroom door is closed behind me before flicking on the light.

After my shower, I wrap a towel around my body, letting my wet hair drip down my neck. Then I turn off the light and open the bathroom door.

My entire life flashes before my eyes at the sight of an imposing figure looming in front of me until I realize it's Adam, who must have been reaching for the doorknob as I opened the door and somehow grabbed onto my towel instead, right over my right boob. He's close enough that I see his eyes are open but glazed, like he's sleepwalking. I hold my breath knowing I should pull his hand away even as my nipples harden traitorously. "Adam?" I say his name softly. I don't want to freak him out.

He smiles, his fingers splayed across my breast. "Sabrina."

"Yes. It's me." My voice comes out like I'm grasping for air.

His eyes open wide and he blinks at me. "Sabrina?" He drops his hand. "What the fuck." He scrapes a hand down his face. "Shit. I'm so sorry."

"It's okay," I say in a soothing voice. "Were you sleepwalking?" I reach behind me to flick on the bathroom light. When I turn back around and get a closer look at Adam, a pool of heat settles in my center. His chest is bare, and his gray sweatpants ride low on his hips and leave little to the imagination. I summon the strength not to rub against him like a cat.

"I'm not sure. I don't think so, but I wasn't fully awake either." He yawns and stretches his arms over his head while my heart races like a horse in the Kentucky Derby as his sweatpants fall an inch. "I'm sorry if I did anything…" His eyes drop down the length of my body and his Adam's apple bobs as he swallows.

I hitch my towel more securely over my tits. "I was trying not to wake you, so I didn't turn on the light."

He runs a hand through his multihued hair. "You're usually a morning shower person."

This is true, and I can't think of a damn thing to say in response. We stand rooted to the spot in silence. I'm still wearing only a towel and he's wearing gray sweatpants and nothing else. The heat coming from his body is torture.

My choices are escaping to my room or pulling him to the bathroom to relieve the tension. The former is my only real option, but he's blocking my path. I clear my throat. "I should..." I look over his shoulder. "...go to bed and let you use the bathroom?"

His body jolts into motion and he steps to the side. "Oh. Right. Sorry."

I nod. We're getting somewhere. "Okay then. Goodnight. Sorry again."

"Me too. Sorry. Goodnight."

Seriously? How many times are we going to apologize before this torment will end? Has anyone ever died of awkwardness?

More silence.

Enough. "Okay. Goodnight." At last, I scurry past him and manage to walk, not run, into my room. I close the door behind me and lean against it for balance. The image of his sweet smile and the sound of his sleepy voice saying my name while his big hand cupped my tit will most definitely haunt my dreams.

At least I hope so.

Chapter Nineteen

That Friday night is Marcia's first date with a man named Gary. Carley comes over to do her makeup before her show. We're all packed into the kitchen, where Marcia sits on a kitchen chair while Carley stands over her. She wanted to record it, but Marcia wouldn't have it.

"Your generation can share your personal business with the world if you want," Marcia says with her eyes closed. "I'm keeping mine private. Besides, what if Gary's on TikTok and sees me making a big deal of our first date before we've even met?"

Adam snorts. "I seriously doubt he's on TikTok, Grams. But I agree."

"Fingers crossed you like the bar." I offered to choose the venue, and even though I don't think of Marcia as an old lady, I also don't want her first date in years to be loud and packed with twenty-somethings like Keybar. The Flatiron Room is not too far away and described on Yelp as "a mature and relaxing environment." Hopefully, not so mature and relaxed they fall asleep or die of boredom (or anything else). I pour more sparkling wine into my glass. I think I'm more anxious than Marcia.

Adam holds out his glass.

I refill it.

He whispers, "You okay?"

I mouth, "Nervous."

His eyes soften. "Me too."

An empty bottle of prosecco later, Carley finishes doing Marcia's face. Marcia goes to her room to change out of her NYCRUNS Central Park 5k T-shirt and leggings and into her date outfit while the rest of us pace in the kitchen.

"I hope she likes him," I say. "But only if it's mutual." I'd rather her not be into him than want a second date if he doesn't.

"Most first dates don't go well. Keep your expectations low," Adam says.

I'm thinking of how to ask about *his* last first date without sounding like I care when Carley says, "You think Marcia kisses on the first date?"

I ponder this. "I say yes, but only if she likes him."

"Maybe they'll go to Bonetown."

Adam shoots grenades at Carley with his eyes.

She laughs. "Don't be a prude. She's seventy-something years old, which means she's probably had more sex than all of us. And didn't she come of age during the sexual revolution?"

Adam grabs an orange from the bowl of fruit on the kitchen island and fakes throwing it at her. "Please stop talking about my grandma and sex. It's bad enough when she does it."

"Maybe he'll be your new grandpa." I squeal, then duck when Adam launches at me.

Marcia reappears. "I'm not looking for a new husband."

The room turns silent as we take her in. She's wearing a white silky top with large black buttons running down the front, tucked into high-waisted black flare-leg pants and black suede booties.

I softly clap my hands.

Carley checks her from head to toe and nods with approval. "That outfit is snatched."

"I have no idea what that means."

"It means you look good, Grams." Adam beams with pride at his grandma.

Insisting Marcia needs accessories, Carley drags us into her bedroom and rummages through her jewelry collection until she finds the perfect heart-shaped hoop earrings and gold bangles. She also encourages her to switch out her booties for zebra-embellished stilettos she finds in the back of the closet.

This is where Marcia draws the line. "No first date is worth suffering in four-inch heels. I'll reserve those for date three." She winks.

"There's your answer about the first date." I giggle.

"Final warning." Adam glares but quickly laughs along with us while Marcia looks bemused, since she has no idea we were debating on which date she "goes to Bonetown."

Finally, she's ready to go. She walks hesitantly toward the front door in her navy peacoat, a red satin knot bag slung over her shoulder, and pauses with her hand on the knob.

"Just be yourself and have fun," Carley says to her back.

"But not too much fun," Adam mumbles.

I place my hand on my tummy. Nerves have turned to nausea. "Do you want me to call you in an hour in case you need an escape?" I don't get this jittery for my own dates, but if tonight doesn't go well I'm afraid Marcia will give up on the whole idea of getting back out there.

She turns around with a timid smile. "No need. But keep your phones nearby because I might call from the bathroom or text you under the table." She points between me and Adam.

We promise to be on high alert for a phone call or text, and she leaves.

Carley gathers her things. "I'm out too, but text me all the deets tomorrow."

"Of course." We hug.

After we separate, she asks, "What will you two do now?" glancing between us with an annoying glint in her eyes. Annoying to me because I hear the suggestion behind the words. Of course, I told her what happened in the bathroom. Not that anything *did* happen. We were just two roommates passing in the night. Given Adam's condition at the time, who knows if he even remembers the interaction. I, however, recall every moment in torturous detail. My nipples hardening even through the terry-cloth towel, the way his eyes scanned my body, the bulge in his gray... I shake away the arousing visual of a sleepy Adam in sweatpants and empty the remains of my prosecco into my mouth.

"I don't know about Sabrina, but I'll probably stare at the TV from now until my grandma comes home," Adam says.

Carley smirks. "I think you can do better than that."

I debate asking what she and Frank plan to do next time they hang out, but she'd just laugh at my sad attempt to turn the tables. Blessedly, she's out the door before Adam has a chance to ask her for clarification, and we're alone.

Against the backdrop of new silence in the room, my own breath sounds like a marching band. "She's going to have a great time." Whether I'm trying to assure Adam or myself is anyone's guess.

Adam sits on the couch. "Even if they don't like each other, it's healthy for her to be out there."

"One hundred percent!" We nod in agreement, him from the couch, me still standing, and then it's quiet again.

I stare at our empty champagne flutes side by side on the coffee table like they're a couple. "It's not like it's her first date ever."

"Exactly."

"Although she's practically born again."

"Please stop."

I chuckle. "Sorry."

Adam turns on the TV.

Bonding moment over. "I guess I'll go to my room."

He cocks his head. "Do you want to watch with me?"

I practically leap onto the couch. "What are you watching?"

"*The Magicians*." He tips his head at me. "Have you seen it?"

"No, but I read the books."

His lips quirk as he raises the volume. "Of course you did."

I try to focus on the screen, but it's no use. I have a one-track mind and it's 100 percent on Marcia. By now, she's at the bar with Gary, assuming he showed up. If he stands her up, I will hunt him down and kick him in the balls so hard, he won't be able to walk for the next month. I'm positive Adam will help. He's currently staring so intently at the screen, it's obvious he's not watching either. We're quite the pair, overprotective like parents of a fifteen-year-old on their first date. When the comparison makes me chuckle out loud, I throw my hand against my mouth.

Adam swings his head toward me. "Did you say something?"

"Nope."

He squints at me for a beat before turning back to the show.

I do the same. On the screen, Quentin tells Alice he's not good in bed. She says she's just bad at asking for what she wants. She tells him to kiss her. He takes his shirt off and slips into her bed. His hand is on her breast, but she directs it between her legs.

She gasps and…oh shit. This is hot and now I'm all wet and tingly. I squirm and cross my legs before braving a glance at Adam.

His Adam's apple bobs in a heavy gulp a moment before his eyes slide to me and quickly back to the show. He grips the remote. *Hard*.

Of all the shows he could have chosen. Of all the episodes. But we can't change it because it will be so obvious *why* we changed it. It's not a big deal. We can handle this. It's a sex scene. Big whoop. We're grown-ups. Neither of us are virgins. And it will be over soon.

Except now Alice is *riding* Quentin and they're both moaning.

Adam turns to me and licks his lips.

I lick mine.

There's a moment of hesitation before he inches toward me.

Boom. I hurl myself onto his lap.

Chapter Twenty

We kiss like we've been pining for it for decades... *centuries.* It's almost comical how desperate my lips and tongue are to dance with his, and based on his erection pressing into my thigh, I'm not the only one. Are we both turned on by what we saw on *The Magicians*? Is fooling around merely a way to relieve stress over Marcia's date, or are the sparks flying off us finally bursting into flames?

I'm too horny to care.

From beneath me, Adam's lips slide from my mouth to my neck, sucking gently. I moan and readjust my position on his lap so that the soft and wet part of me that is aching with need hits the hard part of him that feels the best... *right there.* Over and over.

He cups my ass and jerks upward while I grind against him, my hands resting on his thighs for balance. All the need I've been holding back—I've been too self-conscious to touch myself since he moved in—is bubbling up and coming to a boil. Adam's hands dip into the back of my jeans until his fingers meet with flesh. He cups my ass and rocks me up and down on top of him. I whimper, my teeth pressing down on my lower lip. I rest one hand on his shoulder and slip the other under his T-shirt, running it along his smooth skin while I pump my hips. I'm fully clothed, yet so close to coming apart at the seams.

Adam surges forward again. He tucks his head into the crook of my neck and groans.

Rocket lets out a loud bark and races to the front door.

I slip off the couch as Adam flings me from his lap without warning.

Standing over me, he looks horrified and runs a hand through his matted hair. "Shit. Sorry, sorry."

I look up at him from the floor in a daze. I'm too consumed with unfulfilled need to comprehend the world around me. I hear mumbling from the hallway and the jingle of keys. My eyes widen.

Marcia!

Adam's sweating. And still hard.

I leap off the floor.

Adam covers his erection and hoofs it to the bathroom.

I hear the sound of a key turning in a lock a moment before Marcia enters. I launch back on the couch and zip my jeans just in time for her to look my way from across the room.

She's back early. I glance at my watch. I'm not wearing one. I plant on a smile. "How was the date?"

Adam exits the bathroom. "Yeah, how was it?" He lost his boner, along with the ability to look at me, it seems.

Her face crumbles. "It was awful!"

"*Ruff, Ruff!*"

Marcia kneels to kiss Rocket. "I'm okay, baby."

Sufficiently reassured of her well-being, Rocket retreats back to Marcia's bedroom.

I press a hand to my heart, the sexual encounter with Adam now behind me, at least for now. "Oh no."

"What did he do?" Angry sparks fly from Adam's eyes.

Marcia drops her purse on the coffee table. "Do we have any of that prosecco left?"

"I'll open a new bottle." I rise from the couch and rush to the kitchen.

A few minutes later, after Marcia changes into pajamas, we reconvene in the kitchen, and she recaps her night over glasses of prosecco.

"When I got to the restaurant, he was already at the table, along with a pile of pills in front of him like he was waiting until I arrived to take them. Before even saying 'Nice to meet you,' he went through the list of all the medications he's on: Crestor for high cholesterol, Monopril for high blood pressure, Celebrex for arthritis, Zoloft for anxiety."

"Hot," Adam deadpans.

Marcia takes a glug from her glass. "We're senior citizens, I get it, but can we at least *pretend* to still be sexy for a first date?"

"You *are* sexy, Marcia! Sexy is not about age. It's about..." I look at Adam. Why am I looking at Adam? Because he's the epitome of sexy. *Snap out of it!* "What about Richard Gere?"

"And Michelle Pfeiffer. She's totally sexy!" Even though this is the perfect time to present a united front while we list some of the sexiest of the over-sixty crowd, Adam avoids eye contact with me as if his own cholesterol, blood pressure, joints, and anxiety depend on it.

"I could have gotten past the meds—even bonded over the side effects of our high blood pressure medication—but then he went on a rant about his last several dates. This one wanted to sleep with him on the first date. He should be so lucky! One had been married twice already, to which I say, so what? I just can't with Judgy McJudgersons." She side-eyes us in annoyance.

A smile slips out in the midst of her rant. I'm a terrible person.

Marcia is in the aftermath of a brutal reentry into the single scene and I'm *smiling*. Yet I can't help but feel a burst of pride for the main-character energy she's bringing to this fiasco.

"Is it always like this?" She glances between us, pleading for us to say no.

At the same time, we say, "NO." Left unsaid is that it's *often* like this.

"Good, because I can't wait to do it again as soon as possible."

I choke on a sip of prosecco. "Wha . . . what?"

Marcia grins. "Tonight was a disaster, for sure, but the excitement? Getting dressed up? The optimism that maybe we'll hit it off? I liked it. I liked it a lot. I want to keep trying."

"That's fabulous!" I raise my glass. "To trying!"

We all take a sip, then Adam shakes his head. "It's all well and good you want to get back out there again, but *I* might need anxiety meds to get through it."

My heart tugs even as a chuckle leaks out. I can't resist sneaking a glance at him. My gaze locks on his lips and my mind flashes to how soft but firm they felt against mine. When I look up, he's watching me too. The room gets hotter.

Marcia walks her glass over to the sink. "It's past my bedtime." She kisses Adam's cheek. "Thank you both for sharing in my excitement. This was the most fun I've had in a long time!" She glances between us with obvious affection before retiring to her room.

Once she's gone, it's me and Adam alone in the kitchen again. The vibe is awkward with a capital *A*. He's on one end by the refrigerator and I'm on the other side by the table. Even though it's a small space, it might as well be the Atlantic Ocean.

Adam scrubs a hand across his face.

I decide to break the ice. "Well, that was a close call!"

He drops his hand and cocks his head at me. "You think?"

"What *are* you thinking?" I don't even know what *I'm* thinking, but it would be nice to get a sense of where he's at. Carley and Gabe are right about one thing: I like Adam. He's kind. He listens. He cares. He *reads*. His yummy appearance doesn't hurt. And *damn* the boy can kiss. He's also packing serious heat between his thick legs.

But nothing's changed. He's still Marcia's grandson. Getting involved with him is probably a lousy idea. If things go bad between us, it could ruin everything. I love my living situation (and Marcia) too much to risk losing it over a boy.

"It shouldn't have happened. We were both worried about Marcia," Adam says before walking to the pantry and predictably removing a bag of Cheetos.

I wonder if that's all it is, but don't dare ask. "True, true. And that scene in *The Magicians*." I whistle.

Adam's hand travels from his pecs down between his legs and his voice is breathy as he impersonates Alice. "Bite me, Quentin. Not there. *Here*."

I breathe out a laugh. "Nothing good can come from doing it again. We live together."

"You're my grandma's roommate."

"And you're my roommate's grandson!"

Adam smiles. "We're in agreement then? It was a one-time slip?"

"Yes." I answer quickly, though my brain, heart, and other parts are one step behind and not as convinced. I'm dying to know if he's struggling with the same thing, but it wouldn't change anything.

"Goodnight, Brina."

My heart skips a beat. "What did you call me?"

He frowns. "Brina."

"Why?"

"It just slipped out." His eyebrows furrow. "No one calls you that?"

I drop my gaze to my feet and back up at him. "Only my grandparents." Nana Lena and Grandpa Lou called me Brina Bear. My mom does too, but only when she's feeling sentimental.

His mouth forms an *O*, but he doesn't comment.

"Goodnight, Adam." I turn and walk away before he can respond.

Back in my room, I change into my pajamas. I skip washing my face and brushing my teeth because I'm afraid to run into him in the bathroom. I slip into bed. I try to read for school, but the words blur on the page as my eyes close. It's been a day.

Behind my lids, Adam is everywhere. Straightening chairs in the library at work, snacking on Cheetos at home, under me on the couch, his eyes hooded as we rock together.

I flip to the fetal position. Considering we work and live together, keeping our distance to the extent we can is smart. It's a good thing we both decided fooling around again is a bad idea.

Now to figure out how to stop thinking about his mouth on mine and daydreaming about a repeat performance, only minus our clothes this time.

Chapter Twenty-One

The following weekend, I'm at my childhood home in northern Connecticut to celebrate Passover and my mom's birthday. It's just the three of us tonight because Mom's long-term boyfriend, Bob, is out of town.

My family isn't religious. For the most part, Jewish holidays are limited to presents on Hanukkah and consuming large dinners on Rosh Hashanah and Passover. We don't do a full seder or keep kosher, but we have our own Passover traditions, like reading short passages from the same children's Haggadahs that Audrina and I colored in as kids, playing hide-and-seek with a piece of matzo (the afikomen) to win a special "jumbo size" matzo ball, and, most recently, celebrating our mom's birthday at the same time. We started combining the occasions after Audrina and I moved out and it became harder to visit twice in the same month. It works great for everyone except Mom, who has to cook her own birthday meal.

When we're done with the main course, I stand from the table. "Can you help me with something, Audrina?" I cock my head knowingly.

She gives me a blank look before understanding washes over her face. "Oh, yes. Of course." We giggle and race toward Mom's second freezer in the garage like excited children.

"Whatever could my daughters be doing?" Mom wonders out loud behind us, even though she knows *exactly* what we're doing since we've done it every year before.

Together we remove the Carvel ice cream cake from the freezer and bring it into the kitchen. "Cover your eyes, Mom!"

When we're sure she's not watching, we light birthday candles with the numbers five and four and bring the cake over to her. "You can look now!"

She opens her eyes, and we sing an exaggeratedly off-key version of "Happy Birthday." To clarify, *I'm* exaggerating. No one would mistake me for Billie Eilish, but Audrina's natural singing voice sounds like a screaming cat in a horror movie.

During cake, we laud our mom's cooking skills. Growing up, Nana Lena's meals were a given and therefore taken for granted. She'd spend hours cooking five-course meals with pleasure, yet we'd beg our mom to make her special ziti, which was only special because she made it.

Mom shrugs. "I can only take credit for the soup and chicken this year. Audrina made all the side dishes."

"Did you like the maple-roasted carrots?" Audrina's eyes, the same honey shade of brown as mine, widen at me with the expectation of praise, and it's like looking at a slightly older version of myself except she dyed the golden hair we were both born with a dark auburn and wears it longer.

"I did."

She smirks. "And yet you gave me such a hard time."

"Because it breaks tradition." I complained when I learned she was substituting the standard tzimmes, a Jewish stew made from carrots and dried fruits like raisins and prunes, with a new, "healthier" recipe she stole from Joy Bauer's website. Tasty or not, maple-roasted carrots are not tzimmes. But it's not like I have a right to complain about anything since my one measly contribution every year is the charoset—chopped apples and walnuts mixed with sweet wine. It takes skill to mess it up, something I did only once, when I substituted Riesling for sweet dessert wine so I'd have something palatable to drink during the arduous chopping process.

As if reading my mind, Audrina says, "The charoset was impressive this year."

I beam. "We can thank Marcia's food processor for the consistency and the lack of Band-Aids on my fingers. Speaking of Marcia," I say, cutting into my slice of cake and making sure to include some of the sweet blue frosting and chocolate crunchies with the ice cream, "she had her first date in a decade last week. Carley did her makeup so she looked gorgeous."

Mom's eyes widen in interest. "How was the date?"

"Awful, but at least she's trying."

"Good for her. Maybe you can follow her example, Aud."

Audrina responds to our mom's suggestion with a noncommittal "Maybe" while using her fork to fiddle with the melting ice cream on her plate.

My heart splinters for my sister. She loved Kevin with every fiber of her being and still does. Three years into their marriage, they legally separated when he claimed he felt trapped and needed to experience independence before he could start a life and family with her. Last we heard, he was in El Salvador working as a long-term volunteer for Habitat for Humanity.

To change the subject, I say, "Nana Lena would be impressed with this dinner, Mom."

"You don't think she'd be jealous?" Mom chuckles.

"Oh, she'd be jealous, but also proud of you." Nana loved to complain about how hard she worked in the kitchen, but she also lived for the praise and wanted to be the only person who cooked for us. One of my favorite ways to punish her was turning down a second serving even when I *really* wanted it. My heart races and my throat feels full like I'm about to cry, but I'm not the only one.

When Mom meets my gaze, her eyes are wet too.

I'm poised to spoon another bite of ice cream cake into my mouth but drop my fork. "Are you okay?"

She wipes away her tears. "I'm fine. Just... she never treated me like I was her ex-daughter-in-law. I was her daughter. And she was my mom long after my own mother was gone. I miss her all the time but the grief comes in waves."

"Me too," Audrina says.

We're silent for a moment until I speak up again. "I hate the way I treated her."

Audrina leans forward. "What do you mean?" She was in college and out of the house for most of it.

"She loved me so much and I acted like I didn't want her around half the time." *Half* is generous.

Mom's gaze penetrates mine. "You're being too hard on yourself."

"I don't think I am." I swallow the lump in my throat.

Audrina hands me a clean napkin, her expression rife with concern.

"What? Do I have ice cream on my face?"

"Probably..." Her lips quirk up. "But also... you're crying."

I touch a finger to my wet cheek. "Oh, for fuck's sake. Every time."

"Talk to us," Mom says.

I'd prefer to shrug it off like I usually do, but I already opened the door and the only way out is through. My tears would make a hostile witness for the defense anyway. I tell them everything: about rebuking her embrace the last time I saw her and how guilty I feel for refusing to spend real quality time with her during the last years of her life. "I blamed her for what Dad did. Or didn't do."

Audrina squeezes my hand under the table.

I squeeze back out of reflex, not because I think the support is justified. "She didn't deserve it. She loved me so much. I never stopped loving her either, but I..." My throat chokes up again. "It was like I had no control over my anger." And then Mom called me at college to tell me she was gone and I immediately regretted everything. But it was too late.

Mom's features soften as she steadies her gaze on me. "Lena wasn't clueless about her son's behavior. She wrongly blamed herself for not being able to rein him in, and she was a willing punching bag if it meant you had somewhere to direct your feelings of abandonment."

Adam said something similar, but I don't mention it out of reluctance to bring him up in conversation. I shouldn't be thinking about him at all. Except not thinking about a crush you live *and* work with is not an easy feat. I try to keep my distance at the library and in the apartment. When I can't, I force my brain to turn off the memory of kissing him and the feel of his hands on my ass. Was it naïve of me to hope for an "out of sight, out of mind" weekend?

"I should have sent you girls to a therapist, but I naïvely thought you were doing fine... that you didn't need a father because you had me, Nana, and each other. But there's no substitute for a father's love." She mutters "asshole" under her breath. "It was his loss. I hope you know that. But while we're being open and honest, I carry a lot of guilt myself."

Audrina and I look at our mom with matching expressions of confusion.

She tosses her napkin over the liquid remains of her ice cream cake. "Your grandparents rescued me when your father disappeared, and I let her practically raise you girls from preschool through high school while I worked all the time."

"She wanted to help!" I argue.

"She was so proud of how hard you worked," Audrina insists.

"Audrina's right. She bragged about you all the time."

"I just wish I thanked her more," Mom says.

It never occurred to me that my mom also struggled with feelings of guilt over Nana's death. I hate this for her. "She knew you appreciated her. You thanked her by killing it at work. All those promotions proved it wasn't all for nothing." My mother had a reason for not being able to attend our parent–teacher conferences or chaperone school trips and leaving us in the care of Nana. The best reason of all—making sure we had a roof over our heads and food on the table. She *would* have shared this responsibility with our dad if he weren't a garbage human who eschewed his parental obligations at every turn.

"With my own parents already gone since before we were married, I needed her desperately at the beginning. She and your grandpa paid off the mortgage on this home. I'm just glad by the time she died, it was me taking care of her financially rather than the other way around. But I'm grateful she was there when I needed her."

I study my mom. Her given name is "Dina," which comically and, believe-it-or-not, coincidentally, rhymes with Audrina and Sabrina. Tall and larger boned with jet black hair (now dyed to cover the gray), she looks nothing like Audrina or me, who take after the human trash can, at least physically. She's deservedly proud of how far she's come while acknowledging she couldn't have done it without the financial support of my father's parents, at least initially. Maybe she'd be willing...*happy*...to pay it forward to me with a small financial cushion.

She walks her dishes to the sink. "In her day, women relied on their husbands for everything. I didn't have that luxury."

"Neither do I. Not anymore, anyway." Audrina covers her mouth with her hand, but not quickly enough to hide the beginning of a tremble.

"Single here too!" I say.

"Not forever, unless it's what you want. In the meantime, you must be able to take care of yourself, partnered or not. And don't think of it as a burden. Be independent and proud." She sits back down and glances between us, her expression businesslike. "I hope I've taught you at least that much."

Has she ever. I decide not to ask for that cushion.

"How about tomorrow, we visit Nana's grave and then celebrate her life over dinner at Fleming's?"

I love this idea. The steak house was Nana's favorite.

"Can we watch *That's Entertainment!* after?"

I smile at my sister. Nana looked out for *That's Entertainment!* on TCM and other cable networks every year and would have delighted in knowing it was available for streaming at our whim now. I'm choosing to believe we'd watch it together, cuddled in her bed, if she were alive. There's even a trace of her signature scent—coconut oil and cocoa butter, like she bathed in suntan lotion—in the air right now, as if she's here with us in spirit. The guilt hasn't disappeared completely, but it's muted thanks to talking it through with my family and discovering I'm not alone.

* * *

The next day is all about Nana. We visit her and Grandpa Lou at a Jewish cemetery not too far away and leave rocks on their graves, as per Jewish custom. We give each other space to talk to them in private.

When it's my turn, I kneel on the grass by Nana's grave and tell her I love and miss her. I apologize for taking my dad's behavior out on her. I promise if I had the chance to go back in time, I'd spend so much more of it with her—reading all the books, eating all her home-cooked food, and hugging her with everything I had the day I left for college, simply making sure she knew how much I loved her. I acknowledge that it wasn't only me who lost a father when he bailed, but her who lost a son, and that she deserved better. I also tell her I understand why she never stopped loving him despite everything. I cry. A lot. But rather than forcing myself to get it together or hiding it like I usually do, I let the tears fall down my cheeks with abandon until her granite headstone is a blur. Then I hug it out with my mom and sister. It's a release I desperately need.

After dinner, we watch *That's Entertainment!* on Apple TV, all three of us huddled on the couch under a giant lavender-and-pink knit blanket, a Nana Lena original. Then Mom announces the conclusion of Nana Lena Remembrance Day and goes to bed. I'm about ready to head to my childhood bedroom too.

Audrina catches me mid–yawn and stretch. "Not you too! Please stay up a little longer."

I haven't slept well since before Marcia's date, but after spending the last thirty-six hours lamenting taking Nana for granted, I can't say no to hanging out with my big sister a little longer. The opportunities lately are few and far between. "Okay. I need a drink to stay up though."

"Hold that thought!" She bounds from the couch with the energy of a five-year-old on Christmas morning and returns a minute later with two glasses of chilled white wine.

We arrange ourselves so we're both stretched out on either side of the couch with the blanket covering our legs. We say a collective cheers and lean forward to clink glasses.

"So what's it like living here again? And with Mom?"

"Same as it ever was." Audrina takes a sip of her wine. "Mom still keeps the house ridiculously cold, and I have to turn up the heat when she's not watching."

I chuckle. No matter how much money Mom earns from her various promotions, she treats money like it could be taken away from her at any moment. Case in point, keeping the thermostat just high enough to avoid frostbite.

"She still leaves early for work and gets home late, so I rarely see her. Only now, I don't have Nana Lena skulking around or my little sister following me like a puppy."

I kick her foot with mine. "Can you believe what she said about Nana? I had no idea she felt guilty."

She frowns. "Me neither."

"The whole 'Nana Lena Remembrance Day' was her idea. Maybe she's mellowing in her old age."

We ponder the possibility in silence for a moment then collectively say, "Na!"

"And don't let her hear you call her *old*. She prefers 'middle-aged.' " Audrina smirks.

I bring my glass to my mouth. "Does Bob stay over?" Mom didn't meet him until after Nana died and I was already out of the house.

"Not since I moved in." She wrinkles her nose. "Do you think they fuck?"

I'm mid sip and wine dribbles out of my nose. "Gross." I shake my head to erase the visual. "Although even one of Marcia's reasons for wanting to meet someone is because she misses sex."

"Respect. I hope I'm still horny at seventy." She waggles her eyebrows. "What about you? Getting any?"

I want to deny it but can feel the heat rush to my face and a goofy smile slip out at the memory of my almost-fuck with Adam.

Audrina shoots up. "Don't you dare hold out on me! I need to live vicariously through you. Who is he?"

"Adam. We didn't have sex... but we kissed."

"Just kissed? You're blushing awfully hard over a kiss."

"Kissed with some light petting."

Audrina raises an eyebrow, clearly not buying it.

"*Fine*, we dry humped the fuck out of each other on the couch in plain sight and almost got busted by Marcia when she returned home early from her first date."

Audrina howls, her glass of wine shaking in her hand. I join her.

My sister stops laughing and pins her eyes on me all thoughtful-like. "You like him, don't you?"

I scratch my fingers up and down the blanket. "Even if I do, it's too complicated with us living together and him being Marcia's grandson. We already agreed it was a one-time slipup."

Audrina lies back down and tugs her end of the blanket up to her chin. "That's too bad. It's tough out there. What's a more convenient way to find your person than him sleeping in your living room? Aside from work, and he's there too." She kicks my foot. "All that proximity. You sure it won't happen again?"

The truth is that I'm *not* sure it won't happen again. I'm definitely not sure I don't want it to. But I've hit a wall in terms of thinking about Adam. It's time to move on. "Enough about me. How's your job? Have you heard from Kevin lately? Should I even ask?"

She grins. "The job is great. Glenn Close and Justin Long came into the spa last week—separately, but two famous people in the same week was exciting." Her face turns serious. "As for Kevin, we spoke a few months ago. I miss him, but we're legally separated and he's not ready to come home. Maybe I'll try dating again. If Marcia can do it, so can I."

"You should!"

"So should you. Since you're determined to stay away from Adam and everything."

She's right. I *should*. But I'm pretty certain I won't.

Chapter Twenty-Two

The following week, I'm on a folding chair at the library leading my first-ever story time while a dozen or so tiny humans sit crisscross applesauce at my feet on a bright multicolor rug.

I'm not sure who's more excited to be here: me or them. The children's shining faces look up at me in awe with their mouths hanging open as I read *Lola at the Library*. I channel Nana Lena reading to me and vary the tone of my voice while pointing at the pictures. Joy fills me like helium in a fresh balloon, but I freeze when I look beyond the children toward the back of the room, where Adam has stopped shelving middle-grade books to watch me. Our eyes lock and I stumble over my words. I quickly return my attention to the kids who, aside from one little girl who's staring at the ceiling and bouncing on the mat like there are ants in her pants, are engaged with the story and answering my questions in that adorable high-pitched voice I adore.

Except now that I know Adam's listening, I can't get my mind or body to focus and it's unnerving. We've kept to our agreement not to fool around again, and there have been no postmidnight semi-naked rendezvous in the bathroom. But it doesn't mean I don't play back every sensation and observation of that night at the end of each day when I lie down for bed—his mouth hungry against mine, my frenzied need while I ground against him, the black dots of his eyes dilating with desire, the soft moans I couldn't hold back.

Somehow I make it to the end of the book and watch as the children race back to their parents, who I can tell wish I'd "babysit" a little longer. The guardian of Bouncing Girl in particular gives me a pleading look as she tries to gently pry a bunch of the girl's hair out of her mouth. I offer a sympathetic glance and turn away, making eye contact with Adam, who's approaching me all smiley.

Butterflies take flight in my belly, and I silently tell them to go fuck themselves. I mirror his expression and pretend I'm not at all affected when he closes the space between us to kissing distance.

"Great job."

"You think?"

"You had them riveted." He wrinkles his nose. "Except for that one girl."

I breathe out a laugh. "You can't please everyone."

His cheeks dimple. "I've almost finished *The Hunger Games*. Any time this week to discuss again? I already put *Catching Fire* on hold."

Despite the satisfaction I feel over making a match between person and book, disappointment settles in. There's no way Adam would follow up on our buddy read if he was also struggling in the aftermath of our dry humping. I don't know if I can sit with him on the couch and debate the worst district and why it's obviously district two and not climb on his lap again, but he clearly doesn't share my concern. "Um. I'm not sure..."

I'm saved from making up an excuse when a little girl races by us. Right on her tail is a little boy around the same age. They're both shrieking in what looks like a game of chase.

"No running in the library," I call after them. To Adam I say, "Where are their guardians?"

He shrugs and watches in awe as the kids, who appear to be about six years old with matching sandy-colored curly hair, hers spilling out of a ponytail, race up and down the aisle. I consider getting Penny, whose years as a youth librarian have presumably trained her in how to deal with rowdy, misbehaving children but want to prove I've got this on my own.

They finally stop running, huddled together by the picture books, but continue to squeal in decidedly not library-appropriate volumes.

I approach them with a calm smile. "I'm glad you're both enjoying yourselves but remember to use your library voices," I whisper, aiming to teach by example. My eyes catch on the practically full Kool-Aid juice pouches in both of their hands.

The girl looks at her juice and back to me. "You want?"

I don't bother telling her that food and drink are prohibited at the library, but I'll remind their guardian if they ever make an appearance. "No thank you, but it's very nice of you to offer."

"Aren't you thirsty?" she asks while her partner in crime watches with rapt interest.

The hairs on my arms stand up. "No."

"Your shirt is!" She aims the juice pouch at my slouchy boatneck pale yellow sweater and squeezes out red liquid like it's an art project and my shirt is her canvas. While I'm still rooted to the spot in apparent shock, she yells to her friend, "Do him! Do him!"

I watch in horror as the little boy, following the instructions of his leader, shoots his juice pouch right at Adam's face. Juice hits his forehead and neck. He opens his mouth as if to protest and is rewarded with a healthy shot of fruit punch. The girl returns her attention to me, and by the time my defensive instincts spark up and I think to shield my chest with my hands, it's too late.

"I never liked this sweater much anyway," I say to Adam, though I'm lying.

The children's father finally showed up, conveniently after both juice pouches were already empty. He apologized profusely and, while forgiveness didn't come easy while looking and smelling like a fruit punch experiment gone wrong, Adam and I handled ourselves gracefully and are now in the employee bathroom cleaning up.

"I'm seeing boarding school for those kids in the future," Adam says, leaning his hip against the sink.

"For her, definitely. Maybe he can be saved." I catch Adam's reflection in the mirror and wince. The front of his hair is matted from juice. I pull a paper towel from the dispenser and wet it with water. Then I stand on my tippy-toes and clean it off before it dries and gets sticky. My eyes meet his. "You'll live."

He does a circle of my face with his eyes and smiles softly. "I suspect you will too."

As a blush warms my cheeks, I lower my gaze to the balls of my feet and look down at my sweater. "I can't wear this all day. Maybe Jenny will let me..."

Before I can finish the sentence, Adam pulls off his midnight-blue Henley. The movement causes the white T-shirt underneath to ride over his belly and display a glimpse of tight bare skin. While I'm still recovering from that, he pulls the T-shirt off over his head as well and hands it to me. "Wear this."

I stare at it...at him. Once again we're in a small bathroom, and Adam's not wearing a shirt.

"It's fresh out of the laundry, aside from the few hours I wore it this morning."

His eyes are up here. I raise my head. "What will you wear?" I practically pant.

He pulls the Henley back over his head. "He didn't get this too bad and it's dark enough that the stains won't show. I can wear it for a couple of hours until I get home."

"Thank you." The guy literally gave me the shirt off his back. I reach for the bottom of my soiled sweater to pull it over my head when it hits me that I'm about to undress in front of Adam, which is not the same as him doing it in front of me. I turn so that my back's to him and then realize he can still see me in the mirror. I should probably tell him to turn around. I watch as he comes to the same conclusion and does a double take.

He clears his throat. "I'll give you some privacy and meet you back on the floor."

I smile. "Thanks, Adam."

When the door closes behind him, I breathe for what feels like the first time in ages. Then I whip off my soaked sweater. As I absently bring the T-shirt to my nose and inhale Adam's signature scent, I stare at my own reflection in my pale-pink lace bra. My cheeks are only a shade lighter than the stains on my sweater and my nipples are hard as a rock. Who knew fruit punch could be so sexy?

Chapter Twenty-Three

I pull Adam's shirt over my head and return to the circulation desk.

Gabe ends his call when he sees me. "I heard what happened. I'm so"—he presses a finger to his lips—"sorry." His voice quakes and shoulders shake, belying his words.

I grunt. "You're not sorry at all."

He points at my T-shirt. "Where'd you pick that up? The big-and-tall shop?"

I knot Adam's admittedly large shirt at the bottom so it rests, hopefully more attractively, at my waist. "It's Adam's." I regret the admission immediately when Gabe's mouth drops open.

"He gave you his shirt?" He asks the question slowly, drawing out each word as if he can't believe what he's saying.

I sink into my chair. "Yes. He didn't want me to have to wear my dirty sweater all day. It's not a big deal. He was wearing it under his Henley." I pull up the hold list on the computer to avoid eye contact with Gabe, but I feel his stare on my cheek.

"You were in the bathroom together when all this lending of shirts went down?"

"Yes."

"So he took off his shirt to give it to you?"

I swing my head to face him. "Yes! It's not the first time I've seen him with his shirt off." I wince. "I just mean because we live together and all. It's bound to happen."

"*Something's* bound to happen, I'm sure." He barks out another laugh, creating temporary wrinkles on his otherwise smooth brown skin.

I glare at him. Gabe doesn't know about my moment with Adam on the couch because I only told Carley and Audrina. He *also* doesn't know about our accidental trip to second base in the bathroom at home, and I'm definitely not telling him now. I ignore him and eventually he stops laughing.

The eventful morning morphs into a quiet afternoon, aside from a small group of tweens sitting at a table in the YA section. So far they've spent more time debating which K-pop star is the cutest and giggling than studying, but we've refrained from "shushing" them since the remaining tables in the area are uninhabited.

I smile tentatively at one of the kids, a white girl with freckles and mousy brown hair in waves who got up to use the bathroom, but instead of returning to her classmates has been pacing in front of the desk, alternating her gaze between me and her phone for the last few minutes. I asked if she needed anything and she said no, but she's still standing a few feet away, looking lost.

The girl, who's wearing a soft-pink top and flower-patterned wide-leg jeans, looks up from her phone again and wipes her dark eyes. They're red and puffy, and although it could be seasonal allergies, based on her averted gaze I'm guessing she's been crying. In a fit of protectiveness over this stranger, I tense up in fear the other girls are leaving her out or otherwise being mean. Girls that age can be cruel.

She tosses yet another pitiful glance my way.

"Are you sure you're okay?" I ask the question gently, hoping it's clear I'm not accusing her of anything but simply offering help if she needs it.

She chews on an unpainted fingernail and gives a slight nod of her head.

Though I'm sure she's lying, I nod and return my attention to next month's programming schedule on the computer.

"Actually…" She approaches the desk and whispers, "I just… um…" She looks behind me in the direction of where her friends are sitting at a long table, then to Gabe, who's tapping the keys of his computer pretending he's not eavesdropping, and back to me.

My hands clench in apprehension over what she'll say next.

She whispers, "I got my period for the first time, and I don't know what to do."

I gasp. This is not what I expected her to say.

Gabe stops typing but keeps his eyes down.

She blinks and her eyes fill with tears. "My mom is at work in a meeting, and my friends don't know I've never had it before." She frowns. "I didn't lie. I just never said."

I suck in a breath, the memory of my own first period fresh like it was yesterday and not twelve years ago. My mom was also at work that day, and Nana picked me up at school. "Do you have something?"

She shakes her head slightly and tugs on the navy hoodie wrapped around her waist. "There's nothing in the bathroom. I used toilet paper." She wipes her eyes.

I sigh and mentally add "have awkward conversation with Jenny about putting a pad and tampon dispenser in the public bathroom" on my to-do list. "Come with me." I stand and, without a word to Gabe, guide her to the staff bathroom where I unlock the door and use my own money to extract a pad. Teaching this girl how to use a tampon is not in my job description. Handing her the small box, I say, "Do you know what to do?"

She accepts the package and nods. "I've practiced." Her cheeks flush red.

A smile escapes. "Did you read *Are You There God? It's Me, Margaret* by any chance?"

"I saw the movie." She giggles.

I grin. "Okay. I'll leave you to it, but I'll be right outside if you need me."

I lean against the wall and wait. My mind wanders back in time to when Nana came to the school and sat in the nurse's office while I used the pad she brought from Audrina's stash at home. She let me leave school early and treated me to Dairy Queen on our way home. I miss her so much I ache from it. I change the subject in my mind to a shirtless Adam in the same bathroom just a few hours earlier, except now I ache in other places.

A few minutes later, the girl comes out. Her eyes are no longer red and she actually looks delighted.

"Everything good?"

She nods excitedly.

I grin, assuming her experience so far has not included cramps. "Good. Do you need anything else?"

Her phone vibrates before she can answer. She whispers, "I'm fine, Mom. The librarian helped me."

I stand up straighter at the librarian moniker.

"Gross, Mom!" She rolls her eyes, and I guess her mom probably said something about being a woman now. I hold in a chuckle. "I will." She looks up from her phone and smiles shyly. "Thank you for your help."

"You're welcome." With a pat on her shoulder, I return to the desk. Delighted there's no queue of patrons, I relax into my chair and close my eyes.

"Look alive, Finkelstein."

Gabe's voice wakes me out of my resting state. "I'm not dead. Just mentally exhausted." Getting "juiced" by miniature patrons, almost taking off my shirt in front of Adam in the bathroom, and providing emotional support to a newly menstruating girl seems like a lot for one day in the life of a library assistant.

"Helping a girl with her menses wasn't on your bingo card for today?" His eyes twinkle.

I open my mouth to tease him about his use of the word "menses," but the words get trapped in my throat when a woman enters the library. She's about my age with long blond hair, wearing a plaid shirt jacket over cropped jeans and brown suede booties. Something about her hits a familiar nerve, but I can't place it. She gives Gabe and me a passing glance before heading to the adult section and walking up and down the aisles without looking at any of the bookshelves. Then she peers her head into the teen section, where the girls are now debating the best Taylor Swift song.

"Why are you following that patron's every move?" Gabe whispers, lifting his chin in her direction.

"She looks familiar," I whisper back. Where have I seen her before? The answer is just beyond my reach. Then it hits me, and I gasp.

"What is it?"

In a hushed tone, I say, "She's the girl from Keybar! The one who was with Adam."

Gabe's mouth drops open and he gives her an extended once-over. "Oh, yeah. I see it now. She's cute." He cocks his head. "You jealous?"

My stomach tightens. "No! Of course not." *Rude.*

"I think the lady doth protest too much."

I ignore this comment. "I bet she's looking for him."

She can walk the aisles all she wants, but she won't find Adam on the floor since he's behind us in the back room sorting supplies for our upcoming May-flowers craft event for tweens and teens. I'm tempted to wait her out until she gives up and leaves, but I'm also curious what their deal is. Adam came with her to Keybar but he left with me. He's never mentioned her or brought her around the apartment, and it's only been two weeks since I fooled around with him, which means nothing unless they're exclusive, but still. I'm dying to know who she is to him, even while acknowledging I might not like the answer.

I find his contact in my phone.

Sabrina: I think you have a guest

Adam: Who is it?

I'd rather not admit to recognizing her in writing, but he'll find out soon enough when he sees for himself who it is.

Sabrina: The girl you were with at Keybar is strolling the aisles and she's not looking for books

He appears approximately thirty seconds later. "Where is she?" He scans the room. "Oh." When he sees her, his expression turns pinched. This could be attributed to a number of factors, including but not limited to: his displeasure at seeing her, him wishing he didn't have a juice stain on his sweatshirt, or him rethinking his decision to eat sour-cream-and-onion potato chips with lunch. My vote is for option one.

When he joins her on the floor, her face lights up and she draws him into a hug. He hugs her back but seems stiff…like he's not comfortable with the affection…but this could also be due to his breath reeking of the chips he ate with lunch. Either way, it's none of my business.

He glances over his shoulder and catches me watching them.

I quickly look down. When I raise my head again, they're no longer in my line of vision.

"They went upstairs."

"Who?"

Gabe smirks.

"I hate you."

I try to focus on work, but my mind would rather be tortured with images of Adam making out with Keybar Girl in the bathroom, break room, or even against the new "Spring into Reading" display I helped create upstairs on the early readers floor, since that's where Gabe said they went. Maybe Adam's secretly an exhibitionist except for when it comes to being caught in the act by his grandma.

The desk is quiet so I walk the floor, straightening chairs, reminding kids to use their library voices, and confirming none of the patrons using the computers need my help. Then I stroll the aisles searching for colored strips of paper peeking out of books. As part of his training, Adam leaves them so we can double check he's shelving the books in the right spots.

"When can we take off my training wheels?"

I startle at the sound of Adam's voice and roll my shoulders back, pretending I haven't been concentrating on not thinking about him for the past twenty minutes. "It's not my decision, but I think soon." As subtly as possible, I skim the floor behind him. There's no sign of the girl.

Adam's eyes drop to my waist and back up. "My shirt looks good on you."

My first thought is, *Not as good as it looks* off *of you*, but by some miracle, I don't say it out loud. "Thanks again for lending it to me."

He smiles, then checks the clock on the wall. "Almost closing time. No class later, right?"

A pleasant hum vibrates under my skin at the unexpected knowledge Adam keeps track of my schedule and knows I don't have school on Wednesdays. "Correct."

"Walk home together?"

"Sure." We nod to seal the deal, and I turn away mere seconds before cracking a smile I'd prefer he doesn't see. We go our separate ways for the last twenty-five minutes of work.

If there are no issues with the 6 Train, the commute from the library to our apartment by subway takes less than five minutes, but unless it's raining, snowing, 100 percent humidity, or the wind chill is in the single digits, I walk.

It's none of the above today so we walk, the route dependent on the color of the stoplights we hit along the way. Adam easily keeps the pace of a born-and-bred New Yorker, expertly dodging other pedestrians. I focus on silently chanting: *I'm not going to ask about the girl. Not going to ask about the girl.*

"Cool about you having a visitor today." *Fuck me.* I bend to tighten my shoelace even though it's already double knotted.

"Cool isn't the word I'd use."

I straighten. "No?"

"I'm not a fan of unplanned pop-ins at work."

"Was it important?"

"She said she was in the neighborhood and remembered I worked there." He tucks his hands in the pockets of his beige bomber jacket.

"Aha. The old 'in the neighborhood' line. Your girlfriend isn't the most creative at the writers' table." I hold my breath. I have no business being thirsty since our agreement to keep things platonic between us was mutual—at least outwardly.

"She's not my girlfriend." He looks at me and quickly away.

"None of my business." We keep walking. She's not his girlfriend. I smile, and though I can't bring myself to look at him, I feel him smiling too.

The air is charged when we arrive at our building and ride the elevator to our floor, like we're on the precipice of something. It's an effort to remind myself we both agreed to keep things platonic. I can no longer remember why we did that.

The elevator doors open, and the sound of Rocket's barking fills the air. It's not his regular excited bark. It's higher-pitched and sounds frantic. We race down the hall and Adam opens the door, calling out, "We're home! Grams?"

Rocket darts out of the kitchen, into the living room, and back so quickly, I'd think I imagined it if he weren't barking so fast and furious.

We glance at each other and follow Rocket.

Marcia's on the floor, holding her chest. "Call 911," she gasps.

Chapter Twenty-Four

My head whips toward the swinging doors again. *Please be Marcia's doctor coming to update us. Better yet, please be Marcia herself, no worse for wear and ready to go home.*

I release my breath. It's not Marcia or her doctor. It's the same energetic intern with the Jessica Day bangs and braid bopping down her back who's been in and out of the waiting room multiple times over the last hour. I'm not actually sure she's an intern. She might be a resident or an attending. After more than a decade watching *Grey's Anatomy*, I still don't know the difference.

I rub a small circle over my roiling stomach. The hospital smell doesn't help. It's a combination of sick people and antiseptic meant to disguise the smell of sick people, like hospital-scented Febreze.

I bounce at the sensation of Adam's hand on my knee.

"You're fidgeting."

I slump in my leather chair. "Sorry."

"Don't apologize. Just stop." He smiles wryly.

I appreciate his attempt at humor when I know he's as terrified as me. His hair is standing up on top from pulling on it and he has the purple half-moons under his eyes of a person who hasn't slept in days, even though it's only been about two hours since Marcia's incident.

When we found her on the kitchen floor, she said she was lightheaded, her chest was tight, and she was having trouble breathing. But her words came out jumbled. While waiting for the ambulance, all I could do was hold her hand and pray she wasn't having a stroke.

I dig my fingernails into my palms to keep myself alert and focus my attention on *The Real Housewives of Potomac* playing out on one of the many flat screens affixed to the walls of the ER waiting room. It's not a show in my rotation, but its mindless cattiness and vanity are more welcome than MSNBC or CNN, which are broadcast on the other televisions. With my own personal village in turmoil, I don't have the emotional bandwidth to handle the politics of the world at large right now.

"Should you let your dad know what's happening?" I ask Adam, even while my eyes drift between the TV and the doors. *Any second now.*

"I already did."

"Good." It occurs to me I might have to meet the man who shunned wonderful Marcia, his own mother, because of her sexual preferences, and kept her from her only grandchild.

"Jeffrey said, 'Keep me posted.'"

I mutter "dick" under my breath before I can stop myself.

Next to me, Adam laughs. "Agreed."

Deciding a watched door doesn't open, I angle my body to face Adam and try to read his thoughts. If I'm scared...and make no mistake, my fear threatens to drown me...how must he feel? My vocal cords ache to assure him Marcia will be okay, but I don't know if this is true—it was a stroke that killed Nana—and lying won't help anyone.

"I'm not with Ashley."

I push my lips together. "Who?"

"The girl from the library . . . and Keybar."

My face heats up. "Oh. Okay. Thanks for telling me." I tap my fingers along my thigh. "Your timing is weird though."

"Yeah, well, it's a distraction from . . ." He waves his hand around the waiting room. "All this."

I nod. Since he opened it up, I'll see his distraction and raise it with a nosy question. "Does *she* know you're not with her?"

"She does now."

My eyebrows lift.

"I let her down easily." He pins his eyes on me. "I have a crush on someone else."

I blink hard. He means me. I like this boy so much and I'm also so afraid for Marcia. The storm of emotions brewing inside me is overwhelming.

Adam takes my hand and squeezes. "Thank you for being there for my grandma when I wasn't."

I squeeze back. "You're here now." We stare meaningfully at each other for a beat before dropping hands and returning to our individual worries about Marcia.

I give up on *TRHOP* and attempt to use the time wisely on a reading assignment for school. I'm on my second read-through of an article on "identifying information need through storytelling"—because I only absorbed every third word the first time—when the door from the restricted area swings open and a middle-aged Black woman in a white lab coat over scrubs approaches us. Her badge identifies her as Dr. Samantha Philips. "You're Marcia Haber's family?"

We stand. "Yes. I'm her grandson. This is her roommate . . . her friend," Adam says, pointing his elbow at me. "How is she?"

The next words out of this doctor's mouth mean everything and my tear ducts activate, prepared to cry in devastation or relief.

"Your grandmother is going to be fine."

Next to me, Adam lets his head drop back and gives thanks to the ceiling.

I cover my eyes with my hands and breathe deeply.

Once our bodies recover from the initial relief response, Adam asks, "What happened?"

"Did she...did she have a stroke? Her words were all jumbled. I read that was a sign of a stroke," I say. *She's going to be fine.*

"I caution you not to rely on WebMD for a medical diagnosis," Dr. Philips says, not unkindly. "Although slurred speech *can* be a sign of a stroke, Marcia went into a hypertensive crisis, which is a sudden, severe increase in blood pressure. The symptoms—chest pain, shortness of breath, slurred speech—can all mimic a stroke. If not treated immediately, it could lead to a heart attack or stroke, so it's lucky you found her when you did and got her here so quickly."

Even though she's going to be fine, my nerves fire up at the knowledge Marcia might not have been as lucky if we hadn't gotten home when we did. Maybe we should have taken the subway.

Dr. Philips studies me. "I can see your brain working overtime. There's nothing you could have or should have done differently. You were perfect. She'll be fine."

"What happens now?" Adam asks.

"I'll work with her internist to monitor the dosage of her blood pressure medication more closely to prevent it from happening again. I'm holding her overnight for observation, but you can see her now."

"You go first," I tell Adam. "You're blood."

He shakes his head. "You're like her best friend. You should go first."

The doctor glances between us in confusion. "You can both see her together if you want."

"Oh, right," I say at the same time Adam says, "I didn't know that was an option." We look at each other and laugh.

Dr. Philips leads us through the doors and down the hallway. After two lefts and a right, we arrive outside her room, and the doctor leaves us alone with a promise to come check on Marcia later.

She's in the bed closest to the door with her eyes closed. There's a sheet midway through the room dividing it in half for another patient. Even in a twin-size bed, Marcia looks tiny in her hospital gown. I'm struck again by how fortunate we are that she can be fixed with medication when others in hospitals meet with much worse fates. My eyes prickle.

Hovering over her sleeping form, Adam whispers, "Should we wake her?"

"I don't think so."

"I'm up," she says, opening her eyes and smiling weakly. "Fancy seeing you two here."

Adam bends to hug her.

I'm riveted to the spot. I want to hug her too, but she's not my grandma. My lips tremble.

When Adam releases her, she cocks her head at me. "Come over here, you."

I embrace her lightly, careful not to pull out any of her tubes, and try unsuccessfully not to cry.

She laughs. "I'm fine. Unless that's why you're crying."

I wipe my eyes. "Stop it."

Adam chuckles.

I jab him lightly in the side. "I cry when I'm happy."

He snorts at this.

Marcia looks between us. "Seriously. I'm in the safest place I can be. They ran the gamut of tests. What I had qualifies as a hypertensive urgency, not emergency, which is much less severe."

"The word *urgent* doesn't strike me as mild," I mutter. Neither does the blood pressure monitor lit up with squiggly lines next to her bed.

"They're only keeping me overnight as a precaution."

A nurse pops in and checks her monitor, nodding at us before ducking back out.

"I should get some sleep," Marcia says.

"Do you want us to stay with you?" Adam asks.

She glances around the tiny space in her half of the room, where we're standing so close to each other I can see a faint red stain of fruit punch on Adam's hairline. Was Fruit Punch–Gate really just this morning? It's been a long day.

"Where? There's only one chair. Go home. Both of you. I'll call you in the morning when I'm being discharged."

Adam scratches his head. "If you're sure."

"I am. I'm in a hospital, Adam. I don't need a babysitter or private health aide." Her tone screams, "I mean business."

After another round of hugs, we do as she says and leave.

Chapter Twenty-Five

Rocket is at the door waiting for us when we get home. Although *waiting* suggests passive, which only describes Rocket when he's sleeping. Current Rocket, who's blocking our entrance to the apartment and barking nonstop, is Rocket on steroids, as if he's been awaiting news of Marcia's fate from the foyer the entire time Adam and I were doing the same thing at the hospital.

Adam assures him his mommy will be home tomorrow in a loud but soothing voice like he's speaking to a human. Rocket, for his part, continues to bark and climb over us for at least a minute until Adam finally manages to sidestep him long enough to grab the dog-walking bag and usher him out the door before he piddles himself in excitement. While he's gone, I update Carley and Audrina on Marcia's status in a group text.

When they're back, Rocket retreats to Marcia's room and Adam heads straight to the kitchen. He asks if I want something to drink, flashing a can of High Noon at me as an example of my options.

There's nothing I'd like more right now. "Yes!"

We fall side by side onto the couch and clink cans, toasting to Marcia.

Adam lifts his feet onto the coffee table.

I kick off my sneakers before doing the same. "I keep thinking about what would have happened if we hadn't come straight home from work."

"Don't go there, Brina. If we weren't home, she would have called 911 herself and someone at the hospital would have let me know."

"Me."

"What?" Adam takes a pull from his can.

"They would have called *me*. I'm her emergency contact."

He wipes his mouth. "Gotcha."

I worry he's offended by this. "I'm sure she'll change it to you if you want."

"No. I'm glad it's you," he says with unwavering eye contact.

"You are?"

He nods decisively. "I'm glad you're here. Period."

"I'm glad you're here . . . period . . . too."

He circles my face with his eyes, lingering at my lips like a magnet on metal.

It occurs to me I'll be alone with Adam in the apartment overnight for the first time ever. My body flushes with heat.

"Nice hole."

I blink. "Do you use that mouth around your grandmother?"

Adam giggles—legit *giggles*—and it's so cute I nearly piss myself. "I meant your socks."

He's right. I have holes in both of my color-blocked crew socks. New socks are a luxury I can't afford right now. I wiggle my toes. "It's my brand."

He laughs. "Come closer."

I don't need to be asked twice. I remove my feet from the coffee table, and though I'm not sure this is what he means by "closer," I crawl into his lap and straddle him.

He tucks a lock of hair behind my ear and caresses my face. "Hi." He looks at me with lovey-dovey eyes.

Suddenly I'm shy, which is inconvenient given our current seating arrangement, but I manage to croak out, "Hi, yourself."

"I really want to kiss you again."

"I love to hear it because I really want to kiss you too."

"I've wanted to kiss you since you carried my bag into the apartment from the hallway."

From this close, I can count the faint freckles on his nose. "You mean the one filled with a million bricks of gold?"

"If I had a million bricks of gold, I'd buy my grandma an apartment with three bedrooms so I wouldn't have to sleep on the couch." He traces his fingers across my lips.

I close my eyes. "Why wouldn't you just buy your own apartment?"

His thumb glides across my chin and up my cheek. "I like living with Grams."

"I'm sure you do but—"

He shuts me up with a kiss. I'd be offended if I hadn't been dreaming about kissing him again since the first time. I press my mouth to his softly at first, but then we make a silent agreement to deepen the kiss, our noses and chins lining up perfectly against each other with each slide of our lips. I tangle my hands through his hair, and he softly brushes my back and tentatively strokes over my bra. All the while his mouth never leaves mine.

I can't tell if my body is heating up from the inside out or if it's actually hot in the room, but it becomes unbearable. "Too much fabric," I mumble into his mouth before coming up for air and lifting his T-shirt over my head. "I almost took my sweater off in front of you in the bathroom earlier. Did you catch that?"

He nods, smiling. "I almost let you. I forgot where I was for a moment. Who knew fruit punch could be so hot?"

"I was thinking the exact same thing!" He's still wearing one shirt too many. "Hands up to the sky," I command.

He raises his arms and I free him from his Henley.

I run my hands across his bare chest, the soft hair a contrast to the taut muscles underneath. "Should we go to my room?"

He answers by standing and taking my hand. Even though we're alone, I close the door behind us before lying back on the bed and pulling him on top of me.

Adam kisses as if kissing is the headline performance. I'm so entirely lost in the sensation of his warm mouth and teasing tongue that I don't even realize he's freed me of my bra until he relocates his mouth and flicks his tongue along one nipple and then the other. When I moan in response, he lingers there. Eventually he crawls farther down the bed and pulls my soaked panties down my legs. Then he pauses.

I lift my head. "Is something wrong?"

He peeks up at me from between my legs. "Absolutely not. I'm just confirming this is okay. Is this okay?"

"Uh-huh." I drop my head back onto the pillow with a sigh of relief. I'm not typically self-conscious, but for some reason, my need for Adam to want me the way I want him is fierce.

At the first slide of his finger inside me, my train of thought disappears like a magic trick. I hitch a breath and gasp in pleasure. He inserts another finger while flicking his tongue over my clit. His hands and mouth continue to work together until I'm bucking off the mattress. I fist the pillow while grinding against his mouth, squeezing my eyes shut and holding my breath as he brings me closer and closer. Finally, my muscles clench and stars explode in my brain. At the moment of release, I shout a string of made-up words and expletives until I'm rendered both silent and boneless. Adam continues to softly work me with his fingers until the quivers stop at last.

Finally, I come back to earth and my breathing returns to normal. "Oh my god. That was...*fuck*."

Adam crawls up the bed and lays his head next to mine on the pillow. "Do you use that mouth around my grandmother?"

I pause...my brain doesn't quite compute in my postorgasmic state, but then I burst out laughing.

Adam joins in and we crack up together. Speaking from real-time experience, coming and laughing are fantastic ways to relieve stress. But it's Adam's turn to come now, and once the giggles cease, I make it my mission.

Using the palm of my hand, I massage him over his jeans until he grows hard beneath me. He's halfway there already so it doesn't take long. Then I free him from his clothes and stroke him, watching his face the entire time. I clock when his breathing gets heavier...when his eyes softly close...when his chest heaves...and when I decide he's ready, I take him into my mouth. I swirl my tongue over the head then take all of him, while my hand continues to pump his shaft.

After a few minutes, he croaks, "Stop."

My heart skips a beat. "Is this not good?"

He chokes out a laugh. "Oh, Sabrina. It feels *amazing*. But I really want to be inside you. If that's okay."

I'd have been willing...*delighted* to take him all the way with my mouth, but I also really want him inside me too. "It's more than okay."

He rips open a condom and puts it on. I climb on top of him and the first sensation of him filling me up is the penthouse level of paradise. I want to take it slow...savor the push and pull of our bodies connecting and drawing apart. But the need for speed is overwhelming. I place my hands on his chest to pace myself, but I can't do it. "Do you want me to go slow, or can I…" I'm panting.

He lifts his head. "Don't think…just do what feels best to you. It all feels good to me. We can take our time in round two."

I grin. *Round two.* Those two words are all I need. I let it rip… riding him for all it's worth, twisting and grinding until I find just the right angle. Then I hit it over and over again before calling out his name as I come right before he does.

"You're amazing," Adam whispers in my ear. It's round two and he's on top, squeezing my ass as he thrusts into me. "Tell me what you want."

"This feels so good." I'm panting, because it does. "But can you slow down? Just a little."

His pace abates…slow and languid. "Better?"

"Yes. Exactly like that." I lick my lips and pull him closer to me. We kiss while he continues to move in and out of me in slow strokes. "Faster now. And harder."

He laughs with his throat. "I thought you'd never ask." He thrusts deep inside me, hard and fast. His balls slap against my ass. I'm so deliriously blissed out, I start giggling.

He laughs too without losing the rhythm.

"You're so good at this!" My fantasies about Adam have nothing on the real thing.

"You're no slacker either!"

"Librarians are fantastic in bed." I gasp. I'm so close.

"Must be all that reading." He chuckles, then slows again. "I'm not sure how much longer I'm gonna last, Sabrina. Almost ready to come for me?"

"God, yes."

"Good girl."

I wrap my legs tighter around him and a few thrusts later, I come hard, grasping his arm so roughly it will probably leave marks.

He's right behind me.

Afterward, I flip onto my stomach and stretch my arms over my head in a dead man's float pose. With the sheets tangled in a bunch at the bottom of the bed, I'm fully naked and 100 percent exposed. I hear Adam shift and then feel his lips on my butt. "I didn't know you had a birthmark." He kisses my lower cheeks once, twice, three times.

"I meant to say something when I was teaching you best customer service practices at work, but it slipped my mind."

He chuckles. "It's adorable."

I flip over. "Carley has the same one on the back of her neck."

"You win."

We make googly eyes at each other. "Why are you single, Sabrina?" He wrinkles his nose. "I'm assuming you're single."

"I hate that question."

He winces. "So do I. Sorry. It just slipped out. But you're pretty great, you know? Funny, smart, caring, patient…"

"Go on." I'm impressed none of the adjectives he's used are about my looks. Except now I wonder if he even finds me physically attractive or if I just have a *nice personality.*

"I've almost congratulated my grandma on scoring such a hot roommate several times."

I'm unashamedly ecstatic about this add-on but play it cool. "But you were too busy warning her I could potentially rob her blind?"

"I thought we were over that." He tickles my arm.

"We are." I run my fingers over the red marks on his. "I'm sorry about that."

"Worth it." He grins. "Another thing…you always smell so good…like roses and something else I can't place."

"Vanilla. It's my shower gel."

His eyes go dreamy. "It's nice."

"Thank you. You always smell like grapefruit. I like it too."

"Thank you back. You've conveniently not answered my question…about being single."

I lie on my side so we're facing each other, our noses practically touching. "I *am* unattached at the moment. I've had two 'serious' boyfriends, one in high school and one in college, but only serious in that we dated for a longish time and were exclusive. We never talked about 'the future' or anything." I genuinely cared about Eric and Seth, but I don't think I *loved* them and was keenly aware neither were my forever person. It's safe to say neither relationship will inspire any second-chance romance novels.

"Reasons for breaking up?"

I hook my leg around his. "Nothing *bad*. In both cases it was graduation, which is entirely void of drama, but I'm not complaining."

"There's been no one since college?" He brushes his foot up and down my leg.

"Less than a handful of hookups. Between work and school, a relationship hasn't been a priority." I poke him in the chest. "Enough about me. Your turn."

"I'm single too."

"Nuh-uh, buddy. You have to give me more than that."

He makes a face, a nonverbal *fine*. "I'm also unattached. I met Ashley at Academy Records and we hung out a few times, but it was casual. I've also had two 'serious' girlfriends. The first one was my college girlfriend."

"And?"

"And..." He brushes hair off my forehead. "We're not together anymore."

"You don't want to get into it. Understood." This is not me being passive aggressive. Having sex with me does not obligate him to divulge details about his romantic history. But I'd be lying if I said I wasn't curious. Would *his* college sweetheart story inspire a second-chance romance novel?

"No, it's fine. She moved back to Seattle after graduation. We tried to make it work long distance, but when I went to visit her the last time, she told me she'd met someone else."

I throw my hand against my mouth. "She let you fly all the way there just to break up with you? Yikes."

He chuckles. "Yikes is right."

"What about the second one?"

"We met on an app and dated for a little over a year but fought when I quit my second job in a row. She accused me of looking for red flags or reasons to quit jobs like other people quit relationships and that she didn't want to be with someone so flakey and incapable of being a grown-up." His face flushes and it's not a delayed reaction to all the fucking. It's clear this is uncomfortable for him. "I asked if she expected me to stay in jobs that made me miserable and she said it wasn't the jobs, it was me."

I grit my teeth. "Savage."

He smiles. "I don't miss her at all."

"Of course you don't. I bet she smells like asparagus."

He scrunches his nose. "Random... but I'll go with it. It's really hard to figure out what you want to do while busy doing something else, so I came here to figure things out while also rebooting my relationship with Grams."

"Have you?"

"Rebooted my relationship with my grandma? We're getting there. But I still don't know what I want to do as far as a career and kind of afraid I never will. In the meantime, I'm having fun working at the library. Aside from the demon kids who weaponize juice pouches." He grins.

I smooth out a lock of his hair that's standing up, figuring that if I'm ever going to take liberties with touching him, a safe time is probably in bed after we've had sex twice. "You can't live on a library page's salary forever, so unless you want to go back to school for your MLIS it's a temporary gig."

He rolls his eyes like a petulant teenager. "Thanks, Dad."

I throw my hand to my mouth. "You did *not* just say that."

"I'm sorry," he says, laughing.

"I am too. I didn't mean to overstep." He already said he was afraid he'd never figure things out and I went ahead and rubbed salt in the wound.

His face turns serious. "I'm aware that I'm delaying the inevitable by living with my grandma and working as a page, but besides wanting to get to know her better, I hope I can make up for what happened between her and my dad."

I open my mouth to argue that it's not his responsibility but clamp it shut because I understand the urge to want to exert control over a situation you have no control over.

"Well, you're definitely not going to figure out your future this minute." I lessen the space between us and raise my leg so it's now wrapped around his waist. If I twist my body an inch, I can be on top of him. "So let's focus on the present. What shall we do right now?" I could sleep for days, but I also really want to take advantage of the man in my bed one more time.

He flips me over and pins me under him. "Round three?"

Chapter Twenty-Six

The next morning, Adam picks Marcia up at the hospital while I stay back to prepare brunch. *Prepare*, in my case, defined as: I set the table with the fresh turkey-and-brie heroes, penne pesto salad, and seedless green and red grapes I bought from the Garden of Eden market next door. After calling Jenny and asking if she'd be okay with us being late to work, she told us to take the day off. Between Fruit Punch–Gate and Marcia's hospitalization, she said we deserved a break and that the library would still be there on Friday.

They get home just as I finish straightening out the mess Adam and I made last night in the living room before we moved things to my bedroom. It's more mayhem than mess, and if you didn't know we'd tossed our shirts on the floor and kicked the cushions off the couch in the heat of passion, it might not make an impression, especially since both shirts are technically Adam's. But the apartment needs to be tidy for Marcia's homecoming. We haven't discussed what last night meant or if it meant anything at all, but we *did* agree to dote on Marcia and make her life as easy as possible from this point forward so she doesn't have another hypertensive urgency... or worse.

Rocket is waiting at the door and Marcia greets him first by bending and lovingly rubbing his ears, then grabbing him by the collar when he tries to make an escape out the door. In a baby voice, she coos, "You lull me into thinking you're happy to see me, but you're really only using my arrival as an excuse to run laps down the hallway and annoy our neighbors. Aren't you, my love?" She stands and smiles at me.

I take her in . . . still wearing the jeggings and button-down chambray shirt we found her in yesterday. She looks tired. Her skin lacks its usual color and there are dark circles under her eyes. Her top is uncharacteristically wrinkled and the ends of her bob are uneven, like her hair hasn't been brushed. I imagine what could have happened to her if we didn't get home in time and start to choke up. But then I collect myself because we *did* get home in time and she's *fine.* I straighten my back. "How are you feeling?"

"Right as rain." She purses her lips. "Maybe a little tired but only because of all the constant beeping and the nurses coming in to check my vitals every five minutes." She walks into the kitchen with me, Adam, and Rocket following behind her and pauses, her eyes sweeping the fully set table and the containers of food on the island. "You didn't have to do this."

"We wanted to," I say.

"We figured you'd be hungry for something besides Jell-O or whatever they fed you at the hospital," Adam says.

She pats his cheek. "Thank you. Do you mind if I shower first?"

"Of course not," Adam says. "Lunch can wait."

"Can I draw you a bath?"

She looks at me funny.

"A bubble bath can be relaxing. For your blood pressure." I defend my offer even though I'm reeling because, seriously, *Can I draw you a bath?* What am I, her lady's maid?

"If you say so, but no thanks." She furrows her eyebrows as if she's contemplating saying more but thinks better of it. "I'll be a few minutes."

"Take your time, Grams."

As soon as we hear the click of her bedroom door, Adam leans over the kitchen island on his elbows and closes his eyes.

"You all right, Adam?"

He doesn't move at first... just nods... but then he opens his eyes and straightens his back. "It's all just hitting me now how differently things could have played out."

I release a breath. "Same. She's okay though. Try to focus on that."

He chews his lip. "Yeah, I know. It's just... I haven't been in a hospital since my mom was sick."

My heart skips a beat. It hadn't occurred to me that he'd connect the two situations, but of course he would. "I'm so sorry. But Marcia is fine, and we'll make sure she stays that way."

He swallows. "Right."

Feeling helpless and needing a purpose, I walk to the back of the kitchen and pour a cup of coffee. "You look like you could use this," I say, placing it in front of him.

Marcia joins us, fresh out of the shower and wearing a light blue fleece hoodie and matching pants. "Do I smell coffee?"

Adam and I exchange glances.

"How about I make you a cup of decaf tea instead?" I offer.

"Sabrina's right. Caffeine's probably not a good idea," Adam says.

Marcia slides into a chair. "Coffee is fine in moderation, even if you have high blood pressure."

Adam raises an eyebrow. "You literally just left the hospital."

She sighs. "Fine. To be safe, I'll wait until after I see my regular doctor next week."

"I'll have tea too in solidarity." I hate tea, but anything for Marcia.

Adam slides his coffee mug toward the center of the table. "So will I."

Marcia pulls a face. "Don't be ridiculous! Just because *I'm* abstaining from coffee doesn't mean you have to." She pushes to her feet. "I'm starving. Thank you again for making lunch."

At the same time, Adam and I say, "Sit!"

"We've got this. Just relax," I say.

She shrugs and sits back down while I make her a cup of tea and Adam fills her plate with food.

When we're all seated again, she stabs her fork into a piece of penne. "So what did you two do last night?"

"We didn't do anything!" I rush to say, my voice loud and squeaky. I sound guiltier than a shoplifter caught in the act.

Adam side-eyes me quickly before turning back to Marcia. "We watched TV and worried about you."

Her brows furrow. "I'm sorry I worried you over nothing."

"It wasn't nothing, Grams."

She plops a grape in her mouth and her eyes widen with pleasure. "These are so sweet. Much better than last week's batch."

I vault from my chair. "I'll get you more."

Adam stands too. "Do you want more tea? Or water?"

"Sit down. Both of you."

I freeze with my hand inside the refrigerator.

She gestures at our empty chairs. "Go on. We need to talk."

We do as she says.

I choke on a nervous laugh. "Why does it feel like I've been sent to the principal's office?"

"You're not in trouble." She looks affectionately between the two of us. "I appreciate you both taking such good care of me, and I will allow it for today, but starting tomorrow, all this doting needs to stop."

I open my mouth to argue.

Marcia raises a hand. "I'm not *that* old, and although I *do* need your help for certain things, making a cup of tea, putting grapes in a bowl, and 'drawing a bath' are not among them." Her eyes twinkle at that last one. "This is not an assisted-living situation, and I will not allow it to turn into one."

I frown. "I want to be the considerate roommate you deserve is all." It is, of course, so much more than that.

"But it's not *is all* to me. It makes me feel old and useless." She registers my dejected face and her eyes soften. "If my doctor says otherwise at my follow-up next week, I'll let you know, but in the meantime, please just treat me like your friend and roommate. And you," she says, looking at Adam, "I'm supposed to dote on you, not the other way around. Be my grandson, not my caretaker." Her eyes slide between us again. "Can you both do that?"

"Whatever you say, Grams," Adam mumbles rather unconvincingly.

I kick him under the table. "As you wish."

"So what do you want to do for the rest of the day? Let me guess, train for a marathon?" Adam teases.

I laugh.

Marcia rolls her eyes. "I was thinking of scrolling OurTime."

Adam chokes on a bite of his hero. "Seriously? You think maybe you should ask your doctor about that too?"

She levels him with her eyes. "I'm just swiping, Grandson. I'll ask my doctor about more rigorous activities next week." She raises and lowers her eyebrows.

Adam's mouth opens and closes.

She winks at me.

I chuckle.

"You promised you'd both do the same with Tinge or Humble. Any progress?"

I freeze. "Um…I…" *Don't look at Adam. Don't look at Adam.*

"Let's make a deal, Grams. I won't ask about the himbos you swipe right on if you leave my sex life to me."

Marcia leans forward in interest. "What's a himbo?"

I take this one. "It's basically a good-looking, most often big-muscle guy who you assume is a jerk because he's jacked…you know *brawny*…but is actually sweet, naïve, and kind of empty between his ears. Like Jason on *The Good Place*. Or Joey from *Friends*."

Marcia takes a sip of water. "And what makes you think I'm swiping right on Joey from *Friends*? I'm just as likely to swipe right on Phoebe, who, come to think of it, is the female version of Joey. A herbo?" She giggles.

I can't help joining in. The girlish sound coming from seasoned Marcia is delightful and charming, not to mention contagious.

Adam scowls at both of us.

Marcia sighs. "I've had a rough day and all I ask is that the three of us sit quietly and search for our soulmates on our mobile devices. Can you do that for an old lady?"

Adam smirks. "Oh, now you're an 'old lady'? How convenient."

"It's a perk of being eligible for Medicare."

"Fine," Adam says.

"What about you, Sabrina?" she asks.

I stand. "I actually have to shower and get ready for school."

"You have plenty of time," Adam says.

This is true, but scrolling the apps for potential dates and hookups next to the boy I fucked last night while he does the same is not a kink I'm into. Especially when I have no idea what he's thinking about me. Was it a onetime thing to get it out of our systems, or something else? But I can't very well say any of this right now, so I have no choice but to sit back down.

Marcia smiles smugly and turns to her phone, her blue Warby Parker glasses resting on the bridge of her nose.

I watch her for a bit...so serious...she takes her time before swiping in either direction, apparently reading each word of every profile. Unlike Adam, who is frantically scrolling left. Good. I hope his back-to-back left swipes are because it doesn't matter how hot and DTF his matches are, he's thinking about how good I am in bed and when he'd like to get me there again.

My lips curve halfway up before flattening when Adam's fingers freeze. He's staring at a profile as if considering swiping right. What could have him so captivated? Most bios are four sentences long accompanied with basic information about height, education level, and interests. It must be the pictures. My skin prickles with annoyance. He could at least have the decency not to match with another woman when I'm sitting right next to him.

Since two can play at this game, I open my phone to Bumble and a notification immediately comes up.

> **There are 4 amazing people on Bumble who think you're amazing too. Swipe right to meet them.**

Take that, Adam.

My first admirer is Douglas. He's fifty-four.

Swipe left.

The next one is Jeremy. He's twenty-six but double fisting a cigar in one hand and a cigarette in the other.

Swipe left.

The third one is Dan. He's twenty-eight and lives in Brooklyn. He's cute and there's nothing objectionable about his profile. I should swipe right. I glance at Adam. He's back to rapid left swipes... no longer staring intently at one profile.

I return my focus to Dan and swipe left.

The fourth admirer is... my breath hitches. "Interesting."

"See someone you like?" Marcia asks.

"Possibly." I swipe right on the profile, smiling as a notification immediately pops up that I matched with Adam, who also sent me a compliment:

Adam: Whatever perfume you're wearing is driving me wild.

I giggle and type a reply.

Sabrina: I'm not wearing perfume. It must be Marcia's shower gel.

Adam laughs.

Marcia looks up from her phone. "Looks like you're both enjoying yourselves."

"Totally," I say at the same time Adam says, "This was a great idea."

Ping.

Adam: What are you doing later, Sabrina, 24?

I tap my lips.

Sabrina: What do you have in mind, Adam, 25?

"You still going to the co-op board meeting tonight, Grams?"

I jerk my head back. That was random.

Marcia looks up from her phone. "Yes, why? My blood pressure does not render me incapable of voting whether or not to install Nest thermostats in the units."

"Don't get defensive. I was just wondering." He chuckles while typing.

Adam: Down to hang tonight after your class? Around 8?

Oh. Not so random after all. My insides tingle.

Adam cocks his head at me in question. I type my answer.

Sabrina: I'm down.

Chapter Twenty-Seven

The next day, I meet Carley for a late breakfast before my afternoon shift at the library. Friday mornings and early afternoons are one of the rare chunks of time when both of us are consistently free.

Carley is dressed like she's straight off the set of *Emily in Paris* in a pink, black, and gray argyle sweater with a matching pink corduroy skirt and white lace-trim socks. It was also her suggestion to eat at Le Pain Quotidien, a Belgian bakery not too far from the library, but since we sat down, she's been more focused on scrolling travel influencer accounts on Instagram than catching up with me. She's the living, breathing definition of wanderlust.

"Check this out!" From our two-person wood table by a window overlooking Broadway in the Flatiron District, she shows me her phone. It's open to a photo of Laurel from the popular travel account @takemeaway.laurel. She's wearing a multicolor gingham dress and standing in front of a body of water, on the other side of which is a landscape of pastel-colored houses.

My mouth drops open. "It's so beautiful it almost looks like a painting."

"Right? She's in Belgium." Carley runs her thumb along the

phone and coos at the photo like it's a precious newborn baby. She looks up at me with a determined glint in her blue eyes. "My show is closing this summer and I'm going to Europe before my next job."

"Nice!" I take a sip of cappuccino.

"You should come with."

I lower my mug and scoff. "I wish."

"Don't wish. Do."

"I have school, remember?"

She tuts. "We can plan it around the summer schedule."

"You've got something..." I point to her chin, where a bit of chocolate from her pain au chocolat has smeared.

She wipes it off with one motion. "Don't change the subject."

I chuckle. "If this were a rom-com you'd have missed the spot and your love interest would inevitably have to wipe it off for you, leading to a 'will they or won't they kiss' moment."

She freezes with her mug to her mouth. "Are you implying I'd be a shitty rom-com heroine due to my perfect coordination?"

I study her fondly. "In that outfit, you'd be perfect."

She grins. "So... you'll come with me?"

I shake my head. "Even if I didn't have school, I can't afford it. And if I take time off from work, I don't get paid. It's a lose-lose situation."

Carley waves out the window at a toddler being pushed in a stroller, then turns back to me. "Except you'd see the world. With me. Win-fucking-win."

I bite my tongue from arguing more. Carley has an answer for everything, but eventually she'll tire out. *Eventually* being the key word.

She pouts. "You're only twenty-four and all you do is work, go to school, and study. When do you play?"

"I played with Adam last night," I say, waggling my eyebrows.

I rushed home after my class and we had a quickie in my room. By the time Marcia got home from the co-op board meeting, we were fully dressed and on the couch discussing *The Hunger Games*.

"Let's table planning *our* trip to Europe for now." Her eyes twinkle. "And dish about Hot Grandson."

My lips curl into a smile. "What do you want to know?"

She leans forward. "You've hooked up two nights in a row. It's practically a relationship."

I pick off a piece of my apple turnover. "I don't know what it is, but it's definitely *not* a relationship."

"You're allowed to have a strictly sexual relationship, you know. I want to keep it casual with Frank, so we only hook up once a week." She taps my hand. "But what *do* you want?"

I shrug. Based on everything I've learned about Adam in the months we've lived together, if we'd met under different circumstances—like if that message he sent me on Bumble had been real—I'm fairly certain I'd want to pursue something more than sex. Then again, "dating app" Adam and "roommate" Adam might not be the same person. You can write a phony or misleading dating profile and fake who you are over drinks, even dinner, but there's only so much you can hide from the people you live with and, in our case, work with. But why am I even thinking about this? I *didn't* meet Adam on Bumble. He's Marcia's grandson. A knot settles in my gut, though it might be carb overload. "I feel a little scandalous to be honest."

Carley smiles big like this is great news.

I hold up a hand. "Not in a *Bridgerton* sexy-scandalous way. I feel guilty...like I'm betraying the friendship and trust I've built with Marcia over the last almost year by sneaking behind her back to sleep with the grandson she's just getting to know herself." It's the first time I've said it out loud, which makes it more real. I slink down in my chair.

Carley frowns. "What does Adam say about it?"

I fiddle with my napkin. "We haven't discussed it. Between worrying about Marcia's health and then sneaking around, there's been no time to define the relationship. Although that would be premature even in a typical hookup situation, which this is not."

Carley purses her lips. "So what's your plan?"

I shrug. "There is no plan. I assume he'll move out eventually and if we're still—"

"Banging?"

I chuckle. "Right. If we haven't gotten bored of each other by then, we'll need to discuss next steps. But we're not there yet."

"When *is* he moving out? Wasn't this supposed to be temporary? It's been a couple months already."

I recall what he said in bed about not yet having figured out what he wants to do next and focusing on his relationship with Marcia for now. "I don't think he's in any rush. And it's gotten really fun lately, so neither am I!"

We laugh.

I bite down on my lip as that pesky guilt washes over me again. I'm grateful when Carley changes the subject until she brings it back to the old one.

"Okay. Back to Europe. I love that you're having great sex, but you're doing it at *home.* Boring. You need to get out of Manhattan, and not just to Connecticut to visit your mom."

"Like I said, I wish I could." This time, I say it with more force. Discussion over.

Her expression softens. "When was the last time you took a vacation that wasn't a *stay*cation?"

I don't even need to think about it. "Spring break, junior year of college. Destin, Florida. But my mom paid for it." I was still technically her dependent and since she'd paid for Audrina to go to Panama a few years earlier, she said it was only fair. "I'm on my own now."

Carley leans forward in interest. "Was it Sabrina gone wild?"

I recall my five days of bordering-on-hedonistic activities with the vivid yet also cloudy memory made possible with the help of alcohol and lift my chin proudly. "It was." As hedonistic as one can get while remaining faithful to her steady boyfriend at home.

"It will be even better with me," she says assuredly.

"I've no doubt." I look longingly at the slice of quiche lorraine the waitress sets at the table next to us. It was what I wanted but cost three times what I paid for my apple turnover. A girl who budgets breakfast has no business planning a trip to Europe. "I don't see how I can swing it."

Carley looks thoughtful. "I'm going to come up with an economical way. We'll stay at hostels and research cheap eats." She scrolls her phone and frowns. "Clearly, I won't be able to live like these people. When building my TikTok brand, I should have focused my efforts on travel instead of makeup."

"But you're a makeup artist and you love it."

"This is true. But if I were a popular travel influencer, I'd have sponsors paying for my trip and could take you as my guest."

"Unpaid model for makeup tutorials versus travel companion at no cost." I gesture like I'm weighing both options and tsk-tsk. "Yeah, what were you thinking?"

Chapter Twenty-Eight

After Carley leaves me to run errands for a welcome-to-Manhattan party her family is throwing for a cousin who just moved here from the Midwest, I walk to the library with visions of croissants in France, beer in Belgium, and red telephone booths in England dancing in my head. The truth is, I'd love to join Carley on a trip to Europe this summer.

Growing up, we didn't go away much, aside from a few vacations to Florida and one trip to Scottsdale, Arizona when my mom was there for a business conference. While she schmoozed with bigwigs, Audrina and I had our first massage and facial. It was during that vacation when Audrina decided she wanted to work in a spa one day, and she's now the assistant spa manager at a fancy day spa. But I've never been out of the country, not even to the Caribbean.

My shift at the library doesn't start for another hour, but it's raining outside. Adding bulky umbrellas to already congested city streets makes walking in Manhattan a bit of a nightmare. Rather than wander around the neighborhood aimlessly or spend money I don't have on more coffee to justify staying at the bakery longer, I arrive at work early and head straight to the back room.

I open my Rocket Money app hoping there's a way I can swing

Europe with Carley after all. She's right that I'm only twenty-four but live like I'm the single mother of two—like my mom did—sacrificing play for work. But unlike my mom, I don't have dependents relying on me. Taking a break wouldn't hurt anyone except, perhaps, myself. My salary potential will increase once I finish my master's degree, so putting it off will delay my ability to comfortably order quiche lorraine at Le Pain Quotidien that much longer. A vacation will also put me further in credit card debt since I definitely don't have enough money saved to pay for it outright.

I realize while scrolling through my sorted expenses that unfortunately most are nonnegotiable, like rent, phone, and my share of the groceries. I could cancel my NYSC gym membership, but with my student discount, it costs me so little it wouldn't make much of a difference, and if I don't allocate some money for food and drinks with friends, my mental health will suffer.

I tap my nose in thought. Payments on my school loans aren't due until six months after I graduate. Would it be worth it to stop paying the minimum balance early? Or drop to one class a semester? I lower my head to the table in defeat. I'm not going to find a solution right now so I might as well take a nap.

"You're here."

I look up at Adam's smiling face and my belly flips.

"Can I join you?" He waves a cardboard box with a sandwich from Pret and a bag of salt-and-vinegar kettle chips at me.

"Of course." I sigh.

"What was that for?"

"What?"

"The sound you just made." He mimics me by taking a sharp inhale then letting it out *loudly*. "Are you tired or frustrated?"

"Both?" Maybe if I got a different library job with more hours, I could swing Europe. But it was a stroke of luck that I got this one. And I was just promoted! There's no way lightning will strike twice. Besides, I love this library and my colleagues. And now Adam, who's staring at me, waiting expectantly for more details, is here too, at least for now. I don't *love* Adam, but I sure do like him a lot, despite not knowing what we're doing. "I told Carley I can't afford to go with her to Europe this summer."

"And you want to go?" He takes a bite of his egg-salad sandwich.

I point to the budgeting app on my phone. "Yes. If only I had access to my trust fund."

"Does your mom not have the money to help you out?" He holds out his bag of chips.

I take one and bite into it. "Honestly, I don't really know her financial situation. I mean, she's got a very important job at a pharmaceutical company and it's just her. Well, my sister lives with her now, but it's temporary and I don't think it's costing her much extra. She's probably in good shape, but she worked tirelessly for every dollar. When we were choosing majors for college, she urged us to pick something that would easily lend itself to getting a job because she majored in sociology and minored in psychology, neither of which qualified her for much after graduation besides more school. She worked reception and office-manager jobs for little pay and then stayed home when we were first born. But when our dad left, his shark of a divorce lawyer got him the minimum alimony and child support payments, which he barely paid."

"He's as bad as mine."

I shrug. My dad is a nonentity in my life, not worthy of discussion. Audrina has tried to track him down with social media, but I already have too many regrets about the way I treated Nana Lena to waste more energy on him. Considering how little time I had with him, it's easy to forget I even *have* a father sometimes, and also better for my mental health not to dwell on it. "Anyway, my mom did what she had to do and that meant working her ass off."

Adam studies me. "I bet she's a great mom."

I nod. "Not in a television sitcom way, but I think so. I remember her coming home from working late just in time to tuck me into bed. Sometimes I'd be mostly asleep but would feel her kiss me goodnight. She always sounded so tired, but I could feel the love in the kiss she left on my forehead and the way she pulled the blanket up to my chin before leaving the room." I smile at the memory. "She worked so hard to raise me and Audrina. She paid for our college educations on her own. She's helping Audrina out again and that's enough. I want her to be able to retire soon and giving me handouts will make it that much harder. I'd definitely ask if I really needed the money, and I *know* she'd help me out. But I don't think a girlfriend trip to Europe qualifies as a necessity."

Adam's eyebrows knit together. "I guess it depends on your definition of *necessity.* Maybe you should let your mom decide."

"Thanks, Aunty Karen." I don't bother to disguise the snark in my voice in response to the unsolicited advice.

He raises his hands in surrender. "Sorry. You obviously know your mom better than me."

"I just wish my tastes ran to a higher-paying career because the thought of being poor for the rest of my life makes me want to slap my younger self for being all, 'Libraries are the *best*! I want to work at a library when I grow up!'" I contort my face in an expression of disappointment at teenage Sabrina's choices.

Adam chews and swallows. "Careers that pay well are overrated."

I picture him at one of his previous corporate jobs. I'm positive he didn't wear the tattered although extremely well-fitted jeans and

T-shirt he's wearing now when he worked at the bank and probably not at the cruise headquarters or beer distributor either. I'm also fully familiar with the pathetic salary of a library page. "You say that so casually. I assume you took a huge pay cut to work here. That must be hard."

He shrugs. "I was always relatively entry level from switching industries, but yeah, the pay was higher. Not that I have much savings to show for it since it went almost entirely to my rent in Philly. But money seems like a worthy sacrifice for not dreading going to work every day. Then again, it's easy for me to say that while sleeping rent-free on my grandma's couch."

I smirk. "You said it, not me."

He smiles sheepishly. "But what you do is meaningful. Libraries have so much more soul than a commercial building on Market Street in Philly. They're crucial to the community. Maybe that older woman who comes in a few days a week to play solitaire doesn't have a computer at home or just needs a reason to leave the house. And what about the people who are clearly homeless and just need a warm place to sit for a few hours? They don't bother anyone, and we keep them safe." He lifts his chin. "Think about that next time you start doubting your career choices."

His face is positively earnest, and it has the effect of pulling on my heartstrings and my ovaries in equal measure. My throat thickens and I touch two fingers to my mouth to keep my lips from trembling. Adam gets it. He's one of us. When I'm sure I'm not going to cry, I open my mouth to tell him so. What comes out instead is, "I'm so turned on right now, I could climb you like the diving board at the town pool."

Adam's eyes darken. "What's stopping you, Sabrina Finkelstein?"

I clench my thighs. I don't know where the sweet, library-loving boy went but those words in that deep timbre of *this* guy are downright scandalous, and *definitely* in the sexy *Bridgerton* way. But I attempt to play it cool. "Because we're in a *library*, Adam Haber. At *work*."

"Excuses." He laughs.

It's not the charming giggle I've heard before. It's dangerous and so hot I crave a hand fan and might need a fainting couch.

"We have about ten minutes until my lunch break is over. I was thinking of taking an elevator ride first. Would you want to come?" He stares at me unblinking.

I'm momentarily confused since the main portion of the library is only two floors and I always use the stairs to move between them. Then it sinks in and I pulse between my legs. "I'd definitely like to come."

The elevator door closes behind us. We're alone. Adam's hands cup my face, and he presses his lips to mine hungrily. I grasp his shoulders and walk backward a few steps until I hit the wall. I register a sharp pain in the small of my back, but I don't care. Adam pulls my arms over my head and holds them up against the wall. Then he kisses me right there like he's been waiting to kiss me his entire life.

He lowers his right hand and slides it into the back of my jeans. I suck in a breath at the contact. *Snap* goes the flap of the white bodysuit I'm wearing under a hot pink blazer. Or should I say "unsnap"? His fingers trace the slickness between my legs for just a second. "You're so wet," he says before slipping his hand out of my pants way too soon. I press my body against his and grind against his rock-solid thigh instead.

The door opens and we jolt apart. My chest heaves. Is this what a heart attack feels like? There's no one there. I let out a breath. So does Adam. He reaches out his left hand and I'm sure he's going to close the door again to continue what we started, but he presses two. We're currently on the first floor. Disappointment hits me everywhere.

"Thanks for the ride, I guess?" I straighten my blazer, grateful it's long enough to cover the back of my jeans in case it's obvious my bodysuit is unfastened.

"Lunch break is over." He stares straight ahead until the door opens again and turns to me. "After you."

As I pass him, he whispers, "You're such a bad girl, Sabrina. This is a *library*."

Chapter Twenty-Nine

When I walk into the apartment after class almost a week later, Adam's on the couch. "My grandma has a date tonight," he says in greeting.

His deadpan delivery and straight face betray nothing, but I see right through it and nearly collapse to the ground with gratitude. As hopeful as I am for Marcia to find her third-act person, this has nothing to do with her date. It's because over the last six days, Adam and I have had no opportunities to be alone together and finish what we started in the elevator. In the meantime, I've suffered through his relentless teasing, like purposely brushing his arm against mine every time he walks past me. And drawing attention to his mouth by biting or licking his lips whenever I happen to look his way. Not to mention waiting until the last second to put his shirt on before work. He knows how badly I want it—want *him*—and is having way too much fun torturing me.

Pretending that I'm not about to explode with need, I ask him where she's going on her date.

"The lobby bar at the W," Marcia says, stepping from her bedroom into the living room.

My eyes nearly pop out of my head at the sight of my seventy-two-year-old roommate wearing a sexy black V-neck wrap dress and suede boots that come three-quarters to her knees. She's fully made up and her hair is freshly blown out. "Wow... you look... wow. Your dress! And your hair looks *amazing*!"

Her cheeks turn pink. "Thank you. I had a blowout at Drybar earlier." She fluffs her hair.

I manage to temporarily shelve my anticipation over having sex with Adam. "Tell us about your date!"

"Her name is Sharon, but actually, I need to talk to you both about something else first." Her face clouds over.

Worry swirls in my gut. "Is everything okay?" Did she have another health scare? I glance at Adam. Did she somehow find out we had sex? I swallow hard.

"Nothing to panic over, I promise." She gestures for us to follow her into the kitchen.

I pour myself a glass of water. "Anyone need anything? Cheetos, Adam?"

He scoffs. "Why do you assume I want Cheetos, Sabrina? Maybe I'm in the mood for something else, like pretzels or carrot sticks."

"Would you like pretzels or carrot sticks?" I ask in my most patient voice, like I'm speaking to a child.

"Nah. Cheetos are good."

I mumble, "Surprise, surprise," before grabbing the bag from the pantry and joining them at the table.

When we're all settled, Marcia says, "First off, I want to thank you both for listening when I asked you not to treat me like a sick old lady. I have an active life and intend to keep it that way for a long time." She takes a breath and raises and lowers her shoulders as if bracing for her next words.

My heart races.

"That said, I'm not a young woman anymore, and I can't pretend otherwise," she says, glancing between us.

Adam crosses his arms. "What's this about, Grams?"

Marcia clasps her hands together. "I had a follow-up with my doctor today. We talked about my incident and how to avoid another one. She prescribed new blood pressure medication to hopefully curb some of the side effects I've experienced in the past, like swelling of my feet and dizziness upon standing."

"That's good," I say, hoping to ease the tension in the air.

She nods. "Unfortunately, my sugar levels are also a bit high. Not diabetes level but high enough to warrant monitoring. She asked if I've been under any extra stress lately and I said not that I know of. But when I mentioned living with two young people, she... well, she wasn't thrilled."

I frown. "Why?"

She lets out a deep exhale. "She thinks sharing a small apartment with two roommates a third my age might be a bit too much."

Adam and I exchange wide-eyed glances.

"I argued having Sabrina around to help with some of the housework, shopping, and pet care this past year has actually made my life easier."

My cheeks lift as her words warm me up like a mug of hot chocolate on a winter day. "I'm glad you feel that way."

The sound of paper crackling steals my attention and I turn to see Adam opening and closing his grip on the Cheetos bag while his focus remains on his grandmother.

She continues. "I do. But with *both* of you here..." Her face contorts as if the words are causing her pain. "It's been... well... crowded and a bit intense. Lots of activity in such a small space." She licks her lips and blurts, "You know, I hate to say it out loud, but I might be too old for this living arrangement. The late-night comings and goings. The TV on late at night. Which brings me to the reason for this talk." She turns to Adam. "I love having you here. Bonding with you after all these years... over music and politics and everything else... means the world to me and I want it to continue for years to come. But this was supposed to be a temporary living situation while you considered your next steps. Have you considered your next steps?"

Adam drops the Cheetos bag on the table. "Not really, but if the doctor says having two roommates is too much, one of us needs to go." He leans over and kisses Marcia's cheek before rising from the table. "We'll figure something out. Don't worry."

She frowns up at him. "I would never leave you without a place to stay so there's no imminent rush, but maybe it's time to give it some thought."

He pats her shoulder. "Will do, Grams."

As I glance awkwardly between grandmother and grandson, I'm not sure of my place in the moment. I wonder if this should have been discussed between the two of them without me here. I bend to pet Rocket, who's silently taken up residence at my feet like he knows I need the distraction.

Marcia glances at her watch. "I'm so sorry to bring this up and run, but I need to head out." She stands. "We can talk more later."

He pulls her into a hug. "Just have fun tonight!"

We follow her into the foyer, where she removes her coat from the closet and puts it on. "Wish me luck!" she says, slinging her purse over her shoulder.

"May the odds be ever in your favor." I glance at Adam, hoping this inside joke will cut through some of the stress of what just happened, but he doesn't break a smile or even look at me.

When Marcia's gone, he grabs a beer from the refrigerator and brings it into the living room. I worry he's taking the news harder than he let on to his grandma, but he's staring at the television, apparently riveted by Mariska Hargitay on *Law and Order: SVU*.

I join him on the couch and try to read his mind. Of all the worries taking up space in my brain when Marcia pulled us into the kitchen to talk, her asking Adam to leave was not one of them. I really like having him here, now more than ever, but Marcia's health comes first, and if her doctor thinks it's too much for her, we need to heed the warning. It was always supposed to be a temporary situation.

"Do you want to talk about it?"

He takes a pull from his beer bottle. "We probably should."

I chew my lip. "It sucks, but I can help you find a new apartment. Gabe also has a lot of friends who might be looking for a roommate. Or Carley can ask around at the theater!"

Adam mutes the television and whooshes out a breath. When he turns to me, he looks almost apologetic. "One of us needs to go, but I don't think it should be me."

Chapter Thirty

I grip the edge of the couch cushion with both hands. "What are you saying?" I'm pretty sure I know *exactly* what he's saying but hope springs eternal that I'm wrong.

He winces like he'd rather be doing anything else than having this conversation. *Same.* "The doctor told Marcia that living with both of us might be contributing to her health issues, but she didn't say which of us should stay. She's my grandma. I think it should be me."

My pulse speeds up. "But this is my apartment. I have a lease!"

His head jerks back, probably from the aggression in my voice. "It was a one-year lease, which means it should be ending in a few months, right? Marcia said there was no imminent rush."

I haven't been keeping track of the time, assuming that renewing my lease was a no-brainer, but I do the math in my head and I've been here eight and a half months, which leaves three and a half remaining. I take a deep breath through my nose and out my mouth to collect myself. "Okay. Let's pretend for a moment that I agree to move out. Are you sure you want to move in with Marcia permanently? Considering you haven't stuck to much lately, how do I know that you won't change your mind?" This is a low blow and I'm not proud of myself, but it has to be said.

Adam's face betrays no emotion. "With all due respect, Sabrina, that's not your concern."

I remove his beer bottle and take a sip, ignoring his lifted eyebrows. "With all due respect, *Adam*, it *is* my concern when you expect me to uproot my living situation on a whim." I can already hear Gabe saying, "I told you so." *Fucking Gabe.*

Adam's expression softens. "I'm sorry to do this to you. I really am. I know how much you love this apartment—"

"And Marcia."

His eyes do a circle of my face. "And Marcia. But I just got my grandma back, and I don't want to lose her. All those things you do for her, I can do them too."

I smirk. "Says the guy who still uses checks, has probably never heard of Venmo, and thinks pressing control-alt-delete fixes everything." I try not to think about how he built the bookshelf, changed the light bulbs, and did a host of other things since he moved in.

He chokes on a laugh. "Thanks to you, she's all set up. And I'm not suggesting that you never see Marcia again. You can come over all the time. I'd want you to. I like you, Sabrina. A lot." His voice gets husky on those last two words.

I'm not capable of going *there* right now. I have to focus. "By the same token, no one says that by moving out, you would lose her either! If you stay in the city, you can see her every day if you want!"

"It's not the same and you know it." He sighs and rakes a hand through his hair. "If you had a chance to make things up to your grandma, wouldn't you want to?"

The words are like a punch in the gut. "I told you that in confidence and in a moment of weakness. Now you're using it against me?"

"I'm not using it against you, but Brina..." He studies me. "I know you love Marcia like she's your grandmother, but she's not. She's mine."

"Fuck you." The words come out without any forethought and my breath catches in the aftermath. But I'm not regretful. He's gone too far. And to use my nickname to get my guard down wasn't cool.

Adam's eyes widen, but then his features smooth out again. "That was harsh. I'm sorry."

I neither accept nor reject his apology.

"You still have plenty of time to find another roommate. Maybe there's someone else like Marcia on that RoomBridge app." His eyes sparkle with hope.

Except there *is* no one else like Marcia. I can't just replace her or duplicate our relationship with any random septuagenarian.

My stomach sinks as doubts fill my head. Am I being selfish? Is giving up my room the right thing to do? The last thing I want is to keep Marcia from her grandson. But I truly believe defending my right to live here *is* best, not only for me but for Marcia. My plan was to stay as long as she'll have me. Sure, I hoped someday I'd move on—either because I was moving in with a partner or able to better afford being on my own—but that could be years from now! Everything I know about Adam screams that he makes rash decisions and then doesn't follow through. It's why his ex-girlfriend broke up with him! What if I move out and Adam changes his mind and decides he wants to become a flight attendant or volunteer for Habitat for Humanity like Audrina's ex? Or what if he misses his life in Philadelphia? Where would that leave Marcia? I just don't believe he's capable of knowing what he wants, and I'm not going to uproot my own life for nothing.

I stand from the couch so I'm looking down at him. "Marcia made it pretty clear that she was talking about you leaving, not me."

"I'm sure she'd be thrilled."

This stops me momentarily as the doubt creeps back in. But I just don't believe moving out and Adam taking my place would make either of them happy in the long run. Living with a woman who is young enough to be your granddaughter is a different dynamic than actually living with your granddaughter.

Adam's still talking. "How about I ask her tomorrow?"

I shake my head. "If you suggest taking over the guest room while I still have several months on my lease, it's just going to stress her out more because she knows I don't want to leave and I'm not a good actress. You can't tell her now." My brain sparks with an idea. It's bonkers but I go with it. "How about this?" I sit back down and cross my legs. "If you can prove to me in the next few months that you truly are the better roommate and make me believe that you'll stick around, I will bow out gracefully when my lease expires." I raise a finger when Adam opens his mouth to respond. "I'm not done."

He blinks. "Go on. I'm intrigued."

"But I'm also going to be the best roommate *I* can be and if Marcia wants me to stay, you can't argue."

His eyes dance. "So like a contest?"

"More like a battle."

"What are the rules?"

I tap a finger to my chin. "Marcia doesn't get hurt."

"That's a given. Anything else?"

"I don't think so." I extend my hand. "Do we have a deal?" The risk of going through with this is that if Adam ends up the victor, I'll have to follow through and give up the apartment gracefully. But the chances of him winning or even still wanting to stick around by the time we're done are low. And if he *does* win, it will mean that he's the better roommate for Marcia and it's for the best. I selfishly hope it doesn't go that way.

When he takes my hand and gives it a firm shake, a bolt of electricity shoots through me. I know he feels it too because his eyes dilate and he holds it a beat too long. It's a shame we're in this position for many reasons, but one of them is that since we're at war now, sex is most definitely off the table.

Chapter Thirty-One

"What are you doing?"

I look up at Adam from where I'm crouched on the bathroom floor the next morning before work. He's wearing sweatpants that ride low on his hips and a white T-shirt, possibly the same one he lent me the night we slept together for the first time. "Cleaning." I brush a hair off my face. It's damp because I'm sweating. Housework is strenuous exercise.

"With a toothbrush? I thought only Cinderella did that…and Annie and her fellow orphans." He chuckles.

"It's helping me target the hard-to-reach spaces." After we shook on the deal last night, I made a PB&J sandwich for dinner and brought it to my room to strategize. This was the first item on my list. I go back to cleaning until my view of the floor is partially blocked by the gray of his sweatpants as he kneels next to me.

"This definitely qualifies as teacher's pet–level extra credit, but if you're going to put in the overtime, you might want to replace that." He points at the Oral-B toothbrush in my hand. "It's dirty, so you're basically scrubbing the grime off just to put it back on."

If I raise my head even slightly, I'll be staring right at his dick, a temptation I don't need, and so I steady my gaze on his thighs, which, let's face it, are also tempting. "A cleaning expert, are you?" Being snarky with Adam comes surprisingly easy after months of getting along so well, and it seems to be mutual.

His teeth dig into his lips as if he's holding in laughter. "Just trying to help." He stands.

"I'll take it under advisement, but maybe you should stop worrying about me and think about how *you* can prove you're the better roommate. I haven't seen you clean this room once since you moved in." As far as I can tell, he hasn't made any effort at all. Then again, it hasn't even been twenty-four hours. I try to switch positions and wince. I've been sitting here way too long.

"I'll take it under advisement," he mimics.

I return to my scrubbing, expecting him to leave, but he hovers. "Do you need something?"

"The toilet."

I lift my head. "Can't you use Marcia's?"

"Technically, but you look like you could use a break."

I want to argue with him, but my back is aching. He's right. I *do* need a break. I stand. "Thanks." It kills me to say the word, but it just slips out.

"It's a hard-knock life," he says before closing the door in my face.

I go to my room and do toe touches, cat-cow, and other stretches to loosen up while Adam does his business. Even though everything hurts, there's a sense of accomplishment I can't deny. Taking my cleaning up a notch is one way to show both Adam and Marcia how much I care about this apartment. I'm also going to ask Marcia if she wants to do a girls' pottery paint night at Color Me Mine next week for some one-on-one bonding. I have more ideas up my sleeve but need to balance my time with school and work.

When Adam shouts, "Shit!" I fall out of my downward dog and race to the bathroom just as Marcia rushes out of hers.

"What happened?" We ask in unison as Adam peels himself off the bathroom floor.

"I slipped," he says, rubbing his lower back.

"You... *what*? How?" Until now, he's demonstrated more-than-adequate coordination skills.

"The floor was slippery." He darts a glance my way.

My mouth drops open. Is he suggesting his slip had something to do with my cleaning efforts?

Marcia lightly holds his arms one at a time, twisting them from front to back to check for bruises. "Are your legs okay?"

"I'm fine, Grams," he says, fake protesting the attention.

I barely suppress a groan. He's *so* milking this. More likely, he faked the fall to turn my cleaning into a bad thing.

I lift my chin in pride. "Like I told Adam, I'm scrubbing the tiles with a toothbrush... trying to get those hard-to-reach spots the mop can't reach. I'm not sure why the floor was wet considering I was using powder floor cleaner." I gesture to the carton of Spic and Span packets on the sink. I hadn't wanted to shove my efforts in Marcia's face because it would look disingenuous, but if Adam wants to do it for me, damned if I don't use it in my favor. "I'm glad you're okay though," I say begrudgingly. *Faker.*

"That's awfully sweet, but don't bother," Marcia says, patting my arm. "Scrubbing with a toothbrush isn't worth it. The floor will be dirty again in a few hours and you'll have nothing to show for it but achy joints and a dirty toothbrush. I'd know." She laughs and kisses Adam's head before returning to her room.

"*A* for effort." He does finger guns at me on his way out the door, seemingly completely recovered.

Alone again in the bathroom, I rub my achy joints with one hand and toss the filthy brush in the trash with the other.

Later that day, the apartment smells like peanut butter when I get home after work. Before I even drop my purse in my room, I walk into the kitchen expecting to find Marcia with a batch of cookies straight out of the oven. "Inject those cookies right into my..." I gulp as Adam, who's facing the oven with his back to me, turns around.

His eyes light up. "Perfect timing. They're ready."

I take him in and blink. Then I blink again to confirm I'm seeing what I think I'm seeing. But yes, he *is* wearing an apron that says, "My favorite people call me Grandma," and...I take a step closer...there's also an adorable picture of Adam as a baby. I know it's him, not only because he looks exactly the same now, just older, but because below the photo, it says *Adam* in script.

He lowers his chin as if he's forgotten what he's wearing. When he meets my eyes again, he grins. "Can you believe my grandma saved this apron for almost twenty-five years?"

"Cute," I say without emotion since I'm positive his decision to wear it today of all days is some psychological warfare shit meant to undermine my confidence for our battle. But Marcia loving Adam is not in dispute. Him being the better roommate to her is another story, though baking definitely counts as making an effort to prove he's not a useless freeloader.

He turns his back again and bends to open the oven so his ass is practically in my face. I wonder if this too is psychological warfare, since his jeans fit like they were made especially for him by Adriano Goldschmied himself.

I quickly shift my gaze when he straightens his back and faces me again.

Placing a tray of peanut butter squares on the island, he says, "Peanut butter treats. Try one."

I shake my head. "No thanks. I'm not hungry." My mouth is salivating and I absolutely want one... *two*... but isn't eating Adam's treats like helping my opponent win? I'd be a traitor to my own team.

Adam leans against the island and smirks. "I know you want one. You're practically eye-fucking them."

I drag my gaze away from the treats and lock eyes with him. Heat pools below my belly. Until now, he's only ever spoken a derivative of the word "fuck" in my company while he was fucking me.

"Fine." I take a cookie from the tray and bite into it as Marcia joins us in the kitchen.

Her eyes widen. "Did you just offer Sabrina a dog treat?"

WHAT? I spit the bite into my hand and drop the rest of the treat onto the floor. Rocket must have "treat" radar because he races into the kitchen, his tail wagging behind him, and swallows it up within seconds. "Seriously?"

My cheeks are practically baking from embarrassment. I march to the sink and pour a glass of water to wash the taste of dog treat out of my mouth. After I guzzle it down, I face my two roommates again.

Marcia shakes her head at Adam. "What's gotten into you?"

He smiles sheepishly. "The recipe says they're good enough for humans to eat. I was just seeing if that was true."

I cluck my tongue. "Using me as your guinea pig. Nice." From the small taste I got, I agree with the recipe, but I will never admit this to Adam.

The three of us watch Rocket go to town on another treat, but after a few seconds Adam says, "I'm sorry, Sabrina. I couldn't resist, but I swear I wouldn't have let you swallow it."

"I should hope not," Marcia says, her lips twitching. She pats my back. "Are you okay?"

I glance between them, all smiles because I don't want Marcia to suspect anything and also, it's not like he tried to poison me. "Go ahead and laugh. It's all in good fun, right, Adam?"

"Exactly." He pulls his apron over his head. Underneath, he's wearing a black hoodie that he unzips and removes as well, leaving only a T-shirt in such a light shade of blue, it almost looks white. It's so threadbare, I can see his muscles right through it. He might as well be wearing nothing, although this might actually be sexier. Not wanting him to catch me staring, I look away, but it's too late.

"All in good fun." He winks.

I escape to my room to recover. When I come back out about an hour later, Adam's on the living room floor brushing Rocket's hair while the dog leans into his touch with soft eyes. I retreat back to my room and text Carley.

Sabrina: 911

Chapter Thirty-Two

"Adam brushed Rocket's hair?" Carley asks, her voice inflected with disbelief.

"Uh-huh," I say, visualizing the tender moment between man and dog right before I texted her.

"Rocket *let* Adam brush his hair?"

"Rocket must be his angle. Did I mention he baked dog treats too?" *And fed me one.*

After I witnessed Adam grooming a blissed-out Rocket, I had to escape the apartment. I packed an overnight bag and let myself into Carley's studio in Hell's Kitchen using the spare key she gave me in case of an emergency. I binged *Ted Lasso,* the most stress-free show ever, from the comfort of her suede green sofa until she came home from the theater. I'm catching her up on everything now, desperate for her advice.

Carley, who's been talking to me from behind the built-in bookshelves designed to separate her tiny bedroom from her living room and kitchen space while changing out of her work clothes, joins me on the couch, now wearing a pink T-shirt with designs of makeup brushes on it and black drawstring shorts. "What do you mean by angle?"

"He's trying to get into Marcia's good graces through the dog."

Carley frowns and cocks her head from side to side. "But he's already in her good graces. And isn't he supposed to be proving to *you* that he deserves to stay?"

"Yes. Maybe? I don't know!" I rest my elbows on her dark wood coffee table and bury my head in my hands, questioning what I got myself into with this competition. "This was such a bad idea," I mumble.

There's no way Adam is going to play fair, although I'm not sure what playing fair even means. Our only rule was that Marcia wouldn't get hurt in the process.

Carley pats my back. "I'm sure it's not. We just need to strategize."

I sit up and rub my nose. "I did. I got up early to scrub the bathroom with a toothbrush!"

Carley's eyebrows shoot up. "Why do I have a feeling it didn't work out the way you wanted?"

I pout. "It didn't. First Adam 'slipped' and then Marcia said it was a waste of effort." And now I can't get "It's the Hard Knock Life" out of my head.

She touches a finger to her lips. "Was Adam okay?"

"He was fine! He faked it for Marcia's sympathy." The devious side of Adam took me by surprise. What's worse is that it's kind of hot.

"Aah. The grandson card... another angle." She crinkles her nose. "But wait. Back it up a second. Who's the judge of this battle, Marcia or Adam?"

I sigh. "With any luck, Marcia will never even know about it, but essentially, we're all the judges. Marcia already told Adam to start thinking about his next steps, so *his* goal is to convince me that I should be the one to move, not him. *My* goal is to be so wonderful that even if Adam proves to me that he's not a flake and I agree not to renew my lease, Marcia vetoes the decision."

Carley gets up and walks to the refrigerator. Looking at me over her shoulder, she says, "So now Adam is a flake? I thought you liked him." She returns to the couch with half a bottle of white wine and two glasses.

I empty the bottle evenly into them. "I do like him, and I respect his desire to be a good grandson, but he can do that without kicking me out of house and home! I don't think he knows what he wants. His track record for sticking things out is not great. I came up with this idea to buy time. I'm hoping he'll change his mind and prove me right."

"I get it." She takes a sip of wine. "So does this mean you won't be sleeping with him again?"

I slump against her enormous soft-pink heart-shaped throw pillow. "Sadly, yes. I can't afford the distraction. But you should have seen the way he took off his apron. It was like a striptease. And there's no way he didn't know what he was doing when he bent down and practically shook his ass in my face." I finish off half the contents of my wine in one gulp.

She nods. "Sex. Another angle." Her lips curl into a slow smile.

My heart thumps. I know that look. "What are you thinking?"

"Hear me out." She stands and paces the multicolor area rug in front of the couch. "Who says Adam is the only one who can use his sex appeal to distract the enemy? You want him and he knows it and is using it to throw you off your game. But he also wants you. Maybe he thinks you're too sweet to use it against him, but he's forgetting one vital piece of the puzzle." She stops pacing and faces me.

The hair on the back of my neck stands up. "What's that?"

She grins. "Me. I'm a bad influence."

I chuckle. "I sort of like where you're going with this, but let's not lose sight of the goal. It's not a battle of the sexes. This is all for Marcia . . . to prove we're the better roommate *for Marcia*."

Carley flumps back on the couch. "Of course that's part of it, but don't pretend you also don't love living in a luxury apartment building that you don't have to share with three other people for less than $1000 a month."

I dip my chin, unable to deny this. Even if I found another roommate using the RoomBridge app, the apartment probably wouldn't be as conveniently located within walking distance from the library and school. And it might not have perks like a private bathroom, so many streaming channels, and a dishwasher. But appreciating all these extras doesn't make me a bad person. And Marcia is my absolute favorite part of the package!

"I also think it would be fun to tease slash torture Adam. Fun for you, of course. But fun for me secondhand."

I look up at her. "What are you suggesting exactly?"

"It's simple really. You should absolutely focus on Marcia but do it while wearing sexy clothes or as few clothes as possible to make Adam sweat. Tit for tat." She shimmies her chest. "Pun intended."

I grin. This *could* be fun, but there's one problem. "I'm kind of at a loss for how to focus on Marcia in the first place. I think I'm a pretty great roommate as it is."

"You are." She stands again. "But there must be *something* else you can do to make her life easier that you haven't thought of."

I bite my lip. "The one place I'm lacking is the kitchen. Whenever we eat together, Marcia does the cooking and I just set the table and help her wash the dishes."

"That's it then."

I grimace. "But I'm an awful cook!"

Carley grins. "Girl, you are so lucky I love you because *I'm* an amazing cook."

Chapter Thirty-Three

That Sunday, I tell Marcia I'll make dinner (with Carley's help). Carley has three older sisters and about a hundred cousins (no exaggeration). The huge extended family lived on the same street while she was growing up and would rotate preparing meals they'd eat together as one big unit. Suffice it to say, Carley's cooking expertise is on par with her makeup skills. With her guidance via FaceTime, I'm making her family's lasagna recipe. When she texted me the list of ingredients this morning, she promised it was simple... easy for her to say... which is exactly what I told her when she suggested it instead of the more straightforward spaghetti and tomato sauce. But she convinced me to try it, along with garlic bread and a salad, and so far her cooking tutorial has been seamless to follow. I've already made the sauce, boiled the noodles, and assembled the cheese, and now I'm layering everything in a rectangular pan.

Just because cooking doesn't come naturally to me doesn't mean I can't get better with practice, and Marcia is worth the effort. What I'm wearing while doing it, however, is entirely for Adam's benefit (or detriment, depending on how you look at it). During a video tour of my wardrobe, Carley suggested a low-cut, tightly fitted white tank top because it shows off my cleavage. I paired it with short frayed hot-pink denim shorts in case Adam is a leg man. Having slept with him several times, I'm pretty sure he's equally turned on by all my body parts.

"What if he made other dinner plans?"

"As soon as he sees your top, he'll break them," she says without blinking.

Just then, he walks into the kitchen, filling the space with his large frame.

"Gotta go." I end the FaceTime call and remind myself to pretend I'm comfortable using my body to manipulate Adam. It's not like he doesn't have it coming. He did it first! Like Sydney Sweeny said in her interview with *Glamour* magazine, "A woman having large breasts makes men stupid." That's what me and my 34Cs are here for. To that end, I lean over the kitchen island and greet him with a simple "Hey."

Wearing a My Chemical Romance T-shirt and black sweatpants, Adam's sex appeal is less blatant than mine today, which doesn't make him any less hot, but hopefully means he's off his game.

He hops onto a stool on the other side of the counter from me. "Cooking dinner for Marcia tonight?"

I shake an imaginary Magic 8 Ball and pretend to peer into it. "It is decidedly so."

His gaze dips to my cleavage and he swallows hard.

I bite my lip to keep from smiling.

It takes him less than a second to recover and when he looks up again, there's a glint in his eyes. "How's it going?"

I gesture toward the lasagna pan. "I'd say it's going well."

"It's very ambitious of you. I'd have thought you'd start with simple penne and sauce."

"Go big or go home." I push out my breasts and watch his gaze dip again.

His tongue darts out and wets his lower lip. "Great motto."

"You want to join us?"

He doesn't flinch. "If I'm invited."

"The more, the merrier."

I "accidentally" knock a fork off the island and bend down exaggeratedly to retrieve it from the floor.

Adam beats me to it. We lock eyes.

"What are you doing, Sabrina?" His voice is husky as he kneels with his hands on his thighs.

Also kneeling at his eye level, I don't look away. "I'm making dinner, Adam. I thought we established that already."

He hands me the fork. "To me. What are you doing *to me*?"

"I don't know what you're talking about."

We straighten our backs at the same time.

Adam steps closer to me. "I hope your plan doesn't backfire."

I look up at him as my heart threatens to beat out of my chest. "I'm highly confident it won't." I'm such a ginormous liar, my nose is probably growing at this very moment.

"You said yourself that you're a disaster in the kitchen."

"If you can follow a dog treat recipe, I can follow one for lasagna."

We stand off for a few seconds. I will myself not to be the first to break eye contact.

Finally, Adam takes a step back. "Good luck." He smirks and leaves me alone.

I put the lasagna in the oven and start cutting vegetables for the salad, but my hands keep shaking so I put down the knife for a break. What am I even doing? Do I really think making a good meal for Marcia is the key to not losing the apartment to Adam? But I've committed to this plan and, unlike Adam, when I commit to something, I don't quit.

I pick up the knife and resume slicing a cucumber as Adam comes back in, opens the refrigerator, sticks his head inside, and closes it again.

"Don't ruin your appetite or you won't be hungry for dinner."

"Thanks for the advice." He opens the pantry and removes a bag of Cheetos before walking out again.

Rude.

Less than five minutes later, he comes back and returns the Cheetos to the pantry.

A few minutes after *that*, he returns and hovers while I wash leaves of romaine.

"Wet lettuce. Yum."

I let the knife drop to the granite with a thud.

"I'm just saying." He laughs and leaves again.

I'm so close to losing my mind after he comes in and out two more times that I call Carley for reinforcements.

"I have an idea," she says.

I howl when she tells me what it is. "Are you sure? It doesn't seem too sanitary to me."

"It's fine. Just don't put it near the food."

"Okay." I end the call and take a deep breath in and out. *Talk about committing.* I reach behind me with both arms and unsnap my bra. Then I pull it out from under my tank top. After pausing a second to consider, I shove it in a drawer with the take-out menus and turn around just as Adam returns, right on schedule.

"Here to give me more unsolicited advice?"

He lifts his empty glass of water. "Nope. Just need a re—" His eyes drop to my chest and he bangs into a kitchen chair. "*Jesus.*"

Priceless is more like it. I beam. "You all right?"

Marcia enters the kitchen wearing black yoga pants and a baggy yellow hoodie. Her blond hair is pulled off her face with a floral headband. "It smells delicious in here!"

My breath hitches and I quickly wrap my arms around my chest. Carley's brilliant idea didn't account for *Marcia* walking in on me while I'm wearing an obscenely tight tank top without a bra, but it's not like I can put it back on without her noticing. "Thank you! It will be ready in about an hour," I say, attempting to act normal.

"It *does* smell good. I'm so hungry. Can I have a veggie to tide me over?" Adam's eyes dance.

I plant on a smile. "Help yourself."

"Can you hand it to me?"

Ignoring him, I turn to Marcia. "The lasagna is vegetarian for heart health."

"How thoughtful of you." Her eyes drop to my arms still wrapped protectively around my chest and her brows furrow. "Are you cold?"

Adam waves his hand in front of his face like a fan. "It's actually really hot in here. Are you coming down with something?"

"I hope not," Marcia says.

"I'm fine."

Over her head, Adam shakes his head and mouths, "Bad girl."

I shrug. *Guilty.*

Less than an hour later, dinner is ready, and the table is set. I realize I still haven't put my bra back on and am about to remove it from the drawer.

"I'm so excited for this dinner, Sabrina!" Marcia says from behind me.

I throw my arms around my chest, turn around, and face my roommate . . . both of them. She's beaming at me. Adam mirrors my stance with his arms crossed and smiles knowingly.

Fake it till you make it. "Sit! Both of you. I'll be back in a second. Just need to use the bathroom." Covering my tits, I scurry out of the kitchen and to my room, where I whip off the tank top and exchange it for a bra and an oversize sweatshirt. But then I think better of it and put the tank top back on over the bra. Why not make Adam sweat through dinner? Since I really do need to pee, I use the bathroom and join them in the kitchen, where they're both already seated at the table.

"I found this in a drawer," Adam says, dangling my bra in the air. "I assume it's yours?"

Marcia laughs. "It's definitely too sexy to be mine."

"Weird. I wonder how it got there." I remove the garlic bread from the oven while my face burns as hot as the food. "I'm surprised you had enough confidence in me to look forward to this," I say to Marcia, quickly changing the subject.

"I have the utmost faith in you." She makes a move to get up, but I stop her.

"Let me know what you need. I'll get it."

She opens her mouth but I cut her off, knowing what she's going to say. "Not because of your health but because this dinner is my full responsibility from start to finish."

She sighs and sits back down. "If you insist. I was going to get the creamy Italian dressing for the salad."

"Got it," I say, grabbing the dressing from the side compartment of the fridge.

"Do we have Parmesan cheese?" Adam asks.

I snort, recalling how often he shoved his head in the refrigerator while I was preparing dinner. "I'd think you'd have memorized the contents of the refrigerator by now, but yes, we do." I remove the container and bring it to the table.

My butt is about to hit the chair when he says, "How about wine?"

I freeze. "I forgot about it." I bring over a new bottle of malbec and a corkscrew and hand them to him.

Adam looks from me to the bottle and back to me. "Are you going to open it?"

Still standing, I place my palms on the table. "Do you not know how to work a corkscrew?"

His eyes drop to my chest and back up. "It's a twist-off."

I breathe calmly through my nose. "Are you not strong enough to open it?"

His lips twitching, Adam says, "I didn't want to be presumptuous. You said you were responsible for the *entire* dinner."

"What is going on between you two lately?"

I whip my head to the left and Adam whips his to the right so we're both facing Marcia, whose forehead wrinkles are more pronounced as she looks between us in confusion.

"Nothing. He's right. I *did* say I had this entire meal covered." Adam thinks he's being clever, but all he's *really* doing is demonstrating to Marcia that he's an entitled brat. I'll be the bigger person. I reach for the wine.

Except he does too. Our hands touch over the bottle. My skin tingles and I let go first.

"I got it." He pours me a glass and slides it my way with a glint in his eyes. "You worked so hard on dinner, you deserve it."

I lean forward and look at him from under my eyelashes. "Thanks."

A muscle in his jaw twitches.

"I'll take one too," Marcia says.

"Are you sure?" we both ask at the same time.

She rolls her eyes. "I'm not going to dignify that with a response."

Adam and I lock eyes and shrug in a moment of solidarity

that reminds me that we both essentially want the same thing—good health and happiness for Marcia. We *also* want the second bedroom... and each other, but those things are secondary.

Standing, he says, "Let me get you a glass," a subtle reminder that I only brought over two. When he gets up, I snatch the bra from where it's dangled over the edge of his chair and sit on it.

When we're all back at the table, we raise our glasses.

Marcia says, "To Sabrina, for making this delicious meal."

"Maybe you should try it first." I squirm. If Carley were here, she'd tell me to cut out the self-deprecation. I sit up straighter.

"I'm sure it's wonderful and can't wait to find out," Marcia says.

"Even if it's just north of edible, it's still a big deal and you should be proud," Adam says.

My head swings his way, expecting to see a cocky grin or smirk, but his eyes are soft. It's not exactly a glowing prediction, but he's giving my effort more credit than I expect under the circumstances.

"Thanks."

We all drink.

Adam licks his lips. "I needed that."

"Rough day?" I joke. As far as I know, he was either on the couch or spying on me for most of the afternoon.

He leans back in his chair. "Yeah, actually. I changed the filter on Gram's vacuum cleaner and cleaned all the attachments. They were full of hair and other debris. It took over an hour, but it works like new now."

Marcia looks absolutely delighted by this. "I don't think the filter's been changed since I bought the thing years ago! Sabrina tried to do it and couldn't figure it out. Right?"

I take another sip of wine. "Right."

"Glad I could help."

I feel him looking at me but refuse to give him the satisfaction of gloating. Instead, I gesture to the food on the table. "Help yourselves."

I let them each take a piece of garlic bread and spoon portions of salad and lasagna onto their plates. While they take their first bites, I fill my own plate to avoid watching their first reactions. But I hear the crunching of the bread, the clanking of utensils, and chewing and swallowing.

It's only when Marcia says, "This is delicious, Sabrina!" that I dare to look. She's beaming at me.

"Really?"

She nods enthusiastically.

I break into a huge grin. "Yay! Carley deserves some of the credit too. It's her recipe and she walked me through the entire process."

"But you made everything yourself. Take the credit," Marcia insists.

Her soft and encouraging tone reminds me of Nana Lena's when I was little and helped her make latkes at Hanukkah. Even after I got potato pieces all over the floor and cut myself while grating, she said I was the best sous chef ever. "I'm trying to compensate for all my previous failed attempts to prepare anything that requires more than a can opener."

"And it shows. Thank you." Marcia smiles.

I notice Adam hasn't said anything. I dare to look at him.

He meets my gaze and keeps it there while he chews and swallows. I stare back while squirming on the inside. I shouldn't care what he thinks, but I do. Marcia watches the exchange with amusement. Even she can see he's toying with me.

He's *still* staring me down as he wipes his mouth with a napkin then finally drops it to his lap. "It's good."

There's no exclamation point at the end of the most anticlimactic phrase in history, but I'll take it. I'm about to thank him with the same level of enthusiasm when he says it again.

"It's *really* good, Sabrina. Well north of edible."

I smile cautiously at him, afraid he's toying with me. His sincere comments mixed with reminders that our competition is still alive and kicking, not to mention the suffocating sexual tension, is making me dizzy.

He winks.

Not helping.

Dinner continues without drama. Marcia entertains us with tea from her morning spin class: the married thirtysomething guy who stares at the ass of the woman whose bike is in front of him each time she stands in second and third positions; the woman who wears the same smelly heavy sweatshirt and pants to every class; the man who grunts the entire time like he's having painful sex. Soon we're cracking up and I start to forget what truly motivated me to make this dinner in the first place.

"Speaking of smelly gym lady," Marcia says with a chuckle. "She mentioned a dog comedy event in the park tonight."

Adam blinks. "The comedian is a dog?"

At the word "dog," Rocket comes flying into the room and sticks his head on my lap. I lean down and kiss it. "Rocket should headline. He's the funniest pupper ever. Aren't you, sweet boy?"

Rocket bites a piece of cucumber right off of my plate. "Okay, maybe not so sweet, but definitely funny."

Marcia laughs. "It's stand-up *about* dogs with pet participation from the audience. Rocket would love that. Wouldn't you, Rocket Man?" Rocket barks. "You in?"

I open my mouth to accept the invite when Adam says, "I'll go. Unless Sabrina needs help cleaning the kitchen."

I glance around the room and my breath hitches. I'd been so focused on *preparing* the meal, I didn't think about the "after" part or the mess I was making in the process. The room looks like a plane crashed into a train wreck at a bus station. The sink and counters are piled high with all the pots, pans, dishes, and utensils I used. And there's...*fuck*...a sauce stain on the wall by the stove. My heart palpitates. Maybe no one will notice.

"I hope that comes out," Adam says, pointing right at it.

Fuckety fuck fuck fuck.

Marcia follows the direction of his finger with her eyes and low-key cringes.

I vault off my chair. "I'm so sorry. I'll clean it right away."

"It's not a big deal. I can always paint over it if it comes to that. I worked for a house-flipping company one summer during college. Paint is expensive but we might get lucky with a sale," Adam says. Apparently, one of us didn't forget about our competition.

"Or maybe it will come out with soap and water. It's not blood." I stop short of making a dig at yet another of his many short-term jobs.

"Just scrubbing it with soap and water on a paper towel might make it worse. Gently rub it with baking soda and water and let it dry. If it doesn't work, I'll try apple cider vinegar and some ammonia when we get home." His expression softens as he looks at Marcia. "Don't worry about it."

She reaches for his hand across the table. "You're the best."

"So are you." He stands. "I'm gonna change, but then I'm ready for the park whenever you are."

Picturing them enjoying a fun evening in the park, laughing at dog jokes while I stay behind to clean the kitchen, leaves a pit of sadness in my belly. It's something Marcia and I would normally have done together, like when we watched *Forrest Gump* in Bryant Park last summer and a cooking demonstration at the Big Apple BBQ in Madison Square Park. If I end up moving out, will we ever do things like that again?

"I'll help Sabrina with the dishes so she can come with us," Marcia says.

My breath catches. "You will?" I'm probably supposed to turn down her offer to help. I'm the one who insisted I had dinner covered from beginning to end, but I desperately want to come with them.

She stacks her dirty dishes over mine. "Of course. Like I'd really let you stay back and clean up after us while we have a fun evening in the park laughing at dog jokes? *Please.*"

I breathe out a laugh while also blinking back tears. "Thank you."

She furrows her brow. "Are you okay?"

I answer her with a nod and stand to bring more dishes to the sink.

"I'll help too," Adam says.

He's at my side in a moment. "How about Grams clears the table, Sabrina rinses the dishes, and I put them in the dishwasher?"

"Teamwork," Marcia says.

Here is where I should quietly brag that his plan to leave me out of the evening's festivities backfired. But he willingly got with the program, and I have no idea if he's actually cool with it (maybe even secretly happy) or pretending while silently tweaking his strategy to beat me.

"Nicely played," he whispers, his breath tickling my ear.

My muscles tense. I turn to face him and we're so close that my boobs brush against his belly. It wasn't on purpose, but when he sucks in a breath at the contact, I feel victorious just the same. "I wasn't playing anything. Marcia clearly enjoys my company and wants me around."

He places a rinsed plate in the dishwasher. "I'm sure she'll invite you to join us when you move out. Maybe your octogenarian roommate can come too."

"What is this about an octogenarian roommate? I'm not there yet!" Marcia says.

Adam mutters "shit" under his breath while I think quickly on my feet. "I suggested that if Adam wants to stay in New York City on a library page's salary after he moves out of here, he should check out ads on the RoomBridge app. It worked for us, right?"

"It sure did." She glances at her watch. "We should get going in a few minutes. Leave the rest for later." She excuses herself to freshen up.

When she's gone, I turn to Adam. "Now *that* was nicely played."

Chapter Thirty-Four

The dog comedian was no Jim Gaffigan but his jokes, mostly centered on over-the-top dog owners, were funny. The warm feeling in my heart over Marcia refusing to let me stay at home and do dishes while she and Adam enjoyed themselves lasted all night... a reminder that our friendship isn't any less important to her just because her grandson is back in the picture. But the park was crowded, and for the entire hour I was hyperaware of Adam right next to me—his throaty laugh, his long fingers stroking Rocket's fur, his grapefruit scent. My only consolation was that he seemed equally tuned in to my presence. We'd laugh at a joke and catch eyes. Or he'd lean into me so his large body pressed against my side before playing it off as accidental and stepping away, taking his warmth with him.

And now it's two days later and I'm trying to focus on work while he's across the floor shelving returns and wearing jeans that once again make his ass look amazing. I'm well aware, having seen said ass up close and naked, that it's not the jeans, but even Jeremy Allen White's butt doesn't look perfect in *every* pair of pants.

I force my gaze away from him and focus on the patron in front of me at the circulation desk. "Is your last name spelled *o-d-e-r* or *o-e-d-e-r*?" She asked me to check if the branch has a copy of her novel.

"*O-d-e-r*. Gwen Schroder." The woman, who's probably only a few years older than me, bites down on her lower lip. "This is my local branch and I'd be so excited if you had a copy here. I could have checked online, but I wanted to see for myself."

"I totally understand! Let's see." I type her name into the catalog and smile when I see a title come up. "A copy of *Clear for Disbelief* was just returned today. Is that the one?"

Her blue eyes widen. "Yes!" She claps a hand against her heart. "Oh my god. So it's somewhere in the library *right now*? And someone actually took it out?"

I chuckle. Her excitement is endearing. "Yes and yes. Our page is probably shelving it as we speak. Go ask him." I point at Adam. "Tell him I sent you over."

She looks over her shoulder at Adam and back to me. "I will. Thank you!"

"My pleasure. Congratulations on the book!"

Since there's no one else in line, I watch her approach Adam. I can't hear what she says, but I clock the understanding that washes over his face followed by a huge smile before he rummages through the cart, pulls out the copy of her book, and hands it to her. She hugs it to her chest for a second then returns it to Adam, who reads the back. As the two chat, something sour swirls in my gut.

They're two extremely attractive people of similar age who share an interest in books. She's a published author, which is super impressive, and her reaction to seeing her novel at the library was adorable, which probably means she's not an asshole. And Adam is a whole damn meal. Since we're not sleeping together anymore, not that we were even exclusive, he's free to pursue someone else.

Gwen removes something from her purse . . . a bookmark . . . and hands it to Adam. He takes it and . . .

Shit. He's looking at me. They're *both* looking at me. Why? My hands sweat and I wipe them along my jeans, willing myself to pull it together. I square my shoulders and channel the Sabrina of Sunday . . . the Sabrina who absolutely caused Adam to walk into a chair . . . or at least the Sabrina *whose breasts* made Adam walk into a chair. By the time this mental transition from jealous mouse to fierce goddess is complete, they're not looking at me anymore. Adam's returned to his shelving and Gwen is walking in my direction with a huge smile. "That was one of the best moments of my life."

I want to ask if she's referring to seeing her book in a library or meeting Adam. Instead, I offer my congratulations again and resume trying to focus on work and not the perfect fit of his jeans.

After school that night, I pop my head into Marcia's open room to say hi, only to be greeted by a shirtless Adam.

"Seriously?" It comes out before I can stop myself.

Adam grunts and lets the king-size mattress he's raised with his palms fall against the box spring. "Seriously *what*?"

I lean against the doorframe and cross my arms over my chest. "You *had* to take your shirt off to flip Marcia's mattress?"

He swipes his hand against the back of his neck, grinning when he notices me tracking the motion. "It's heavy. I knew I would sweat. Why would I soil a perfectly clean shirt?"

I shrug. I don't have a good answer and refuse to give him the answer I *do* have—that I'm inconveniently turned on by his bare chest.

He crosses the room until he's standing right in front of me. "Does my bare chest bother you, Sabrina?"

I lift my chin, holding my breath. "Not at all." I clench my thighs.

His eyes darken. "Then why won't you look at it?"

I drop my gaze to his chest and right back up. "Done."

He leans forward so we're eye level. "You know what I think?"

I gulp. "What?"

He wets his lips.

My own chest heaves obnoxiously. Logically I know that if I don't breathe soon I might asphyxiate myself, but my lungs won't cooperate.

"I think you're afraid to look at my body because then you'll be forced to admit you want me."

The hypocrisy of what he just said springs my lungs back into action and I take a deep inhale. "Like you admitted to wanting *me* in my tank top the other day?"

He shrugs. "That's easy. I admit it. I wanted you then. I want you now. I even told that Gwen person at the library it wouldn't be fair to give her my number because I'm too into you."

My body goes still. "You did?"

He nods. "Yes."

I'm so unnerved by his sincere expression, all I can manage in response is, "Oh."

"I *like* you, Sabrina."

I hate how much I wanted to hear that. *Needed* to hear it. I drop my gaze to his bare stomach, letting it linger this time. It's too much to resist. "Where's Marcia?" I trace a finger from his belly up his sternum and place my palm over his heart.

It thumps against my hand. "On a date."

I blink. "Another one? Same person as before?"

He cages me against the wall. "Don't change the subject."

My eyes softly close and I feel the heat of his mouth against mine.

He traces my lower lip with his teeth and draws me into a kiss. My legs wobble as I sink into it, raking my hands through his hair, until he breaks away and whispers, "I miss you," in my ear.

I stroke the back of his neck. "I miss you too." My body aches with need.

"If you agree to move out, we can stop this stupid competition and be together."

I jolt out of his embrace while an army of emotions battle for prominence: anger, humiliation, disappointment. "Are you for real?"

"What?" He has the nerve to look all innocent.

My hands curl into fists. "The same is true if *you* move out!" Before he can respond, I wiggle out of his way and into the hallway. "Conceited jerk!"

He laughs at my back. "So I guess you don't want to forfeit?"

"Oh, fuck off." I march to my room and slam the door behind me. I flop onto my bed and scream into my pillow. I can't believe I fell for Adam's tricks. Except I *can* because he's so convincing with his smoldering gazes, romantic declarations, and passionate kisses. It's hard to tell what's real and what's part of the game.

I want to hide out in my room for the rest of the night while I recover from my emotional riptide, but my schoolbag is still in the living room and it's not like I can study without my notes. I'm not in the mood to do homework anyway. What I *want* to do is zone out to trashy television. If I can do that while showing Adam I'm not at all affected by our kiss, even better. With that, I toss the pillow I'm still holding over my face across the bed and stand up.

Adam's conveniently still in Marcia's room so I grab my purse and get comfy on the couch with a blanket around my legs even though it's May and turn on the newest tell-all episode of *Ninety Day Fiancé*. I check my email against a backdrop of the latest season's cast revealing inside scoops that the audience never saw. While scrolling from the bottom up, past emails from the *Skimm*, *Refinery29*, *Library and Information Science News*, the *Newsette*, and *Teen Librarian Toolbox*, a new email message comes in from Verizon at the same time a notification pops up from the app.

I read the notification and my breath hitches. My bank has declined my automatic phone payment this month due to insufficient funds. I sit up and throw the blanket to the floor. This can't be right. I close out of the Verizon app and log in to my online banking app. I should know how much money I have—give or take fifty dollars—but I haven't checked in a while, a nugget of information that would frustrate my mother the way people refusing to leave the library at closing time frustrates me and my fellow librarians. Within seconds, my current balance is displayed prominently on the screen and my pulse races: $98.73.

A chill runs through me. How? It can't be! My first instinct is I've been robbed. Someone has hacked my debit card and stolen all my money! Then reality sets in: no one else is to blame for my money mismanagement except me. I deflate like a faulty air mattress. On the bright side, even Carley can't argue the impossibility of my going to Europe when I don't even have enough money in my checking account to cover automatic phone payments. I curl into the fetal position and try not to cry.

"I see you've made yourself comfortable on my couch."

I raise my head slightly to see Adam standing over me holding Marcia's winter comforter. I heard her ask him to store it at the top of the closet until the fall. I drop my head back to the pillow.

"You're not even going to say something about it not being *my* couch?"

I sniffle.

I hear the comforter drop to the floor. "Shit. Are you okay?"

"Not really," I mumble into the pillow.

He squeezes next to me on the couch. "I'm sorry I was an ass before. You're just a formidable opponent. Funny, sexy, and well-read. The best kind."

I know he's trying to make me laugh but I just can't take the mixed messages on top of everything else. "Stop it. Believe it or not, not everything is about you."

"So tell me what this *is* about." There's not a hint of defensiveness in his tone.

At the risk of falling for his soft-and-gentle act again, I sit up and hand him my phone open to the bank notification. At least he put a shirt on.

He takes it from me, his eyes widening as he reads the message.

"I have less than a hundred dollars in my bank account. Go ahead and say it. If only I'd paid with a check this wouldn't have happened. You know you want to."

"The check would have just bounced. And no, I *don't* want to." He frowns. "Just because we disagree on what living situation is best for Marcia doesn't mean I want the worst for you."

"Oh. Thanks." My voice quakes. I shouldn't have bitten his head off when he was just being nice. I dip my head and rub the back of my neck. "I can't believe I let it get this far." I'm talking about my pathetic bank account, although this could also refer to my competition with Adam.

I make a mental list of where all the money went—groceries for dinner, ice cream at Van Leeuwen for the three of us after the comic show (which I insisted on paying for to prove whatever I was trying to prove), lunch with Carley, Starbucks between work and class, takeout dinner at Westside Market after school. I'd have to look at the app to see what else, but the point is, I spent more money than someone with very little money to begin with should spend, which amounted to *all* the money I had in the bank aside from $98.73.

Adam swallows, then speaks. "You probably don't want to hear this, but maybe you should tell your mom."

My ribs squeeze. He's right. I *don't* want to hear this. Asking my mom for money is a last resort. I'll get paid again before rent is due in a couple of weeks. In the meantime, I'll cool it with the spending, and I have a credit card for emergencies. "The first thing I need to do is call Verizon."

Adam nods. "I'll leave you to it then."

I spend the better part of the next hour alternating between bypassing instructions to press one, two, or three depending on the reason for my call and listening to elevator music on hold. At one point, Adam brings me a Trader Joe's Way More Chocolate Chips cookie. At no point does he raise the volume on the TV or ask me to relocate to my room. Eventually, I get through to a human being and arrange for an extension of time to pay my bill. Late payment fees will apply but at least my coverage won't be interrupted.

Even so, I can't sleep that night. And it has nothing to do with my disastrous financial situation and everything to do with Adam's kindness. I'm more conflicted than ever.

Chapter Thirty-Five

The living room is empty when I get home from school two nights later. Marcia's door is closed, but I can hear muffled voices coming from her room. Adam's in there. Something prompts me to listen in, even though the last time I eavesdropped on their private conversation, I wished I hadn't. But my name isn't mentioned at all this time.

They're debating whether it's better to collect music on vinyl or CD. Marcia is team CD, insisting it's cheaper and the audio quality is superior, but Adam's focus is on the process and how much cooler it is to put a record on a turntable and drop the needle. As far as I know, Marcia doesn't own a record player and if Adam does, he didn't bring it here. The whole exchange is odd but also adorable. Then "Beast of Burden" by the Rolling Stones plays and the conversation stops. They're listening together. My nose prickles as I picture grandma and grandson singing the lyrics duet style.

The guilt over potentially getting between Adam and his grandma haunts me, not constantly, but often enough that I second-guess our battle. This bonding moment doesn't help matters. Maybe Adam's more committed to living with his grandmother than I'm giving him credit for. I assumed switching jobs every six months and delaying making long-term plans meant those plans wouldn't include staying with Marcia. What if I'm wrong?

From the other side of Marcia's door, Adam says, "Night, Grams. See you tomorrow."

Assuming he'll enter the hallway any second, I spring to my room. When I toss my schoolbag on the bed, I knock a small stack of papers onto the floor. I peer at them from my standing position. They weren't there when I left for work this morning. I bend to pick them up, sit on the edge of the bed with my feet dangling, and read the yellow Post-it note on top.

> I printed these out from Roomster during lunch. See anything interesting?

I recognize Adam's loopy and annoyingly neat handwriting from his handwritten grocery lists. *Boomer.* I can guess where this is going and should probably save my mental health by tossing them in the trash, but my curiosity gets the better of me.

> *Midfifties female looking to rent out bathroom in my one-bedroom West Village home. Bathroom is large enough to fit a twin air mattress. I will just need you to remove the mattress whenever I need to use the bathroom. $450 a month.*

I laugh on instinct. The ad is hilarious, unlike the obnoxious note Adam left on top.

> In case you're looking for something more affordable

I read the next one.

> *For rent: Studio apartment in Hell's Kitchen. Red Sox and Patriots fans only. Yankees and Giants fans and friends/relatives of Yankees and Giants fans need not apply.*

> I wasn't sure if as a Connecticuter you were Team Yankees or Red Sox, but maybe? (Go Phillies!)

My muscles tense. I don't need to keep going but read the next one anyway.

> *Roommate wanted: Seeking a roommate for my two-bedroom apartment in Long Island City. Water, heat, and electricity included but must contribute to various streaming channels. Also must agree to keep track of daily bowel movements on shared Excel spreadsheet.*

> This one speaks for itself.

I flop backward on the bed and groan, kicking my feet. Just when I start to feel like the villain, he pulls this crap! I freeze with my legs mid kick as it occurs to me that this is *exactly* what I wanted: to be so annoyed with Adam—quite difficult when he's spewing bullshit like not wanting the worst for me and feeding me chocolate chip cookies—that it reignites my motivation to win this battle. My breathing slows. This is good. I sit up and contemplate whether to confront him or act like it never happened. And then I have an even better idea.

A half hour later, I text him.

> **Sabrina:** See attached links to RoomBridge. Didi sounds sweet and her apartment is centrally located in Turtle Bay. There's a no drinking or pets rule, and she prefers her roommate to be home in the evenings after 10. But it's not like you have much of a social life anyway, right? And Joselyn lives in Rockaway. Isn't that where Patti Smith lives? Maybe you'd be neighbors!

When it's off, I give myself a pat on the back and do a little victory dance. *As you sow, so shall you reap!*

My stomach grumbles. Competition makes me hungry, and also, I haven't eaten since lunch. With a spring in my step, I go to the kitchen, passing Adam in the living room on my way with a smug grin. I pretend to ignore him getting up to follow me and proceed to compile the ingredients for tuna fish while softly singing the chorus to "Because the Night."

"I'm impressed you know where Patti Smith lives."

With my back to him as I use the can opener, I say, "There's this thing called the Internet. You used it too, remember?"

"I was trying to help. Four-fifty a month is a steal."

I roll my eyes, though he can't see me. "To live in someone's bathroom." I stop squeezing the water from the tuna and place the can in the sink. "It was a really messed-up thing to do." I swallow down the tightness in my throat. "Mean."

"What? Printing out roommate ads?" There's an edge of disbelief in his voice.

I turn around. "Yes! After pretending to be all nice after what happened with my phone bill." I lift my chin and work on keeping my face a blank canvas so as not to betray that he hurt my feelings. This competition was my idea. It's not personal, so why does it feel like it is?

His eyes go soft. "I wasn't pretending. It was in the spirit of the battle! All's fair in..." He swallows. "Real estate."

I cross my arms over my chest. "The battle was supposed to be to prove who was a better roommate for Marcia, not play mind games with each other!"

He leans against the island. "I'm playing by your rules, Sabrina. And you said there *weren't* any rules in the competition aside from my grams not getting hurt."

"Why would I get hurt?"

As my heart leaps to my throat, I lock eyes with Adam. At the same time, we swing our heads and face Marcia, who's looking between us with a wrinkled brow and holding what I recognize as the Roomster ads. "I went to your room hoping to catch up... it's been a minute... and I saw these on your bed." She waves the ads with sad eyes. "Are you moving out? And where's the metaverse?"

Adam snorts.

I glare at him. I didn't even see that one. How would that even work?

"And what's this about a competition?" she asks.

Neither of us say anything at first, but then Adam blurts, "I told Sabrina I want to stay here and that she should move out when her lease expires but she refused, so we're battling it out."

I gawk at him. *Seriously?* Wasn't the whole point of competing privately to hopefully come to an agreement ourselves and avoid worrying Marcia and potentially escalating her stress and blood pressure? He didn't even attempt to sidestep the question before folding like a cheap suit. He wouldn't last a minute in an interrogation. But now that it's out, like a fresh comforter out of the tiny bag it comes in, we can't put it back in. "Based on Adam's track record of not sticking around, I wasn't convinced he'd thought it through and didn't want to uproot my life only for him to change his mind in a few months. I told him if he convinced me he was serious, I'd agree to move out." I chew my cheek. The plan sounded so much better the first time I said it out loud.

Marcia ekes out a laugh. "I don't know if I should be pissed off or flattered. Were either of you planning to ask what *I* wanted?"

Of course, *now* Adam is tight-lipped. "I'm sorry for keeping it from you," I say. "I hoped he'd prove me right and you'd never need to find out. The competition was a delay tactic."

Adam frowns at me, looking genuinely wounded. "It was?"

I shrug.

Marcia shakes her head. "What was the competition anyway?"

Adam sighs. "We've both been trying to prove we're the better roommate."

Marcia slides into a chair and drops the ads onto the table. "So *that's* what this has been about? Cleaning the bathroom with a toothbrush? Making homemade treats for Rocket? The elaborate dinner? All the tension between you two?"

I gulp on that last one. Much of that is *sexual* tension.

"Your intentions are all well and good, but you could have saved yourselves a lot of time and effort if you'd just asked me. The only thing this 'competition' has accomplished is stressing me out more, which is exactly why my doctor was concerned with this living arrangement in the first place." She rubs her temple.

I tuck my elbows to my chest. Our attempts to protect Marcia backfired. A lump forms in my gut. Who am I kidding? As much as we want to say this was all for Marcia's benefit, we were 100 percent also looking out for our own interests. And I enjoyed flaunting my breasts at Adam as much as he relished parading around his six-pack abs. "I'm so sorry."

"Me too, Grams."

She gazes up at Adam. "Take a seat, honey."

Adam, who's resting his arm on a chair, drags it farther away from the table with a loud screech. Then he sits, stretching his long legs in front of him.

Marcia gives him a wistful smile. "I love you, but when I suggested you consider your next steps, they didn't include moving in with me permanently. No matter how old you are, you'll always be my grandson, which means if we live together, I'm always going to want to take care of you... to mother you. And I did that already with your father. I don't want that responsibility again. I'm seventy-two years old. I did the work and now it's my time to be selfish. You need to go."

I gasp, then cover my mouth. My heart races while bracing myself for Adam's reaction to Marcia's order. Will he fight it or go easily?

Adam nods. "I get it. I'll figure something out."

She pushes herself to a standing position and squeezes my arm. "I hope *you'll* stay."

I blink back tears of relief and nod.

"And I promise to never make you document your bowel movements."

I press my lips together as bubbles of laughter rise in my chest.

She walks out of the kitchen leaving me alone with Adam, who's still seated at the table. I return my half-opened can of tuna to the refrigerator to make later. I've lost my appetite. It's over. The threat to my home has been vanquished. But with every winner comes a loser. The air in the room is thick and I don't know what to say. What would Adam do if the tables were turned? He's been so inconsistent the entire time that whether he'd throw his victory in my face or be a gentle good sport about it is a toss-up.

His gaze on the wall in front of him, Adam says, "Congratulations."

"Thanks." I swallow. "I'm sorry. I mean... I'm not sorry I get to stay, but I'm sorry you have to leave... if that makes sense."

He stands and faces me. "We always knew one of us had to leave." His eyes do a circle of my face. "All's fair in real estate, right?"

I bite down on my lip. "Right."

He nods, then scoops the roommate ads off the table and walks out of the kitchen.

Chapter Thirty-Six

About a week later, Gabe's voice calls from behind me in the early-readers section at the library: "It's too bad about your roommate."

My hand freezes around a copy of *Honest June*. "What are you talking about?" I ask, turning away from the bookshelf to face him.

"He quit so now we need to hire another page." Gabe's eyes scroll the handwritten list of books I've leaned against the shelf and he wrinkles his nose. "Children's books with *June* in the title? Not the most creative display idea and a little premature, but not bad."

"I'm not sure if I should defend myself or say thank you, but what is this about Adam quitting? I had no idea." I scan the entirety of the second floor over the four-foot-tall bookshelves looking for him, but if he's here now, I don't see him. I hadn't wanted to ask about his next steps since, as the last one standing, I figured I'm probably the last person he'd want to discuss them with.

I sort of hoped things between Adam and me could go back to the way they were prebattle, at least until he moved out. Now that Marcia has proclaimed me the winner—although she didn't put it that way—we could be friends again, commute to work together, revive our book club, et cetera. And maybe we could resume our friends-with-benefits activities as well. But he's mostly kept to himself since that night and hasn't given off any horny vibes at all. Worst of all, he's suddenly pro-shirt, and I rather miss his bare chest.

"I know nothing beyond what Jenny just told me about him quitting. I figured you'd have the gossip," Gabe says, an eyebrow raised.

I chew my lip. "This is the first I've heard of it." I never told Gabe about our battle because I didn't want to hear him say, "I told you so," since he predicted Adam would want the second bedroom for himself from the very beginning. I figured I would reserve his help for when and if Carley's creative well ran dry and I needed fresh ideas to get the upper hand. But it never came to that.

Gabe pushes a book that's sticking out until it's even with the others on the shelf. "Didn't you say he took this job while figuring out what he wanted to do with his life? Maybe he figured it out. You live with the guy…and more." He grins knowingly. "Ask him and report back. Lane wants to know too."

Not bothering to refute the "and more" part, I say, "I will." I don't know when he'd have had time to do all this "figuring out" over the last few days, but Gabe doesn't need to know this.

In typical friend-to-senior-colleague whiplash, Gabe says, "Now get back to work," before heading downstairs.

I finish pulling the books for the display and leave them behind the desk for later. Then I search the first floor for Adam but he's not there. Finally, I break down and text him.

Sabrina: You quit?

Adam: The library is too long a commute from Philly

* * *

Adam and Marcia are out to dinner for his last night when I get home, because as I quickly learn from text messages from both of them, he's moving back to Philadelphia... *tomorrow*.

I didn't think it would happen so quickly. I don't know why, but I assumed he'd stay in New York City when he left Marcia's. Even when I teasingly sent him links to ads on the RoomBridge app, they were apartments in the boroughs. Maybe it's because he barely mentioned Philadelphia during his time here aside from casual references to sports teams and cheesesteaks. Now that I've had a few hours to let it sink in, it makes sense that he'd want to go back to his home city. At the same time, he talked a convincing game about not wanting to lose his grandmother again. Yet he's choosing to move out of the city where she lives rather than find an apartment nearby so he can see her on a regular basis and continue building their relationship. On the plus side, if I held any guilt over his leaving instead of me, I don't anymore.

I lie back in my beanbag chair and look up at the white painted ceiling until the bulb from the light fixture threatens to give me a headache and I close my eyes. Adam is moving out. He's moving on. We won't be roommates anymore. Or colleagues. Or anything else. No more accidental naked encounters outside the bathroom or risqué ones in the elevator. No more sex.

I open my eyes. It's not a big deal. It was all supposed to be temporary anyway. We had fun, but it's not like we were a couple or anything. I'm sure all those things he said about really liking me were true, but also embellished as part of the game... to make me doubt myself. We weren't on our way to becoming anything real. Our hookups will always be a little secret between us... a good memory... but that's all, and I'm okay with that. I'm sure he and Marcia will figure out where to go from here in terms of their grandmother-grandson relationship, and in the meantime, I'll have the bathroom to myself again. And the living room and TV. Back to normal.

There's a knock on my door. "You decent?"

My pulse speeds up. The man himself. "Never." Nervous laughter escapes. "Kidding. Come in."

The door opens and Adam leans against the doorframe. "Is this a good time?"

I scooch my butt so I'm sitting up. "Sure. Come in."

He closes the door behind him and sits on the edge of my bed. "I wanted to say goodbye now in case we don't get a chance tomorrow."

I rotate my beanbag so I'm facing him. "Philadelphia, huh?"

He taps his foot against the floor. "Yeah. My dad pulled some strings and got me a job at an e-learning company."

This is the last thing I expected him to say. "You want this job?" I recall what he said about craving a job he doesn't dread going to... one that he even has a passion for. Is a job with an e-learning company going to check either of those boxes?

He shrugs. "The education part is intriguing. Plus, it pays well. Has benefits... a 401(k)."

I snort. "What happened to good-paying jobs being overrated?" I immediately wish I could take this back. Though it's not my fault he's losing his free housing, it feels a little like my fault. A job with benefits and a 401(k) is certainly a step up from one without either of those things.

He flashes a sad smile. "I was in my idealistic era when I said that. I was also living rent-free." He bites his lip. "And this job... it's not like the others. My dad doesn't want me to feel trapped again, so he called in a favor and got me a floater position at his friend's company. I'll be moving through the customer service, tech support, and content creation departments to see if anything fits."

My stomach roils. This all sounds great except for the part about his dad. I can't stop myself. "So your dad is a great guy now?"

He sighs. "He's trying to understand me, and I can get him to talk to Marcia... to work things out."

My head jerks back. "What do you mean by *work things out*?"

"I said I'd only accept his help... the job and money toward a few months' rent in a furnished apartment... if he called Grams." He swallows hard. "You told me you wished you had a chance to make things right with your grandmother. Well, maybe this is my chance to help make things right between my dad and Grams."

My mouth drops open while sadness covers me like a black cloud. It's hard to find fault with Adam's plan knowing one of his motives is to help Marcia reconcile with her son. If I believed it would work, I would say bravo. But a Dalmatian doesn't change its spots. I want to be supportive though. "I really hope it works out the way you want."

Adam's shoulders drop. "Me too. I have to try."

"I get it." I awkwardly maneuver myself off the beanbag chair and into a standing position. "Well, it was fun being your roommate while it lasted. It worked out better than I expected." I scrunch my face. "Aside from that one week where you fed me dog treats, faked slipping in the bathroom, pointed out a sauce stain in the kitchen, and walked around without a shirt on." My skin burns hot at that last one, reminding me of our more intimate moments. Should I say something about those or are we pretending they didn't happen?

He smirks. "Don't forget the week you wouldn't talk to me because you thought I accused you of robbing Grams blind."

I giggle. "Yeah, that too. But otherwise, it's been great."

He stands. "Well, I enjoyed every second of being your roommate."

"Right. Aside from when—"

"Every second."

I suck in a breath. "Oh. Thanks." My knees wobble and I wish I was still sitting down. Is this my opening to say something about "us"? Why is this so hard?

He nods. "Besides my grandma and the Strand.... and Academy Records, you were my favorite part of my short vacation from life."

Over the lump in my throat, I joke, "I'm so happy to come in fourth place."

His cheeks split wide open. "Well, bye, Brina. Thanks for being so welcoming." He holds out his arms.

I fall into them and hug him hard. But he hugs me harder. I inhale his grapefruit scent for the last time... or at least for the last time in a while... and wipe my eyes just in time for him to pull back. Thankfully. I do *not* want him to see me cry.

"Take care of my grandma for me, okay?"

"Of course." I consider asking him to sneak into my room later for a proper goodbye, but ultimately chicken out. It's better this way. A clean break.

And then he kisses the top of my head, whispers, "I'll miss you," and walks past me into the living room. When I wake up the next morning, he's gone.

Chapter Thirty-Seven

"When using highlighter on more mature skin," Carley says, while applying illuminating serum under Marcia's eyes, "you want to draw attention to the highest points of your face."

Standing next to me in Marcia's en suite, her date Sharon takes a sip of wine. "Where is the highest point on *my* face?"

Carley smiles but doesn't answer because she's filming a video. Her latest project is a demonstration of how to apply highlighter for all generations. She used me as her model for Gen Z before Marcia took her turn as boomer. Her models for millennial, Gen X, and the silent generation are her cousin, mom, and great aunt, respectively, but thankfully they aren't here because Marcia's bathroom is already crowded enough.

I turn to Sharon, who I just met an hour ago but like already. "The highest points are the ones that stick out farthest from your cheeks." She looks impressed and I feel myself blush. "I only know this because I asked the same question."

"Hmm." Sharon stands and peers at her reflection in the mirror over the sink while stretching out the skin on her cheeks with her fingers.

Short and solid with chin-length reddish brown hair, dark eyes the color of acorns, and medium-toned skin, Sharon is adorable. She's also only sixty-six, which means Marcia's dating a younger woman, something Carley and I enjoyed teasing her about before Sharon got here tonight.

The two went out for the first time the same night Marcia told me and Adam her doctor wasn't thrilled about both of us living with her and have been seeing each other regularly ever since. I'm happy for her. I think Adam would like Sharon too—after an intense interrogation as to her intentions toward his grams, that is. I picture his round of twenty questions as a scene in my head and laugh to myself.

Adam's been gone almost two weeks now, and the transition has been fine. The apartment is noticeably quieter without him roughhousing with Rocket or watching television in the living room. It makes it much easier to focus on my homework. I can watch *Love Is Blind* without him interrupting me with unwanted commentary on the contestants' true motives. The bathroom is also much tidier now that he's gone, and I never noticed how spacious the vanity was until he took his shaving supplies and deodorant back to Philadelphia with him. If I have to pee in the middle of the night, I can turn on the lights instead of tiptoeing in the dark to avoid waking him up, and I don't have to worry about going number two while he's right outside! So yeah, it's been fine . . . good, in fact.

Marcia moped around at first. I'd catch her peering out her bedroom door into the living room as if expecting to see Adam on the couch, but then her face would fall when she remembered he doesn't live here anymore. I suggested some of the activities we did alone together before he moved in as a distraction, like yoga classes and walks around the park, but I think Sharon is the one who ultimately pulled her out of her funk. I know she still misses him, but she's not overtly sad about it anymore.

I haven't spoken to him, but Marcia said he's doing well at his new job. Though an online learning platform does seem more up his alley than a bank—and he did enjoy the library events focused on tweens and teens—I have trouble picturing him working in customer service or tech support *anywhere*. But all that matters is that he's happy.

"All finished," Carley says, standing back and surveying her work.

I straighten my back and focus on Marcia. "Looking good!"

She's glowing, although it's unclear whether it's the makeup or Sharon that's causing it. "Where are you two off to tonight?" I ask.

Marcia glances at her diamond-studded vintage Timex watch. "Nonna Dora's, and we'd better hurry or we'll lose our reservation."

"I wish you'd have warned me you'd be all glammed up," Sharon says, placing her empty wineglass on the vanity. Then she raises her palms in the air and bends down then back up again while chanting, "I'm not worthy! I'm not worthy!"

Marcia pushes her gently. "Oh, stop it, Garth!"

Sharon juts a hip. "I'm Wayne, *you're* Garth."

"Why am *I* Garth?"

"He's a blond, like you."

"Dana Carvey is not a blond!"

"He's closer to it than Mike Myers!"

While the two playfully argue back and forth, I lock eyes with Carley.

She places a hand on her heart and mouths, "Ca-*yoot*!"

I mouth back, "I know!" A smitten Marcia is an adorable sight to behold. If Adam were here, he'd grumble before grudgingly agreeing with me. I shake off the image and plant on a smile. "Have the best time, ladies!"

After the two leave, I refill my wineglass with the remains of the bottle of Riesling Sharon brought over and collapse onto the couch next to Carley. Rocket's resting on the rug by our feet. Every once in a while, he sits up and makes sad eyes at me. I take a long sip of wine when my first thought is that he must miss Adam.

"Check this out," Carley says, handing me her phone.

It's an advertisement for an *Emily in Paris* guided tour in Paris. "Oh, this looks super fun!"

"It's only thirty-nine dollars a person, but we can do an unofficial one if you want to save money." Carley says this nonchalantly, as if *acting* like my coming along on her trip to Europe is a foregone conclusion will make it so.

"Hmm," I mutter passive-aggressively.

"Think of it as your reward for winning!"

"Winning what?"

Carley looks at me funny and sweeps her arms around the living room. "The battle with Adam!"

My shoulders drop. "Oh. Right."

Her forehead crinkles. "You're here and he's not. So why don't you look happier?"

"Because he's not here." I whisper the words, hoping that if I say them quietly enough, even *I* might not hear them.

Carley's face falls. "Oh, fuck."

My eyes tear up, no longer able to deny the undeniable. "I miss him, Carley."

I've been focusing on all the positives but suspect they are secretly negatives. Sure, I can turn on the light when I use the bathroom at night, but it just makes it harder to fall back asleep. Watching television without Adam's background commentary is boring. Studying in complete silence is overrated. In fact, the only true positive is that I don't have to plan the timing of my number twos for when he's out of smell-shot.

I sag against the couch cushion. "I keep telling myself it's what I wanted, and it is, but I didn't think he'd move to *Philadelphia*."

Carley leans in closer to me. "Move *back* to Philadelphia, you mean?"

I rub my hands along my jeans. "While we were fighting, he... he said that if I moved out we could date for real. I assumed he was trying to manipulate me into surrendering." *I enjoyed every second of being your roommate. Every second.*

She studies me. "Do you wish you did? Surrender, I mean?"

I take a sip of wine. "Of course not. And Marcia said herself that she didn't want to live with him on a permanent basis because then she'd be a grandmother twenty-four seven instead of a queen."

Carley places a hand over her heart. "I love that she called herself a queen!"

I chuckle. "She didn't. I'm just paraphrasing. Anyway, I don't wish I gave in, but I can't help wondering, *what if*?"

She wraps an arm around me in a side hug. "Well, if ever you needed a European vacation, it's now."

I snort. "Of course you'd find a way to bring this back to your trip."

"It's my gift." She kicks her foot against mine. "Just promise me you'll think about it?"

She insists I make this promise every time I see her. Unwilling to take no for an answer, she's put off booking the trip, but this is the final week of her show so I'm running out of time. If I go with her, I can cancel my registration for summer school, which starts next week, for a full refund, but I'll need to tell Jenny right away so she can organize coverage at the library in my absence. The good news is, jobs in libraries, even temporary, are in high demand. It only took a few days to find Adam's replacement, a college student getting her BA in library and information science. She's *fine*, but she's not Adam. (Although at least I'm not distracted by the perfect fit of *her* jeans or tempted to get to third base with *her* in the elevator.)

I break myself out of that particular train of thought and back to the issue at hand. Why am I even thinking about who would cover for me at work? I'm not going with Carley. I *can't* go with Carley. But lately, my outward insistence of this fact to the woman herself has been sorely lacking conviction.

"Shit. Work." Carley vaults off the couch. "I need to get to the theater!" She runs to Marcia's bedroom and returns with her bag of equipment slung over her shoulder. "Don't think about Adam. Think about Paris and visiting the Pont des Arts and Palais-Royal Garden! Pain au chocolat at Boulangerie Moderne!" Then she kisses me on both cheeks European style and leaves.

My phone pings with a text.

Audrina: come home this wknd

Sabrina: Why?

Audrina: I won free massage appointments in the company raffle

I place my phone on the coffee table and consider the offer. The round-trip train ticket would mean more charges on my credit card that I can't afford to pay off, but otherwise staying at my mom's usually costs me nothing because either we eat at her house or she takes us out. Between adjusting to life post-Adam and getting an F in adulting, I could definitely use a massage, and considering I'm in the financial doghouse, I can only afford a free one.

Sabrina: Make appointments for Sunday. I'm working Saturday morning but I'll leave straight from the library. Don't eat dinner without me

Audrina: Bossy, much? But yes

In slightly better spirits, I rise to walk Rocket. He needs to go out and I need to do something that doesn't cost any money.

Chapter Thirty-Eight

All tension has left my body post massage. My muscles feel like Jell-O. Wanting to extend this afterglow as long as possible, I take the glass of cucumber water my masseuse, Gary, handed me into the waiting room and fill a cup with a mixture of raw nuts, banana chips, and dried fruit. Then, still in my robe and slippers, I sink onto a beige suede reclining chair next to my mom and sister, who it seems aren't in any rush to return to reality either. I breathe in the scent of eucalyptus oil as a feeling of well-being washes over me.

My mom's eyes open halfway. "How was it?" The words come out drowsy, almost like she's on drugs.

"Amazing," I whisper back. "Yours?"

"Same." She closes her eyes again and smiles contentedly.

For the next several minutes, the room is silent as the three of us enjoy the blissful aftermath of our treatments. The version of Sabrina who walked into the spa two hours earlier, wound up and heavy-hearted, no longer exists. Thanks to Gary's long, kneading strokes along my body with jojoba oil, I have a new outlook on life. Living with Adam was a learning experience. It taught me I'm capable of compromise and flexible with my space and routine. And yes, it was also fun. I hadn't made time for boys and sex, and he got me out of my drought.

But it was the *idea* of him that I liked—a smart, funny, kind...okay, *hot*, man who loves books, dogs, and his grandmother, and isn't too alpha to admit he's horrible at techie stuff—not him specifically. Now I know those men exist and I will meet someone else eventually.

I suddenly feel a burst of gratitude for my big sister for unknowingly coming to my rescue by offering this all-expenses-paid experience (minus the tip) to put things into perspective.

I sit up. Keeping my voice quiet, I say, "Thanks again, Aud. This was just what I needed."

Audrina remains still, and for a second I wonder if she's fallen asleep. After a moment, she says, "Same. And you're welcome."

"And I love spending time with my two daughters even if we're in separate rooms and not speaking."

Audrina and I share a skeptical look. Our mom's affection for us has never been in question, but the demonstrative statements aren't her brand.

To counter the vicarious cringe of her sentimentality, I joke, "I'd think you'd be sick of Audrina by now. She's best in small doses."

Audrina pouts. "How quickly gratitude turns to ridicule in this family."

I chuckle.

"Girls," Mom says sternly, proving she can still scold us with her eyes closed (and probably hands tied behind her back too).

"If Mom is sick of me, which is *highly* unlikely, the good news is I've saved enough money to rent my own place again."

"That's great!" I'm happy for my sister (if not also a bit envious) and assume our mother is both relieved and pleased by Audrina's refound independence.

"Thanks! I'm going to stay another few months to boost my cushion though."

Mom says nothing, insinuating this isn't news to her.

And just like that, my sense of calm disappears and I burst into tears, shocking my mother, sister, and myself in one fell swoop.

Audrina shoots up in her chair. "Oh my God. What's wrong?"

"Are you hurt?" Mom asks, alarm in her voice.

"I'm fine," I choke out, but the uncontrollable sobbing makes me a liar, as do the big fat tears pouring out of my eyes. My chest heaves with them and I can't stop.

The blurry blob that is my sister says, "Is this about Adam?"

Because I can't speak at the moment, I shake my head in answer.

It's not about Adam. At least it's not *all* about him (because who am I kidding? I didn't like the *idea* of him. I liked *him*). It's everything: Adam, my bank account, the trip to Europe I didn't know how much I wanted to take until I realized I couldn't. But the true cause of my breakdown, without a shadow of a doubt, is the ease with which Audrina asks for and accepts our mom's financial support while I can't, or more accurately, *won't*. While my sister manages to float through her period of economic distress using my mom as a raft, I'm drowning and it's no one's fault but my own.

"Massages have a way of releasing emotions you don't even know you're carrying," Audrina says, now at my side rubbing my back.

"You can talk about sex with me, you know. We're all grown-ups here," Mom says.

Another spa client walks into the room, and we pause speaking while she pours a cup of tea and sits on an empty chair.

"It's not about sex," I hiss as quietly as possible. My gaze darts to my mom and quickly away. I've stopped actively crying, but my chin trembles in the aftermath.

"Then what is it about?" she asks.

Through my teeth, I say, "Not now." I lift my chin toward the stranger in the room. "People come here to relax and treatments aren't cheap. I won't ruin it for them by doing this here."

Mom pulls me up by the arm. "Then come with me." She drags me toward the exit while Audrina looks on with a bemused expression.

"We're in our robes!" I flash a timid, apologetic smile at the receptionist.

To the person at the front desk, Mom says, "I promise we're not going any farther than the parking lot." She removes her credit card from the pocket of her robe and hands it over. "This is collateral."

I frown. "You brought your credit card into the massage with you? Isn't that what the lockers are for?"

"I see you've regained the ability to communicate. Good. That will come in handy. Besides, your sister works here. They'll know how to find us. Let's go." She pulls me out the door, where it's a perfect June day—dry with a pleasant temperature of about seventy degrees. Too bad there's a storm brewing inside me.

The spa is located in a small strip mall housing two other stores: a fancy sandwich shop and a bougie boutique. Fortunately, neither are heavily populated today and no one else is outside save for two women who just left the sandwich shop and are walking to their car. We wait for them to pull out before facing each other.

"This is about me, isn't it?" Mom says, all knowing as ever.

The vision of my mother standing in a public parking lot wearing a fluffy white robe and towel-cloth slippers with her hair standing up at weird intervals and a postmassage pink glow to her face would make me laugh if we were out here to talk about anything else. "Sort of. You and Audrina."

Her eyebrows draw together. "What about us?"

I wrap my robe tighter around me. I'm going commando underneath. "You always lectured us on doing whatever it took to be financially independent and then you let her move back home with you rent-free."

"Yes," she says, as if it were a question to be answered.

I lick my lips. *Fuck*, this is hard. "Since graduating college, I've never asked you for anything. I didn't think I could, and I also didn't want to. I wanted to prove to you I could take care of myself like you did. But the thing is, I'm really struggling."

She reaches for me.

"Please let me finish." I take a deep breath and let it out. "My job pays crap, but it's all I ever wanted to do so I don't complain, except that I need to spread that money over a lot of things. My rent is cheap comparatively speaking, but it eats up most of my paycheck, and there are other expenses. I'm also paying off my school loans already because you put the fear of credit card debt in me growing up."

"Guilty."

"Carley is *begging* me to go to Europe with her this summer—she says I'm only young once and deserve a break from working and studying. I desperately want to go, but it's not the responsible move for a struggling grad student whose automatic phone payment was declined for insufficient funds."

Mom's face goes white. "What?"

I gulp. "I worked it out with them to pay late, but yeah." I take a deep breath and let it out. "Adam thought I should ask you for help right from the start, when I missed out on the scholarship..." I chew my lip. I never told her about that. "But I didn't want to involve you because I'm a grown woman living on my own. Then you let Audrina move home, and of course I wouldn't deny her that, but there were no lectures about her getting her act together and being independent. So here *I* am, unwilling to ask you for help because you worked so hard for every cent and I don't want you to use any of your well-earned retirement money when I'm an adult capable of taking caring of myself, while *Audrina* says she'll stay even longer than she needs to for a *cushion* and you're totally okay with it with zero stern talk...and well, I'm just so tired of trying to figure out everything on my own and could really use a cushion too!" I burst into tears again.

Mom blinks. She takes a step back and does a half turn. I think she's going to walk away from me but then she faces me again with tears in *her* eyes and pulls me into the tightest hug of my entire life. She squeezes me so hard like she's afraid I'll try to wriggle out of her embrace and chants, "I'm so sorry, baby. I'm so sorry!" over and over again into my hair. When she finally lets me go, her formerly dewy pink skin is blotchy and her eyes are red. "You've been afraid to ask me for help all this time?"

I shrug. "Not afraid as much as...proud maybe? I can't explain it. You did it yourself. Shouldn't I try to do the same?" I flash a sheepish smile. "But yes, kind of afraid too."

She groans. "I didn't do it all by myself, Brina Bear. I had your grandparents! With both of my parents gone, your father's were all I had. I didn't want their help, but I was desperate for it and they were desperate to give it. They couldn't control their son's actions, but they could control what happened to his family and begged me to let them help." Her eyes turn heavy. "They loved you girls so much and were afraid they'd lose you too."

My eyes well up again. So much for resolving my grandma issues.

As if reading my mind, she says, "We talked about you, you know."

My breath hitches. "Who? You and Nana?"

She smiles softly. "Yes. She knew you were working through your father issues on some sort of delayed schedule and she hated it."

My shoulders sag with the weight of my guilt.

"She was less concerned with her own feelings... though of course, she missed your closeness... than knowing you were in pain. We both knew you'd come through the other end eventually."

"You did?" I wipe my nose.

She nods. "Remember that card you made her? The one where you matched compliments to the letters in her name? Lovely..."

"Energetic!"

"Nice. Angelic."

I snort. "I was such a dork!"

"You sure were."

We laugh.

"She knew you loved her. Through all of it."

Mom's expression is so earnest, I'm forced to trust her. I *want* to trust her.

"Back to the topic at hand. Don't put me on a pedestal. I would have lost the house if Lena and Lou hadn't helped pay the mortgage. And I wouldn't have eventually built up my own savings if she hadn't taken care of you girls so I could go to work." She shakes her head. "I hate that my own daughter isn't comfortable enough to tell me when she's struggling. I relied on my mother-in-law the same way you can rely on me."

I shuffle my feet. "But you always taught us to be independent and not need anyone."

She sighs. "I was mostly talking about not relying on a romantic partner because I don't want what happened to me to happen to you, but regardless, financial independence *is* something I want for both of my girls. And I want you to want it as well! I know I drilled it into you and I'm glad you listened to an extent. But it's rarely something you can achieve uninterrupted over a lifetime. And if you're lucky enough to have someone to support you when you're struggling, you accept it. Why do you think I've worked this hard? For you!" She raises and drops her shoulders. "This is a failure on my part. I should have known. I should have asked. I'm asking now. How much do you need?"

My instinct, out of sheer habit, is to insist I don't need her help or at the most give her a lowball number. I recall Adam saying rather than assume my mom wants me to figure everything out on my own instead of supporting me financially, to give her a chance to decide for herself. I also know she's serious about wanting to help me. Her tears don't lie, and also, what's in it for her to be dishonest? *If you're lucky enough to have someone to support you, you accept it.* "An extra few thousand dollars in my bank account would legit help me sleep at night."

"Done."

"And maybe a bit more so I can go to Europe with Carley next month?" I grit my teeth, afraid I took her generosity too far.

"Yes. Definitely." She takes both of my hands in hers. "Listen... none of this means you should stop working hard toward financial independence. I don't intend to bankroll you through life, but Carley is right that you deserve a break, and even if it means taking time off from work this summer, or pushing back classes until the fall, you should do it. You have your whole life to do the 'responsible thing,' and I trust you will. Today, let me be the mom. I won't always have this opportunity. If it makes it easier for you to say yes, think of it as doing *me* a favor." She gives me a wry grin and lets go of my hands.

I hurl myself at her and this time, it's me squeezing so hard she couldn't escape my embrace if she tried.

Chapter Thirty-Nine

From: Sabrina F. <SFinkelsteinreads@gmail.com>
To: Adam Haber <Adam.Haber@gmail.com>
Date: July 11, 5:01 p.m.
Subject: Hi

Hey Adam,

Hello from Paris! Yes, I went with Carley on her trip. I finally caved and told my mom about my financial troubles and she offered to help.

I know what you're thinking. I TOLD YOU SO. You did.

But that's not why I'm emailing you. It's because I miss you and am not sure if I'm supposed to miss you like a friend, a roommate, or something more. We never talked about "us." It probably doesn't matter since you moved back to Philadelphia but I...

Ugh. This is so cringe. I'm covering my face like you can see me. I can't send this. But I do miss you. And I do think you should know about my mom so I'm going to start over and try to be normal. Maybe I'll ease into the more personal stuff if you email me back. I don't know why I'm still writing this. Bye!

This email was written but not sent and will save as Draft until further action.

From: Sabrina F. <SFinkelsteinreads@gmail.com>
To: Adam Haber <Adam.Haber@gmail.com>
Date: July 11, 5:32 p.m.
Subject: Guess where I am

From: Adam Haber <Adam.Haber@gmail.com>
To: Sabrina F. <SFinkelsteinreads@gmail.com>
Date: July 11, 5:44 p.m.
Subject: Re: Guess where I am

Epcot? Vegas?

From: Sabrina F. <SFinkelsteinreads@gmail.com>
To: Adam Haber <Adam.Haber@gmail.com>
Date: July 11, 6:08 p.m.
Subject: Re: Guess where I am

I can't tell if you're joking, but no! It's the real Eiffel Tower. I'm in Paris with Carley!

From: Adam Haber <Adam.Haber@gmail.com>
To: Sabrina F. <SFinkelsteinreads@gmail.com>
Date: July 11, 6:14 p.m.
Subject: Re: Guess where I am

Nice! Did you rob a bank?

Guess where *I* am.

From: Sabrina F. <SFinkelsteinreads@gmail.com>
To: Adam Haber <Adam.Haber@gmail.com>
Date: July 11, 6:20 p.m.
Subject: Re: Guess where I am

A parking lot? Wow. That's so cool. Way better than the Louvre.

No banks were robbed in the planning of this trip. But the Nigerian prince scam really works!

JK

I asked my mom for help. Well, more accurately, she *offered*. We had a long talk in a parking lot wearing robes and slippers but…you had to be there. Long story short, I told her I was broke. She was upset that I kept it from her and offered to pay for this trip to Europe (along with a cushion to help get me back on my feet).

Your turn. How are you? I hope it's okay I reached out. It's been a while, but I thought you should know that you were right. My mom wanted to help. Go on, say it: I TOLD YOU SO.

Gotta run. I'm dragging Carley to Shakespeare and Co. before cocktails at a floating hotel! The goal was to spend $100 a day at the most, but Carley has expensive taste. Let's blame it on her, shall we?

From: Adam Haber <Adam.Haber@gmail.com>
To: Sabrina F. <SFinkelsteinreads@gmail.com>
Date: July 13, 9:12 a.m.
Subject: Re: Guess where I am

How was Shakespeare and Co? Do you need another suitcase for all the new books you bought?

I'm glad you told your mom while wearing slippers, although she might have treated you to new socks if she saw your holes. Also, I TOLD YOU SO. Kidding.

It's the middle of the night here. I can't sleep. Tell me more about this trip. Is it only Paris or are you on one of those fast-paced "ten cities in ten days" tours?

Doing ok. I don't love this job, but it's not the worst. And so far, no demon kids have attacked me with their juice pouches. My apartment's not in the metaverse but the dishwasher is in the bathroom. Manhattan doesn't have a monopoly on weird setups. And there's a great indie bookstore across the street called A Novel Idea. You'd love it. I go to all their author events.

From: Sabrina F. <SFinkelsteinreads@gmail.com>
To: Adam Haber <Adam.Haber@gmail.com>
Date: July 13, 8:33 p.m.
Subject: Re: Guess where I am

We're in Brussels now! See attached photo of us and some new friends at the Cantillon Brewery. The city is so charming. Lots of cobblestone streets and gorgeous architecture. We're splitting our trip between Paris, Brussels, London, and Rome. I bought the French version of *The Perks of Being a Wallflower*. Pic attached.

That bookstore looks so cute and cozy. I hope you were joking about the dishwasher in the bathroom. At least you have an actual bed now. I assume you have an actual bed now?

I'm sorry you don't love the new job, but at least it's not the worst. It had some big shoes to fill. Everyone knows librarians make the best co-workers.

From: Adam Haber <Adam.Haber@gmail.com>
To: Sabrina F. <SFinkelsteinreads@gmail.com>
Date: July 14, 4:08 a.m.
Subject: Re: Guess where I am?

You look happy. The jacked guy on your left with the lion, tiger, and bear tattoos must really like animals. Did you show him your bunny-rabbit birthmark?

I have a bed now. A waterbed.

Yes, librarians make pretty great co-workers. But nothing gold can stay, right?

From: Sabrina F. <SFinkelsteinreads@gmail.com>
To: Adam Haber <Adam.Haber@gmail.com>
Date: July 14, 10:34 a.m.
Subject: Re: Guess where I am

Who says nothing gold can stay (besides Robert Frost and Ponyboy)? No one forced you to quit the library and leave the city! I could have helped you find an apartment. Marcia hasn't mentioned Jeffrey. Has he even called her yet?

This email was written but not sent and will save as Draft until further action.

From: Sabrina F. <SFinkelsteinreads@gmail.com>
To: Adam Haber <Adam.Haber@gmail.com>
Date: July 14, 10:36 a.m.
Subject: Re: Guess where I am

Jacked Guy (Dean) does love animals. He also has a tattoo of a golden retriever. No comment on my birthmark. Are you jealous?

Is a waterbed like a personal bounce house? I heard it was bad for your back, but you should be used to that from sleeping on a pull-out couch for months.

Today's our last full day in Brussels. On to Rome next. I can't wait to stare at the Sistine Chapel, but mostly, I want to eat and drink my way through the city.

From: Sabrina F. <SFinkelsteinreads@gmail.com>
To: Adam Haber <Adam.Haber@gmail.com>
Date: July 15, 9:37 p.m.
Subject: Re: Guess where I am

Hi!

Just making sure you got my last message. I'm in Italy! Which makes the subject line pointless. Do we need a new string?

This email was written but not sent and will save as Draft until further action.

From: Adam Haber <Adam.Haber@gmail.com>
To: Sabrina F. <SFinkelsteinreads@gmail.com>
Date: July 16, 6:12 a.m.
Subject: New email

We needed a new string.

I was joking about the waterbed. Do they even make them anymore?

Are you in Rome now?

Yes. I'm jealous of Jacked Guy. But not because he's jacked. And not because he has animal tattoos. Also not because he's in Brussels and I'm stuck in Philadelphia, where it smells like weed, hot sewer air, cheesesteak, and garbage. But because he gets to hang out with you (and possibly see your birthmark).

I miss you.

From: Sabrina F. <SFinkelsteinreads@gmail.com>
To: Adam Haber <Adam.Haber@gmail.com>
Date: July 17, 1:01 a.m.
Subject: Re: New email

I miss you too. Since you brought it up, I have to ask. Was it just sex or were we on our way to being something more? Because it didn't feel like just sex to me. But then you just left and neither of us said anything. Would things be different if you stayed?

This email was written but not sent and will save as Draft until further action.

From: Sabrina F. <SFinkelsteinreads@gmail.com>
To: Adam Haber <Adam.Haber@gmail.com>
Date: July 17, 1:03 a.m.
Subject: Re: New email

See picture of me eating the best pizza of my entire life.

I miss you too.

From: Adam Haber <Adam.Haber@gmail.com>
To: Sabrina F. <SFinkelsteinreads@gmail.com>
Date: July 17, 10:52 p.m.
Subject: Re: New email

That pizza looks almost as good as Una Pizza's. Did you take one of those pizza-making classes? Or do you only cook in battle?

In London yet? I'm sure you'll do the touristy things like the changing of the guard at Buckingham Palace and all the museums, but I've attached a list of the best bookstores. Not that you can't do your own research and I'm sure you have, but I curated this one based on several different sources. (I'm bored.)

I did the same with record shops, which is more my thing than yours, but I couldn't resist, and pet shops because I know you'll want to spend some of your daily budget on Rocket.

Send more pictures even if Jacked Guy is in them. (Douchebag)

From: Sabrina F. <SFinkelsteinreads@gmail.com>
To: Adam Haber <Adam.Haber@gmail.com>
Date: July 18, 10:16 a.m.
Subject: Re: New email

I don't only cook in battle! Okay, yes, I do 💀 I'm not spending my first ever European trip taking a class! I'm already a student in my real life.

Thank you for the bookstore list. That was so nice of you!

You're probably joking about being jealous of Dean, but I'm

just going to ask because I might literally explode if I don't. Was any of it real? Or was it just sex and then mind games to mess with my head?

From: Adam Haber <Adam.Haber@gmail.com>
To: Sabrina F. <SFinkelsteinreads@gmail.com>
Date: July 19, 10:52 p.m.
Subject: Re: New email

It wasn't just sex and mind games.

From: Sabrina F. <SFinkelsteinreads@gmail.com>
To: Adam Haber <Adam.Haber@gmail.com>
Date: July 19th, 10:56 p.m.
Subject: Re: New email

But was it real?

This email was written but not sent and will save as Draft until further action.

From: Adam Haber <Adam.Haber@gmail.com>
To: Sabrina F. <SFinkelsteinreads@gmail.com>
Date: July 19th, 11:01 p.m.
Subject: Re: New email

It was real.

Chapter Forty

I stop on the street in front of the Target two blocks from my apartment and as gently as possible place four brimming grocery bags on the ground at my feet. I wipe the sweat from the back of my neck and shake out my arms. They're sore from carrying two heavy bags each. I also have red marks on the underside of both elbows from where the plastic straps slid off my shoulders and down my arms. In a word, I'm a mess. Taking an Uber from a supermarket that's literally down the street from my home felt extravagant at the time, but now I regret the decision to walk. Blocks feel like miles when carrying a hundred pounds of food.

I remove my phone from my purse and text Marcia.

Sabrina: Are you around tonight? I bought shrimp, scallops, and fresh veggies and thought I'd make us dinner

Something I should have asked before *I added the expensive ingredients to my cart.*

Since getting home from Europe a week and a half ago, I've noticed Marcia's been spending more and more time with Sharon, which is great, but if they already have plans tonight, I'll save this attempt at stir-fry for another night—hopefully within the next two days since according to Google that's about how long fresh shrimp and scallops last in the fridge.

Thanks to my mom's generosity, my checking account has surplus funds and while I'm determined to save most of it, splurging feels less like a foolish indulgence when shared with someone else. Also, I decided to take the summer off from school. The session started while I was on vacation and most of the classes conflicted with my schedule at the library anyway. I'm happy with the choice, other than a smidge of pesky guilt over delaying the completion of my master's degree, but it leaves me with nothing to do several nights a week. Why not fill some of it by exercising my cooking muscles and spending time with my roommate? Seriously. It's time to move forward and remember all the reasons I loved when it was just me and Marcia...before Adam showed up and made it even better.

The bubbles dance on my screen while Marcia writes me back.

Marcia: Hi Sabrina. I'd love that! 🙂 🥳 👏

I chuckle at her overuse of emojis and return my phone to my purse. I glance at the groceries at my feet and frown. With a longing gaze at my building still a ways down the block, I huff and lift the bags back over my shoulder, where they immediately slide down my elbows again. The sweat from the early August heat has left my skin damp and more conducive to slippage. My sunglasses slide down my nose and when I raise my hand to push them back up, the weight of the bags follow me.

Ping.

Happy for the excuse, I free my arms once again and check my phone.

Marcia: How about we cook together? ? 👩‍🍳👩‍🍳

I clap my hands. Dinner is guaranteed to taste good now!

Sabrina: Fun! I'll pick up a bottle of wine

Right after pressing send, I look over my shoulder at the liquor store I *just* passed and curse my offer to add yet more pounds to my already heavy load. But an offer made cannot be rescinded. New York is a great walkable city, but sometimes walking sucks!

By the time I finally get home and release the four grocery bags hanging on my elbows, purse over my shoulder, and bottle of wine in my hands, my arms feel bloodless. Though I could use a drink, I doubt my ability to hold a glass right now without dropping it, and I'm sweating like I personally picked the grapes for the wine.

After a desperately needed shower, I join Marcia in the kitchen. She's already chopped the vegetables and laid out the seafood for the stir-fry. I handle the rice. It's boil-in-a-bag and completely within my range of abilities. Soon, the combined aromas of garlic, ginger, and onions fill the air.

Marcia and I dance around each other to the cooking playlist I helped her create on Spotify.

"Did I ever tell you I saw Earth, Wind and Fire live during their Spirit tour in seventy-six? Life-changing!"

I stop watching the rice boil and turn to her. "Yeah? How so?" I love Marcia's stories of partying in the seventies. I imagine her in a satin pantsuit grooving to the Hustle on a dance floor of flashing multicolor lights like in *Boogie Nights*.

"It was right before I got pregnant and—"

Beep beep beep. Beep beep beep.

Marcia groans over the noise. "Every damn time!" She opens a kitchen window to let the smoke out.

I race into the living room calling, "I'll get the front door," behind me.

The smoke detector goes off whenever we fry. The high screech of the alarm is like nails on a chalkboard. All we can do is open the windows and the front door and wait until the apartment cools down enough for it to stop.

I don't even notice Rocket behind me until he flies out in the hallway to the other side of the floor, barking all the way. *Sneaky little fucker.* "Rocket!" I call his name only once before giving up. Let him tire out. He'll come back inside when he's ready. It will be a while, but thankfully, our neighbors love the rascal and don't complain.

I lean against the open door and face Marcia, who's now standing at the edge of the kitchen where it meets the living room. "If Adam were here, he'd sweet-talk Rocket back inside in no time," I say, with a glance behind me to make sure Rocket hasn't entered another apartment or gotten on the elevator.

Marcia looks at me funny. "Are you okay?"

"Yeah. Why?" I blink and feel a tear slide down my cheek. I wipe it off. "Must be the onions." It's a flimsy excuse since Marcia cut the onions, not me. Cooking was a nice distraction from thinking about Adam, but one mention of his name and he's front and center on my mind again. *It was real.*

When Carley asked who I was emailing whenever we had Wi-Fi

and I told her it was Adam, she gently suggested (okay, more like on-the-verge-of bullied me into) asking if his feelings for me were real from the safety of a different continent. I whined in protest, but she insisted if I didn't do it, I'd always wonder. She also banned me from telling him that Dean (Jacked Guy) is gay because, in her words, "let Hot Ex-Roommate be jealous!" Except rather than his answer satisfying a curiosity, it might have made things worse because real or not, Adam moved back to Philadelphia and now I worry I'll never like anyone else as much for the rest of my life.

Marcia's eyes soften knowingly, although the content of her knowledge is unclear. "I'll finish dinner. You wait for Rocket," she says.

Eventually, running up and down the hallway loses its appeal and Rocket comes back inside. He finishes his own dinner before settling under the kitchen table while we eat ours, no doubt waiting for crumbs to fall to the floor.

I bite into a tender and buttery scallop and moan. "This is so good."

Marcia bites into a shrimp. "Perfectly crisp."

I stand, remembering the bottle of wine I bought that's waiting on the island. After suffering through getting it home, I intend to enjoy every sip.

"Have you spoken to Adam lately?"

I freeze with my back to Marcia and squeeze my eyes shut. "Not in a bit."

I return to the table with the bottle and pour us both glasses.

"He told me you sent him photos from Europe."

Back in my seat, I rearrange the veggies on my plate. "Yeah. He'd urged me to be honest with my mom that I was struggling financially and needed her help. I thought he should know the outcome."

I don't mention that I never replied to his last email. What was I supposed to say? It was real for me too? I'm in Manhattan and he's in Philadelphia, where he has an apartment and a job that's "not the worst." Considering the way his last long-distance relationship ended, I doubt he'd want to do that again.

Marcia's forehead crinkles. "I didn't know you were struggling financially."

I swirl my wine and take a sip. "It's not the kind of thing you want to tell your landlord."

Marcia's face falls. "I'm more than your landlord. I'm your friend!"

"You definitely are!" I dip my chin as my chest tightens with guilt. I'd be beyond hurt if Marcia ever introduced me to someone as just her tenant, but I didn't want her to worry about whether I'd be able to pay my rent. "Honestly, it's not something I was proud of. I only told Adam because he was always around when it came up." First at Keybar when I realized I missed the deadline to apply for the scholarship. Then in the library when I complained about not being able to afford Europe. And finally in Marcia's room flipping her mattress when my automatic payment was declined. He was consistently supportive and listened without trying to fix it for me... aside from urging me to tell my mom, that is.

"Well, I'm glad your mom helped you out."

"Me too!"

She tops off my wine. "Have you ever been to Philadelphia?"

"Interesting segue." I chuckle. "I don't think so. Other than possibly driving through it."

"It's a great little city. But Adam fell in love with the energy here and fit right in."

She's right. When I moved to Manhattan, there was a learning curve while I figured out how to *be* a New Yorker. For most of us, *living* here is only half the journey. It's big and crowded. The subway system is like a giant obstacle course with unplanned detours, local trains running on express tracks, and impossible-to-decipher announcements. The pace is lightning fast and either you move with the crowd or it buries you like an avalanche. The locals have a certain swagger. *If you know, you know.* Then one day, if you're lucky, it just clicks... like it did for me. Adam might have been an awkward teenager but after our first walk to the Strand, when he was wide-eyed and in awe, he caught on to the fast pace and heightened energy of the city like a boss.

Still, Marcia's words come as a surprise since I thought she was on board with him moving back to Philadelphia. "What about his new job? It's a floating position so he can see what he likes best. That's perfect for him, right?" If I'm being honest, I'm playing devil's advocate and hoping Marcia comes back with something to prove me wrong.

"I'll give credit where it's due. My son's heart was in the right place this time, and it was an impressive attempt to think outside of the box. But I don't think Adam will be happy there in the long run. Unlike Jeffrey, I don't see any rush for him to settle into a permanent career as long as he's doing *something*."

Since she brought him up, I open my mouth to ask whether she's spoken to Jeffrey when her next words stop me in my tracks.

"I can't think of anyone I'd rather see Adam settle down with than you."

Say what? All thoughts of Jeffrey fly south as Marcia's left field comment pierces my brain like a lightning bolt. She didn't just say what I think she said.

"You heard me right." She leans forward. "If you get married, I'll be your real grandma."

I stop breathing. "M-married? W-what do you mean?"

Marcia smirks. "I have eyes and ears, dear. I saw the way you looked at each other... pining like Elizabeth and Darcy. And then suddenly you were more like Maddie and Addison."

"Who?" I have no idea who these people are.

Her eyes widen. "From *Moonlighting*!"

I shrug. It's like Patti Smith all over again.

She sighs. "It was a TV show in the eighties. David and Maddie fought all the time but also wanted to tear off each other's clothes. It was magic. They finally did and the show jumped the shark. Shame." She takes a bite of shrimp.

I dip my head so my hair covers my flaming face. Marcia talking about me and her grandson in the context of tearing each other's clothes off is... well, awkward. "The fighting was only because of the battle for the bedroom."

She rolls her eyes. "I still can't believe you did that."

I pick up my fork and then drop it back on the plate. My appetite is gone. "I'm so sorry."

Marcia frowns. "What are you sorry for?"

"For all of it. For falling for your grandson when he moved here for you. For coming up with that stupid competition. I didn't want to lose this place... lose you. And I didn't trust that Adam knew what he wanted."

She pats my hand across the table. "You don't need to apologize. I might be biased but I think Adam is worth falling for. I also agree that he doesn't have the best track record for sticking through things. But if you'd only come to me first, I could have saved you time, energy, and a toothbrush."

I frown. Toothbrush? *Oh.* "Ha."

Her lips quirk. "Anyway, my relationship with Adam is not mutually exclusive with yours. We managed to bond quite well all while the two of you got to know each other separately."

My stomach drops. Rehashing Adam's and my history is ruining the vibe of what was supposed to be a girls' night dinner. I take my dishes to the sink. "Why are we even having this conversation? He's not here anymore."

"I kicked him out, remember?"

Facing her again, I say, "He's a grown man who was living on his grandma's pull-out couch rent-free for months! It was time to get his own place. But he couldn't get out of Manhattan fast enough."

"His deal with his father was time sensitive, as were the job and apartment on the bargaining table."

My eyes open wide. "You knew about that too?" I sit back down.

"I heard from Jeffrey a few days after Adam moved out. The timing was too convenient. Jeffrey told me everything but said he'd been wanting to call me anyway... that it had been too long."

Hope fills my heart. Maybe it wasn't all for nothing then. "And?"

She shakes her head.

I deflate. "Oh, Marcia. I'm so sorry."

"He apologized for keeping me from Adam for so many years, which was something." She slides a broccoli floret from one side of her plate to the other.

"For sure." I feel a *but* coming on.

"But he downplayed the harm that was done, suggesting the months we spent together now make up for the ten years we were apart."

"Every minute counts," I whisper, thinking of Nana. We had more good years than bad, but the bad doesn't cancel out the good and the good doesn't cancel out the bad. All the moments have meaning.

"He also assumed I was at an age where my sexuality didn't matter anymore. I questioned whether he thought he'd still be sleeping with his wife when he was seventy, and he said he hoped so. I said, 'Well, there you go.' "

"You tell him, Marcia!" I clink my wineglass against hers.

She smiles before taking a sip. "He asked if I was dating someone and when I said yes, he asked me his name. I answered, 'Sharon.' The air got so quiet, like dead-of-night quiet. He didn't say anything negative, but the silence spoke volumes. We ended the call with some promises to all get together soon. I guess it's progress, but not the outcome Adam wanted."

I study her heavy eyes and dropped shoulders. "Is it fair to say it's not what *you* wanted either?"

She tosses her napkin over her plate. "I didn't have my hopes up. I'm more sorry about Adam. If he'd told me this was his plan, I'd have warned him he was setting himself up for disappointment."

"I understand why he thought he needed to go, and I can't fault him for wanting to facilitate peace between you and Jeffrey." I fiddle with my napkin. "My grandmother and father were also estranged, and while I want nothing to do with him . . . and the feeling appears to be mutual . . . he's her son and I know it killed her not to have a relationship with him." I give Marcia the back cover–copy version of my family's history, including my regrets about Nana.

Her eyes are wet when I'm done. "I can't believe I didn't know this."

I'd love to say I didn't purposely keep the information from her, but it would be a lie. "I was too ashamed to confess my crimes against my grandmother to another grandmother." I rearrange the vegetables on my plate. "I was also afraid you'd look at me differently." My throat closes up and my nose tickles. I can't bear the idea of Marcia hating me.

Her face falls. "Oh, honey. In the short time you've been in my life, you've added so much good. Your heart is pure. There's very little you could tell me to make me think otherwise. And this isn't it." She goes on to assure me that Nana Lena knew I was working through my issues and would come back to her eventually. By the time she's rested her case, I'm so much lighter and wish I'd confided in her months earlier. Then she stands and insists on a hug. There's no resistance on my part.

When we're seated again, Marcia puts her hand on mine. "Let's get back to you and my grandson. You miss him."

I nod, although it wasn't a question. There's no sense denying the undeniable. "I do. We bonded pretty quickly, but it was purely platonic. Then you had your health scare and told him to move out, which led to our battle, and now he's gone."

Marcia raises an eyebrow. "I'm pretty sure that's the redacted version, but I understand."

My cheeks burn. "Anyway . . . somewhere in the middle of all that, we caught feelings for each other, but it's too late now."

"Why is it too late?"

"Because he left!"

Marcia places her elbows on the table. "So? Philadelphia is less than two hours away."

I push my lips out. "True. But his last long-distance relationship didn't end well."

"How long ago was that?"

"Right after college."

She waves a hand. "Different time, different girl. Did you even ask him to stay in New York rather than move back to Philly?"

I shake my head. "It wasn't my place. He's not my boyfriend. Did *you*?"

"I did. But I'm his grandma. Not a pretty girl his own age who *wants* to be his girlfriend."

Another truth not worth the energy of refuting. "He had a job and an apartment waiting for him. Not to mention his deal with your son."

"He agreed to move back to Philly in exchange for Jeffrey calling me. Both men held up their end of the bargain. No one said it had to be a permanent move." She quirks an eyebrow.

I chew on my cuticle. "I think you're giving me too much credit. Your grandson likes me, but asking him to quit yet another job and move back here for me seems like a bridge too far." My stomach knots at the thought of being that vulnerable with Adam. "Wouldn't I also be enabling his quitting habit?" Even through my protests, my mind is whirring. What if I'd asked him to stay that night in my bedroom when he said goodbye? I hadn't been brave enough, but would it have made a difference?

Marcia doesn't bat an eyelash before responding. "There's a difference between running *away* from something and running *toward* something...or *someone* else. And he'd be moving back for both of us." Her expression turns serious. "If things continue to progress with Sharon, we might move in together at some point."

My eyes widen. "Wow! I'm so happy for you guys!" After everything I went through to secure my place here, I might have to get back on the roommate app anyway, but I can't think of a better reason. No matter what happens, Marcia will always be my friend and, *fine*, my surrogate grandma, and that's all that really matters.

She pats my hand. "Don't start packing your things yet. I'm not kicking you out, but perhaps keep your mind open about your next move. Three might be a crowd, but maybe it's you and Adam who are meant to live together without me."

Chapter Forty-One

I take a step back and study my "book it to the beach" display in progress. I'm happy with it, except the left side is too blue. I pluck a book with a yellow cover from the top shelf and reposition it to the middle to break up the color scheme.

There's a difference between running away *from something and running* toward *something... or someone else.*

I love you, Marcia, but STFU!

Since last night at dinner, I can't get those words out of my head or stop thinking about Adam. Am I giving up on him... on *us* too easily by assuming that his moving to Philadelphia means we can't be together? He had his reasons for going. But his deal with Jeffrey didn't change things, and like Marcia said, he held up his end of the bargain. He can come home now... to Marcia and to me. Or he can stay in Philadelphia, and we can try a long-distance relationship. I tap my lips. Would I even want that? Long distance is *hard*.

"Sabrina!"

I jolt and turn to face Gabe, whose expression is a cross between amused and pissed off. "You scared me. What's up?"

"I should ask you the same question. I called your name twice."

I clench my teeth. "Sorry. I was focusing on my work and didn't hear you."

Gabe runs his dark eyes up and down the four-sided wooden display in the center of the floor and presses his lips together. "Focusing, you say?" He turns back to me and raises an eyebrow. "Tell me, Sabrina . . . which book on here does not belong on a 'beach' display?"

Starting from the top shelf, I read the book titles out loud. "*The Five-Star Weekend*, *One Summer in Savannah*, *Summer Romance*, *Snow Road Station* . . . Oh! Oops." I smile wryly and remove that last one from the second shelf from the bottom. "Good catch."

Gabe does a circle of my face with his eyes. "What's with you today?"

I frown. "Nothing. It was an accident."

"Was directing a patron to the employee bathroom earlier an accident too? And what was with sitting on my chair before? I was in it!" He waggles his eyebrows. "Are you trying to tell me something? Do you have *feelings* for me?"

I roll my lips. "You wish. I don't have *feelings* for you. This is about Adam."

"Of course it is. Spill." He glances around the room, still crowded with patrons who lingered after the 11:45 knitting and crocheting club meeting. "Just make it fast and do it quietly."

In a low voice, I summarize everything that happened with Adam, concluding with my conversation with Marcia the night before. "She seems to think Adam would be happier here and that I could convince him to move back. What do you think?"

Gabe sets his elbow on the edge of a shelf and presses a hand to his ear. "Damn. I don't know. Do you want to show your cards like that?"

I scratch my head. "Not really, but if Marcia's right, the only thing standing between me and Adam is me. If he still lived here, I could torture him with my cleavage until he begged for it, but with him all the way in Philly, it's either the direct route or accept that it's over. I can't really afford to play it cool." I've never had to put myself out there for a guy before. I've always known where I stood. Adam wrote that his feelings were real, but never expressed any desire to resume things, which means it's up to me to start the conversation.

Gabe stares at me blankly.

"Well? What do you think?"

He shakes his head. "Sorry. I was stuck on the 'torture him with my cleavage' part."

I nudge him.

He throws his hands up in surrender with a cheek-splitting smile. "You walked right into it!"

I glare at him.

His expression softens. "You should go for it. What have you got to lose?"

"He has a stable job and a furnished apartment. What if he's happy? I don't want to ruin that for him." I sigh dejectedly. "I need a sign telling me what to do!"

A patron approaches and clears his throat to get our attention. "Excuse me."

I do a double take and break into a huge grin. It's Chloe's grandpa! And he looks so dapper in a gray pin-striped suit with a red-and-white gingham tie and matching pocket square. This time he left the umbrella at home. "Nice to see you again! How can I assist you?"

"You and that handsome fellow helped me with my granddaughter a few months ago. She's visiting again and I was hoping for another recommendation. We really bonded over *The Selection*." He beams.

"I'll leave you to it then." Gabe nods at the man, gives me a "to be continued" look, and walks off.

"I'd be happy to help you!" I walk him over to the YA section and search the shelves for more YA dystopian fiction. The Divergent trilogy is out, so I recommend *The Dividing Sky* by Jill Tew, a more recent addition to the subgenre that I thoroughly enjoyed. The entire time, I think about how during our first meeting with Chloe's grandpa, he assumed Adam and I were a couple and Adam didn't correct him. It's because of him that we buddy-read *The Hunger Games*. For a moment I wonder if *this* is the sign I was asking for. But I dismiss it. There's no such thing as signs!

I check him out and wish him good luck with Chloe. Then I turn to Gabe sitting next to me... on a different chair... and grin. "Helping people bond through reading is one of the reasons I became a librarian."

Gabe snorts. "When you're done being cheesy, want to have lunch with me and Lane?"

"Sure!"

"We're going to Citizens of Gramercy."

My mouth opens and closes.

Worry lines appear on Gabe's forehead. "What? Is it bad? I've never been, but my date this weekend recommended it."

Under normal circumstances, I'd interrogate him about his date, but I'm too busy having a minor inner meltdown. Adam took me to Citizens of Gramercy to thank me for getting him the page job at the library. Could it be? I shake my head. Just a coincidence.

"I've lost you. Are you thinking about Adam again?"

"No." *Bold-faced lie.* "I'm in. The food is great there."

Lane joins us. "Ready?"

Gabe checks his watch. "As soon as my coverage gets here."

While he waits for one of the other assistants to cover the desk, I use the bathroom. On my way back, I toss the paper towel I used to open the bathroom door in the trash. I'm about to walk away when my eyes lock on a small two-tone orange bag lying at the top of the heap. I swallow hard. *It can't be.* I take a closer look, and it can be, in fact it is, an empty bag of Cheetos, still dusted with crumbs.

My legs wobble. I breathe in and out with purpose to center myself. I don't have time to freak out about yet another "coincidental" Adam-adjacent occurrence less than an hour after asking the universe for a sign. Gabe and Lane are waiting for me. Besides, Cheetos are a very popular snack. I do a quick check with Google on my phone, delaying myself even further, where it is confirmed that Cheetos are the top-ranked cheese snack in the United States. I'm certain it's a fluke.

I'm actually not certain at all, but a hangry Gabe is scary. My phone pings with a text message proving my point.

Gabe: Leaving in 5, 4, 3...

I quicken my step and meet them at the entrance with a second to spare. When we arrive at the restaurant a few minutes later, I hold my breath as we pass Adam's and my stools at the counter and sit at a table underneath the STAY GORGEOUS, GRAMERCY sign.

"I think I want a burger," Lane says.

Gabe scrunches his face. "This place is known for its authentic Australian brekky and you're gonna have a burger?"

"Don't burger-shame me," Lane says.

A waiter drops off the menus. "Hi, I'm Adam and I'll be your server today."

I gasp. My head falls back and I shake my palms in the air. "Message received, Universe. Message received!"

Lane and Gabe stop bickering to gawk at me.

"I'll give you a few minutes," the waiter says to Gabe and Lane while blatantly avoiding eye contact with the weirdo at the table.

"I'm worried about you, Sabrina," Gabe says.

"Don't be." I click the app store on my phone and download Amtrak.

"What are you doing?" Lane asks.

I look up from my phone. "Going to Philadelphia."

Chapter Forty-Two

I can't believe I'm doing this.

I tuck my purse closer to my side to leave room in case someone sits next to me, and I look out the train window as the world zips by. I close my eyes and try to relax, but my body and mind are not having it. I brought a paperback and my Kindle to keep me occupied for the eighty-nine-minute train ride, but I can't stop thinking about the purpose of my trip long enough to surrender my mind to a fictional world.

The universe, who I think might actually be my nana, was loud and clear with her signs—four of them, according to my count. She wants me to fight for Adam. And so, taking my cues from romantic comedies, I'm on my way to deliver a grand gesture.

I sit up straight as the conductor announces the next stop is the William H. Gray III Thirtieth Street station in Philadelphia—my stop.

Fear wraps its cold, tight grip around me. Unless I use my return trip ticket immediately to turn around and go home, this is really happening. Adam doesn't know I'm coming. I didn't call or text him because I can't think of a single romance where the grand gesture was delivered over the phone. Adam mentioned going to all the author events at the bookstore across the street from his new place. According to the store's website, there's one tonight for the launch of a YA fantasy novel, and I'm going to surprise him there. Given our history, a library might have been more fitting (and romantic), but we'd have to keep our voices down, which is hard to do when declaring your love for someone. Because I love Adam. I've loved him for a while now.

When we first hooked up, we didn't have to think about what it *meant* because we had the luxury of seeing each other every day at home and at work. But now that we're separated by approximately one hundred miles, we no longer have the convenience of just seeing where things go naturally. We have to *decide*. Well, I've decided that I want to be with him for real and give what we have a chance to bloom into something even more. Long distance isn't the best-case scenario, but I just want to be with him. Period. I don't know if Adam feels the same way, and I can either wonder forever or until I stop caring—whichever comes first—or I can listen to the universe/Nana and ask him. Forever is a very long time, and I don't want to wait another day.

The train comes to a stop and people immediately crowd the aisle to get to the exit. In no rush to take the biggest risk of my life so far, I stand and gather my things while manifesting the events of the next hour. Adam will see me and break into a surprised but enormous smile that grows even bigger when I tell him I love him. He'll say he loves me too. We'll skip the author talk and race across the street hand in hand back to his apartment and frantically kick over his coffee table and smash right there on the rug like David and Maddie on *Moonlighting*. (I watched the scene on YouTube. 😅)

My hot feelings turn cold as I'm suddenly flooded with doubts. What if these events have lost their novelty by now and he doesn't show up? What if he has to work late tonight or is traveling out of state? I'm positive this is the most poorly planned grand gesture in the history of grand gestures. And then my heart leaps into my throat. What if he skips this one because he has a date? Or worse, what if he shows up *with* a date? My stomach dips and swirls like the ocean at high tide.

A space opens up in the aisle, and I join the queue on autopilot. Once off the train, I follow signs to the Twenty-Ninth Street exit, where Google said I'd find a taxi line. When I reach the front, I get inside the cab and give the driver the address for A Novel Idea bookstore, which, also according to Google, is an approximately twenty-minute drive. The event starts at six and it's 5:42 p.m. I had to leave work early, but Jenny was totally okay with it when I told her I was meeting Adam. (I didn't mention Adam has no idea he's meeting *me*.)

The driver says the best route is via I-76. This means nothing to me so I agree. I'd like to see the sights as I pass them by to get a vibe for Philadelphia—architecture, bars and restaurants, shopping—but I-76 is a highway not unlike New York City's FDR Drive, and also not unlike the FDR, congested with traffic. It's rush hour after all. What did I expect?

The cab finally drops me off at 6:15 p.m. Before entering the store, I check out my surroundings. It's a cute neighborhood with narrow streets lined with brownstones and trinity houses in assorted colors, many with stores or restaurants on the ground floor. Adam might live in one of the apartments above these businesses. Does he like the pizza at Marra's or has Una Pizza Napoletana ruined him for pizza from anywhere else?

I walk across the bluish-gray carpet set outside the entrance and through the periwinkle-blue door into the bookstore. It's a small space but cozy, with charming exposed-brick walls. The area behind the checkout counter is painted in a greener shade of blue with "A Novel Idea" written in white script and adorned with little pink star designs. It's perfect and I can see why Adam comes here often.

A woman behind the counter around my age with long red hair in a side ponytail and short, straight bangs greets me, and when I tell her I'm here for the event, she points to the back, past a set of comfy-looking blue chairs. I ignore the temptation to stop at the "popular reading" and "new release" tables as a further delay tactic.

I step quietly into the back room, a narrow space with large brown wood bookshelves set against both side walls. It's a full house, with guests on about ten rows of black folding chairs and two people, the author and the person she's in conversation with, at the front.

It's standing room only. From behind the back row of chairs, I half listen to the author talk about what inspired her world building while skimming the crowd for a familiar head of short multi-shade brown hair. But no one here looks like Adam. I repeat the process, going slower this time, until I'm convinced he's not here.

My shoulders slump with the weight of disappointment, but it's no one's fault but my own. What was I thinking coming all this way on a whim?

The audience laughs at something the author said and I wish I were one of them—a reader merely excited to meet a favorite author in person and get a book signed.

I could go home... get back on the train and pretend this never happened. Only I won't be able to live with myself if I don't try at least a tiny bit harder to connect with him tonight.

I contemplate returning to the main room but don't want the author to see me leave and take it personally. Instead, I casually slide my phone out of my purse to text Adam I'm in Philly. The element of surprise seemed like the most swoony way to go, but maybe Nana wants me to take the direct route.

Only there's a new text waiting for me. From *him*.

Adam: Your doppelganger?

Attached is a photo of the back of a blond-haired girl wearing jeans, a cropped white short-sleeve sweater, and sneakers. My pulse races. It's me.

I snap my head and look behind me, sucking in a breath when I see him—Adam—leaning against a bookshelf and staring right at me. He must have slipped in after I did. He gives me a slow wave like a beauty contestant in the Miss Universe pageant.

My face breaks into a smile.

He returns the expression and we remain eyes locked until he eventually points his thumb behind him toward the main room.

Though I'm desperate to get closer to him, I chew my lip and send a text first.

Sabrina: Is it rude for both of us to walk out at the same time?

I watch Adam read the text. He looks up and shakes his head at me, then sighs. He types out a response with a slight quirk of his lips.

Adam: We can't have that. I'll go first. Count to 60 and follow

I nod and watch him slip out.

I turn toward the front, mentally count to sixty, and as quietly as possible, step out into the main room.

Adam's back is to me while he peruses books on a small round table in the center of the room allowing me to appreciate his defined delts through the thin fabric of his brown graphic T-shirt.

As if sensing me staring at him, he turns around and his eyes light up. "Did you make it out without offending anyone?"

"The audience didn't boo my exit and the author didn't burst into tears—"

"That you know of." His blue eyes twinkle.

"Right." I place a hand over my frantically beating heart willing it to slow down.

"So what's up?" His tone is not unfriendly, but based on the way he's studying me, his question is casual code for "What are you doing here?"

My face goes hot under the scrutiny. "You know . . . the yuzh."

He narrows his eyes. "Bookstore events in Philly are *the yuzh* now?"

I tuck a strand of hair behind my ears. I should have rehearsed my speech better. *Or at all.* "No . . . I'm just . . . um . . . I came to see you."

His eyebrows furrow. "How did you know I'd be here?"

I shrug like it's no big deal. "One of the emails you sent me while I was in Europe . . . you mentioned this store and said you went to all the author events, so I thought I'd—"

"Surprise me?"

"Surprise!" I do dorky jazz hands before I can stop myself. "I didn't see you in the crowd and thought you weren't here but then you—"

"Texted?"

I jut a hip. "Are you planning to complete *all* my sentences tonight?" I'm not really annoyed. The teasing banter is good. It allows us to ease back into our dynamic rather than blurting out my feelings.

His lips quirk. "Sorry."

"I have things to say that I'd rather say in person than over text."

He looks at me with focus. "Go on."

I take a deep breath in and out. "The thing is, when I fought you to stay with Marcia, I didn't realize that winning the apartment would mean losing *you*. I sort of assumed you'd stay in New York and that maybe we could continue what we started. I also don't think I even realized how much I liked you... *loved* you... until it was too late." I lower my gaze for a beat before raising my head again.

Adam's eyes are wide, but he remains silent, probably assuming I have more to say.

I swallow hard. "There's more to my speech, but please put me out of my misery if you don't feel at all the same way." My heart is still thumping frantically.

His lips curl up in the hint of a smile. "I've missed you, Brina."

"Yeah?" The word comes out choked and I hold a breath, bracing for the *but* that I pray doesn't follow. That he used my nickname is a good sign. It's more intimate and less likely to be followed by a rejection. Right?

He nods. "I miss watching trashy television with you. You've made me believe the people on *Love Is Blind* are actually there for the right reasons and not just to collect followers. I miss the way the bathroom smells like Valentine's Day after you shower because of your body wash. I miss the way you blush when I take my shirt off. I miss how easily I can make you blush in general. Like right now." His eyes dance. "You're such a good friend to my grandma. You love reading. You're smart and tech savvy. You put up a good fight when you believe in something. And you're really hot!" This time *he* blushes. "I didn't expect to fall for my grandmother's roommate, but that's exactly what I did." He licks his lips. "Which is to say, I love you too."

Because I'm temporarily mesmerized by the quick flash of his tongue, I hear his words on a brief delay. But when they sink in, my rib cage expands and my cheeks spontaneously stretch into a huge grin. He loves me too!

It's my turn again. "When you came to my room to say goodbye, I was too afraid to ask you to stay, but I wish I had." I swallow hard. "If you're settled here, would you consider trying a long-distance relationship?"

Adam reacts to this with a shake of his head. "I don't want to do long distance."

The air whooshes out of me like a faulty tire. "Does that mean that you don't—"

"I'm moving back to Manhattan."

My breath hitches. "You are?" His words warm my heart like a cozy wool sweater. I have so many questions, but he's still talking.

"Moving back here didn't magically change my dad's relationship with my grandma or who he is and likely always will be."

"Marcia filled me in. I'm sorry it didn't work out the way you hoped." I reach for his hand and lock it with mine.

"Win some, lose some." He rubs a finger along my knuckle. "But in the meantime, you're not the only one who has been regretting things they didn't say that night in your bedroom. I also want to date for real, and I've finally figured out what I want to do when I grow up."

My mouth drops open. "And?"

He smiles.

"Wait." My body hums with excitement. "Do you want to be a librarian too?"

His gaze wanders the length of my body. "We'd make a very sexy pair of librarians, no doubt, but as much as I enjoy being a page, the answer is no. I want to be a middle school English teacher . . . like my grams. It's not a whim this time. Going back to school is not just an excuse to avoid another job. I mean it. Maybe *The Outsiders* will be in the curriculum," he says with a crooked grin.

My hand flies to my mouth. This fills me with so much joy, I could burst. There's a round of applause from the event room, almost like they're happy for Adam too. It's perfect. Adam always enjoyed the tween and teen programs at the library best and is an advocate in the fight against book banning in schools.

"I've already applied to the master's programs at Fordham, Hunter, and Columbia." He grins sheepishly. "I haven't even told Grams. I was planning to do my own grand gesture if I got accepted somewhere."

"Of course you'll get in somewhere!" The man already has an Ivy League education. I'm positive he'll make a brilliant teacher—as long as his students are able to put aside their crushes long enough to listen to his lessons. I stroke the soft skin of his arm below the sleeve of his T-shirt.

"I should know in a few weeks. After that, there's only one thing left to figure out."

"What's that?" I lower my hand and move out of the way to give a customer access to the books on the table.

Adam gestures for me to slide closer to the bookshelves. "My living arrangements. You think I can find something on RoomBridge?"

I cluck my tongue. "Possibly, but I have a better idea."

He raises an eyebrow.

"Marcia thinks she might move in with Sharon at some point."

His eyes widen in mock horror. "My grandma? Living in sin? No!"

I giggle. "You're missing the point. If they shack up, I'm going to need a new apartment and roommate. Are you interested? Or is it too soon? It's not happening immediately so we have time to date like regular people who don't live together first."

He lessens the distance between us and takes both of my hands in his. "We've already lived together, so not too soon. But I have some conditions this time around."

I lace my fingers through his and squeeze. God, how I love holding hands. People underestimate how electrifying it can feel when you're in love. *We're in love!* "Lay them on me."

He strokes my thumb. "We share a bed."

Heat pools down my stomach and lower. "No brainer. What else?"

He shrugs sheepishly. "Actually, that's it."

"Well, I have a few conditions of my own."

"Do tell."

I drop his hand and straighten my back to emphasize the seriousness of this conversation. "We have to buddy-read *Sunrise on the Reaping.*"

Adam flicks his wrist. "Easy. What else?"

"I'm not sure you're going to like this one." I bite my lip.

His gaze travels to my mouth and stays there. "Let me be the judge."

"You can't wear a shirt while flipping our mattress. Or while baking dog and non-dog treats. In fact..." I say, tilting my head back and forth and tapping a finger to my lips. "You'll be prohibited from wearing a shirt about seventy-five percent of the time."

He nods. "Like when I'm really, really cold."

"Yup. And when we have guests over." I wave my hand in front of his chest. "I don't want you flaunting all *this* to other people." I assume a serious expression and shrug. "You in or out?"

Without hesitation, he says, "I'm in." Then he drops my hands and scratches his head. "What will my grams say?"

Normally, bringing up one's grandma in the midst of a grand gesture would be a turnoff, or at least awkward, but not this time. "It was her idea."

His cheeks glow. "She's so smart."

"The smartest." I can't stop smiling. "I can't stop smiling."

"I have a solution for that." He pins his eyes on me, heavy lidded and smoldering.

I know where this is going and check my left and right for spectators, but when I turn back to Adam, he's only looking at me. "No sneaking around anymore." He lowers his head and brushes his lips against mine, at first feathery light but then deeper and more passionately, releasing one of his hands to place it on the back of my head. I use mine to tug his T-shirt and draw him even closer.

I picture the scene as captured through the window of the bookstore. Two people kissing in a room surrounded by books with pages and pages of fictional love scenes and happily-ever-afters.

But none are more romantic than ours.

READING GROUP GUIDE

Discussion Questions

1. Sabrina struggles to forgive herself for the way she treated her nana toward the end of her life. Do you think Nana Lena understood why Sabrina acted out? Is there anyone you wish you'd treated better while you had the chance?

2. When Sabrina learns that Adam called Marcia after so long, her first instinct is to blame Adam for not being in his grandmother's life, which comes up again later. Do you think Adam should have made more effort earlier? Do you think Marcia should have pushed more? Or do you place the blame for the decade-long pause in their relationship squarely on Jeffrey? Is there someone in your

life you wish you'd made more effort with to maintain a relationship?

3. Sabrina is hurt and angry after overhearing Adam caution Marcia about sharing her passwords with Sabrina (a stranger) until he explains that his mother was a victim of identity theft. How did you feel during this scene? Were you offended along with Sabrina or, like Adam, did you think Marcia was naïve to trust a non-relative with such personal information?

4. When Adam gets angry with Sabrina for reading his copy of *The Outsiders* without asking her permission, she says he's acting like a six-year-old. Later, he explains that the book has sentimental value because it was his mother's and her mother's before that. Do you keep any books (or something else) for sentimental reasons that you feel extremely protective of?

5. Adam and Sabrina have a lot in common between their love of reading, complicated relationship with their fathers, and guilt toward their grandmothers. How much of a part in their mutual attraction do you think these commonalities played? Do you believe it's important to have things in common, or do you think "opposites attract"?

6. While Adam and Sabrina encourage Marcia to use dating apps, they assume she wouldn't be interested in more casual "hookup" situations, but Marcia surprises them by saying she misses sex. Do you think society wrongly assumes

women over a certain age don't care about sex anymore? If so, why do you think that is? What do you think older people should say to younger friends and family in these situations to set the record straight?

7. Relationships with grandparents are a strong theme throughout the book. Are your grandparents still alive? What is/was your relationship with them? Are you a grandparent and if so, how close are you with your grandchildren?

8. Carley tries to talk Sabrina into going to Europe with her. When Sabrina argues that she can't afford it, Carley encourages her to enjoy being young while she can. Do you agree with Carley that Sabrina worries too much about money for such a young woman, or do you admire that she's practical and wants to put career and education first?

9. Sabrina clearly has a lot of respect for her mother and loves her very much despite her not being around that much when she was growing up. Yet Dina feels guilty that she left her mother-in-law to practically raise her daughters. Are you a working parent? How about your own parents? Were either of them home when you got out of school every day? If not, do you wish they had been?

10. When Marcia shares her doctor's concerns about living with two younger roommates, Sabrina is shocked when Adam says he wants to stay. What did you think of their solution to make it a competition? Who do you think had more of a right to be there?

11. Sabrina struggles financially but is reluctant to ask her mom for help because Dina always stressed that her daughters should be financially independent. But when Audrina says she's going to live with their mom a little longer even after saving enough to move out, Sabrina finally admits that she needs a monetary cushion. Do you think there is a limit to how long a parent should financially support their child? Where do you think that line should be drawn?

12. Sabrina receives what she believes are four signs from the universe that she should be honest with Adam about her feelings for him: Chloe's grandpa comes to the library, Gabe suggests eating lunch at the same restaurant she went to with Adam, she sees the Cheetos wrapper in the trash, and the waiter's name is Adam. Do you think these were signs or just coincidences? Do you believe in signs?

13. The book ends with a HFN. Where do you think Adam and Sabrina will be in five years?

Acknowledgments

Roommating felt like the easiest book to write while drafting, but in hindsight it was the hardest, both artistically and emotionally. Even as the words and story flowed out of me, there was a sense of anxiety I didn't experience with the others. Authors talk about the Second Novel Syndrome, but I've always been a late bloomer, so it doesn't surprise me that I'm on a delayed schedule. In the end, I'm so proud of the final product, but I could not have done it alone. If gushing makes you uncomfortable, please skip these pages.

To my agent, Melissa Edwards. Thank you for always having my back, for seeing things objectively, and for giving me the hard truths. Though you don't sugarcoat, you somehow always know when I need a tiny bit more "squish" and deliver. There is no one else I'd rather partner with through the highs and lows of this journey. I can't wait to celebrate more highs but sleep better at night because you stand by me through the lows.

To my editor, Leah Hultenschmidt. When you calmly suggested that I "rework the premise," I had a mini-meltdown, but those words, along with our video call to brainstorm, turned everything around for this book. It's so much better now, thanks to you! It's truly been an honor to work with you on three rom-coms.

Without the entirety of Team Forever, *Roommating* would just be a saved document on my computer, but together you brought it to life in paperback, ebook, and audio. It's you who got it into bookstores and libraries, and to readers. It's you who spread the word far greater than I could ever do on my own. Thank you to everyone in editorial, design, production, marketing and publicity, and sales, including (but not limited to) Leah Hultenschmidt, Jordyn Penner, Sam Brody, Alli Rosenthal, Estelle Hallick, Dana Cuadrado, Luria Rittenberg, and Alayna Johnson.

To my cover designers, Daniela Medina and Janelle Barone. Thank you for designing the gorgeous cover. Forever has always knocked it out of the park with my covers, but this one exceeded all of my wildest dreams!

Some authors can write a book and confidently send it directly to their agent/editor. I'm not one of those people. Enormous gratitude goes to my critique partner, Samantha M. Bailey, and beta readers, Lindsay Hameroff and Margot Ryan. Thank you for seeing and pointing out what I couldn't see myself.

Thank you to Melissa Stock, Sarah T. Dubb, and Jennifer Jumba for generously answering all of my questions regarding librarians, your individual library systems, and information regarding the MLIS. You seriously went above and beyond, allowing me to confidently create that part of Sabrina's world. Any mistakes or small liberties taken for the sake of the story are my own.

For authors like me who are hopeless at creating eye-catching and clever posts and reels, I highly recommend Booked With the Emilys for extra support.

There's so much outside of an author's control and it can take a mental toll. The first person I call when I need a pep talk or just to vent is my author bestie, critique partner, travel buddy, and personal cheerleader, Samantha M. Bailey. This happens weekly (sometimes—okay, *often*—daily). Sam: thanks for always being there for me, for never judging, and for telling me what I both want *and* need to hear on demand. In short, thank you for being my person. I love you!

To my beach babes: Eileen, Francine, Jen, Josie, Julie, and Sam: Beach, mountain, desert, or jungle, I'll be there for you (because you're there for me too). Beach Babes forever!

Because one group chat is not enough, I'm so grateful for the many friends and fellow authors I regularly chat with (or lurk) via Discord, Slack, IG messenger, and good old-fashioned email for advice, venting, marketing support, and comic relief: NYC Writer Commiseration Station, Team Melissa, Forever Contemporary Romance Authors, Jewish Joy Club, Smutfest 2.0, and Jewish Romance Authors.

To my parents, Susan and Michael. Thank you for telling everyone you know about your youngest daughter, the "famous" author. I hope it will be a true statement one day, but in the meantime, I'm so grateful for your confidence in me, for reading my books, and for sharing them with all your friends. (I'm fortunate that you have so many of them!)

Thanks to Deborah and my other colleagues at my day job for supporting this journey. And to all of my non-writer friends, including but not limited to Ronni, Shanna, Megan, Vanessa, Lorraine, Phyllis, and Dee, I appreciate you asking about my books and your patience for my too-long answers! Your presence at my events and signings means everything.

I'm not going to thank individual bookstagrammers/readers by name this time because the risk of inadvertently leaving someone out and hurting their feelings is too great. If you're reading this and have been a support to me, this paragraph is for you. Maybe you helped share my cover or partnered with me for giveaways or both—you know who you are—if you consistently include my books in roundups and recommend them to your followers, this paragraph is for you. I am so enormously grateful to *you*. As an author who consistently struggles with anxiety and impostor syndrome, your enthusiasm and excitement for my books and your eagerness to spread the word help me fight those demons every single day.

Thank you to Finkelstein Memorial Library in Spring Valley, New York, for being my favorite place to go every weekend when I was growing up. The name Sabrina Finkelstein was not a random choice!

Finally, in memory of Alan Blum. You've been gone more than ten years, but your words of encouragement have stayed with me. I revisit them often. I promised to always thank you and I always will.

About the Author

A born-and-bred New Yorker and lifelong daydreamer, **Meredith Schorr** fueled her passion for writing everything from restaurant reviews, original birthday cards, and even work-related emails into a career penning romantic comedies. When she's not writing books filled with grand gestures and hard-earned happily-ever-afters or working as a trademark paralegal, she's most often reading, running, or watching TV... for research, of course.

To learn more, visit her at:

MeredithSchorr.com
Threads @MeredithSchorr
Instagram @MeredithSchorr
Facebook.com/MeredithSchorr/Author